ADIS RIS

A   ler

by

FAITH MORTIMER

The Best Selli g Author of

"On Devil's Brae"
"Behind a Twisted Smile"
& "The Green Room"

About the author:

Faith Mortimer: born in Manchester, England and educated in Singapore, Malaya and Hampshire, England. Qualified as a Registered nurse and later changed careers to oversee a number of travel and sport related companies.

Faith is married with a family. Once the children attended University, she decided to join them in reading for a Science degree. Faith obtained an Honours Science degree in 2005 and believes the dedication and stamina needed to sit for a degree while in full-time employment, gave her the confidence to finish writing her first novel.

She has now written and published 18 novels and a volume of short stories. All are available as eBooks and paperbacks from your favourite online book store.

For more information about Faith and her writing please follow on Facebook.
www.facebook.com/FaithMortimer.Author
http://twitter.com/FaithMortimer
Website: www.faithmortimerauthor.com

Where Faith writes a regular blog about all manner of things!

PARADISE PRISON

A Gripping Psychological Thriller
in the "DARK MINDS" Series

by

FAITH MORTIMER

ISBN-13: 978-1541376373

ISBN-10: 1541376374

This edition published 2017 by Topsails Charter, Southampton

Acknowledgements

A Big Thank You to my editor Catherine and to my husband Chris for their invaluable assistance and patient support

A big thank you to my Beta and ARC reader/reviewers plus THE Book Club, especially Tracy Fenton and her administration team for their wonderful support.

Cover picture with kind permission of Robert Finlay

Paradise Prison

by Faith Mortimer

Chapter One

It all started with 'that look'.

While Gillian was preparing dinner that evening, a hand touched her shoulder.

"Gill, I'd like a word."

She tried hard not to let him see her shudder or hear the words she whispered to herself. *Oh no! What is it this time?* Lawrence's 'a word' almost always led to ill treatment of some kind.

"Dinner can wait. We need to have a little chat, clear the air." How she hated his public-school voice. When they first met, she found it attractive; it was what drew Gillian to Lawrence in the first place—that and his perfect manners. She could feel his hot breath on the back of her neck. It made her cringe. Gillian turned around from the kitchen hob and faced her boyfriend. Although her heart was beating twice as fast as normal and her legs were in danger of turning to jelly, she knew she had to smile. To frown or look the slightest bit miserable was bound to

1

bring his wrath down on her. Lawrence didn't 'do' miserable.

"Of course, Lawrence. What do you want to talk about?" Although she tried to make out they were about to discuss things on a level footing, Gill knew there was only one point of view that mattered: his.

"It's about Nathan." This time she caught her breath. Nathan was an old friend of Gill's; their friendship went back to their early teens when they both started senior school. Gill didn't have many old friends—just two, in fact: Nathan and Rebecca. She didn't see them often— maybe three times a year if she was lucky—and never alone. Lawrence always made sure he was around and within earshot. But the three had formed a strong bond and kept it going ever since, despite Lawrence. She was sure Nathan hadn't done anything wrong…so what had *she* done now?

"Nathan? I haven't seen him in ages. The last time we got together was at Bex's birthday party. But you were there, remember? You normally hate parties but insisted on going to that one."

Lawrence gave a lazy smile and after flicking a speck of dust from his shirtsleeve, moved closer. His eyes never left her face. "My dear girl, I don't mean that time. I mean last Tuesday. You said you were going to the hairdresser's. I dropped you off and collected you." He ran one finger slowly down the side of her face, and this time she did shudder. "When did you arrange things, my sweet?"

Gill blinked, but didn't dare move away from Lawrence. "And so I did." She smiled her best smile and drew her fingers through her hair which she'd had cut short and dyed dark brown. "I said I fancied a big change, a new look. You took me there and brought me home."

"Yes, but you didn't tell me about meeting Nathan and going for lunch with him. Did you?"

Gill bit her lip. So, that was what it was all about. This could go on for hours. At best, Lawrence would dissect every minute of the time she'd spent in Nathan's company, bit by bit, until she felt wrung out and ended up agreeing with everything he said. His verbal abuse was deadly. At worst, well, it wasn't worth thinking about. How could she have been so stupid to imagine she could have her hair done and slip out for half an hour with Nathan and be back at the salon before Lawrence arrived to take her home? She was never allowed to be alone with Nathan or any other man, for that matter. Not that she often had the chance. Why was Lawrence making this fuss now, anyway?

She needed to defuse the situation once she realised where it would lead. If he said she could no longer see Nathan, she knew the ban would inevitably include Bex. Life wouldn't have been worth living without her two friends. She looked him in the eyes, trying to appear unperturbed. "Oh that! We didn't have lunch, just a quick ten-minute break for coffee."

Lawrence narrowed his eyes. "So he just came along by chance, did he? How very convenient."

Gritting her teeth, she carried on smiling and nodded. "Yes, honest. It wasn't planned. He saw me paying the bill, with the money you gave me, and tapped on the salon window. He said it would be rude not to go and have a coffee with him. Lawrence, you know Nathan's my oldest friend."

"Who no doubt would like to be more," Lawrence sneered.

This time, Gill felt her stomach churn in terror. She knew Lawrence's jealousy was intense, although she ensured she never gave him cause to complain. He just used every opportunity to his advantage.

His rage seemed to come from nowhere. "Slut. Whore," he burst out as one fist smashed against her rib cage, followed up by a second blow to her jaw. "I was watching the whole thing. His leg against yours in the café, his hand on your arm. He couldn't take his eyes off you, and when you parted in the street, he gave you that look which made me certain you were more than just friends."

Gill fought to get her breath under control and tried to answer, her voice coming in painful gasps. Tears slid down her face, mingling with the blood from where she'd bitten through her top lip. "It's true...we're just friends. But, Lawrence, why bring all this up now?"

"Because I've been thinking about it, and I've decided you're a liar! How long, eh? How long has he been sniffing around?"

Battling against agony, Gill raised her eyes to meet Lawrence's. She saw only glacial chips of ice-cold blue, his normally handsome face, ugly and mottled red with anger.

"I swear there's nothing between us. How could there be? You keep me a virtual prisoner here. I'm not allowed to go shopping without you, and you choose my clothes and shoes. You even drag yourself around Tesco's. I don't have a proper job—I take in ironing."

Lawrence's answer was to slap her face. She felt her mouth go numb. "Just as well I do, otherwise where would you be? You need to be taught a lesson. And next time, don't bloody answer back."

She yelped in pain and put up her arms to cover her head. The day was obviously going to be one of the worst. He planted another thump to her vulnerable stomach, and she fell to her knees. Lawrence drew back his right leg and swept her knees from under her. She rolled onto her side, and he aimed another at her stomach.

Gill couldn't move or protect herself. As he delivered the blows to her lower abdomen, all she could think was, not again. The last time ended in a tragedy, for which she'd never forgiven him.

Finally, Lawrence stopped and stood over her, his eyes glazed with lust, his breath laboured. He stood up and glanced towards the hall from the kitchen, and it was then that Gill heard the second knock on the door.

Lawrence shot her a look. "Stay there, and don't say a fucking word," he hissed between his teeth. "I haven't finished with you."

After he'd left the kitchen, Gill staggered to her feet and clung onto the work unit for support. She knew she had to get away. She'd tried in the past, but he was always too clever.

When he first invited her to move in, he'd been nothing but loving and charming. Gill couldn't believe how lucky she was after her miserable childhood to find someone who placed her on a pedestal. All too soon, that pedestal became a chain around her neck. She was never allowed to do anything for herself, go anywhere or meet anyone. Lawrence made her a virtual prisoner in his castle—and he alone kept the keys.

She felt blood trickling down her face. She tore off a piece of kitchen roll to staunch the flow. As she held the pressure pad to her lip with her shaking hand, she heard voices coming from the front door. Her heart leapt as she recognised Nathan's. Could he help her? Then just as quickly as it had risen, her heart plummeted. Lawrence was a seventeen-stone rugby giant of muscle and bone. Nathan was five foot nine, unmuscular, and as slender as a reed. His brains were no match for Lawrence's brawn.

The voices became louder and there was the slam of the door. So much for that, Gill thought as she feared Nathan had left. But then, she heard running footsteps and turned fearfully towards them.

A flushed and panting Nathan burst into the room and rushed over to her. "Gill! My god, what has he done to you?" He spun round to confront Lawrence, who had crept in behind him. "What have you done, you bloody coward. She's your girlfriend, for god's sake. How can you justify hitting someone smaller than you? Are you all right, Gill?" He turned back and laid a gentle hand upon her shoulder. "You're coming with me. I think we need to get you to hospital, get that lip looked at. It might need stitching."

"She's going nowhere. It's just a little cut. Piss off."

"Don't be ridiculous, man. Look at her. She can hardly stand. Gill, did he hit you anywhere else? You might need X-rays."

"I said, get the fuck out of here. This is between me and my fiancée. You're not welcome."

"Gill's my friend. If you've hurt her, you'll pay. I'll make sure of that."

"Will you, you little twerp? I don't think so." As he uttered these words, Lawrence smashed his right fist into Nathan's nose. There was a sickening crunch. In dismay, Gill realised his nose was broken. She screamed when blood trickled down Nathan's shirt front.

"Lawrence, don't! Please!"

Lawrence gave a sickly grin, and in response, aimed at him again, this time connecting with his jaw. Nathan howled and put up his hands to hold him off. Lawrence took hold of Nathan's ears and head-butted him. Nathan slid to the floor.

There was a silence as Gill and Lawrence stared down at the crumpled body lying at Lawrence's feet. Gill couldn't see any signs of breathing, and a cold finger of terror shot up her spine. In her heart, she knew Nathan was dead. Lawrence bunched up his fists and started to turn towards her. In panic, she lifted the heavy frying pan from the cooker and swung it at his head.

Chapter Two - Rebecca

After finding no pulse in Nathan's neck, Gill stood up and looked around in desperation. Nathan was dead, and although she couldn't bring herself to touch or go near Lawrence, she feared the worst. He lay as still as Nathan. What the hell was she to do? She'd be blamed for both deaths. She had to get out, get away.

She didn't have much money of her own, Lawrence saw to that. Every penny she earned from ironing, he'd taken from her, saying it was for their savings account. That was a lie, as she knew full well Lawrence never banked anything if he could get away with it. How he made his money, she never knew, but she reckoned it was illegal. He owned a top-of-the-range car and never stinted on clothes for her or himself. He liked nice things around him, and that included her, too; she always had to look her best.

She staggered out of the kitchen in a daze. If she left, she would need funds. Lawrence kept a stash of cash in his study, under the Persian rug and beneath a square cut into the wooden floor. She sniffed, wiped her lip and then placed her hand on the banister. As her mind cleared, she made a rough plan: pack some essentials into a couple of soft bags; leave everything else; find the money and take it. Where should she go? Abroad? She could hardly turn up at an airport looking like she did. She didn't know anyone well enough to help her...except Rebecca. She pondered her conundrum. Was it fair to enlist her aid? She and Bex had always been best friends. If she didn't go to her, then she knew she'd never be forgiven.

***

"Of course I'll help you," Rebecca said once Gill was seated in her living room in front of a roaring log fire and had told her everything. She was shocked to find a shivering and terrified Gill on her doorstep earlier that night. She hustled her indoors and dealt swiftly with her torn lip before pouring out two generous measures of brandy. "First, we must ring the police and get an ambulance sent round to your house."

Gill gasped in horror. "No! Please don't, we can't do that."

"Why not? Look, the longer we leave it, the worse for you ... us." She corrected herself, thinking that she was now an accessory to the two deaths. Her head swam. She couldn't stop thinking about dear old Nathan. He'd never hurt a fly in his life and now this.

"Please. I'll be blamed for their murders. They'll know I was part of it because my blood's everywhere. I didn't clean any of it up. I just had to get out of there."

Rebecca studied her friend. She was in a state and needed help, but she also knew that if she lifted her phone, Gillian would bolt out of the front door and do something stupid. "Okay. Let's think about this. You're assuming they're both dead. You're positive poor old Nat is because you couldn't find a pulse, and you think

Lawrence is too. Surely they'll identify that Lawrence killed Nat? You had to protect yourself from Lawrence…hence bashing him over the head. I can't see why you're worried."

"I know I'll be accused of both deaths. I'm terrified of facing the police."

Rebecca didn't know for sure why her friend was so scared of the police, but then there was a period of a few years in which they hadn't seen each other. Gill had told her everything she could remember, but Rebecca thought there were a few gaps in her history. The last ghastly incident had been when Gill was pregnant with Lawrence's baby. He was so furious and blind with alcohol that he beat her and kicked her half senseless. She lost the tiny foetus and eventually recovered. Bex's immediate reaction was to report the matter to the police, but Gill had been too frightened, saying he'd find out and kill her. Bex knew Gill was in a dreadful situation, but she had to do as her friend had asked, or she'd be in danger. She didn't agree, but what else could she have done?

"Okay, but at the very least, we have to call the authorities and let them know someone's been hurt. We can call anonymously, but what about when they come looking for you?"

Gill stared into the flames. After a while, she lifted her head and spoke. "I don't want to involve you in all this. I know you said I can stay, but I want to get away. Yes, I know I'll have to face the consequences sometime, but right now, all I can think of is Nat. Let me disappear for a while, and I'll return when I'm ready."

Rebecca looked at Gillian curiously. She seemed calmer than half an hour earlier…almost too calm. Was she still in shock? Not for the first time in her life, she wished she had a partner with whom she could share her problems: a problem shared was a problem halved. "Well, maybe, but let me make that call."

Gill nodded reluctantly. "But don't tell them who you are. Make sure the call's untraceable."

"I have an old mobile and SIM card I use abroad sometimes. I'll use that."

***

The two friends stayed up well into the early hours discussing what to do. Rebecca was sure Gillian would be treated appropriately if she went to the police and told them everything, but she wouldn't be budged. Eventually, after a soothing hot chocolate, they nodded off in the warm room, both too exhausted to do any more. Around six o'clock, Gill awoke, stiff and aching from her beating and feeling chilled, as the fire had died down. She stretched and seeing Rebecca was still asleep, went through to the kitchen to put the kettle on. There was a radio on the work top and she switched it on. A minute later, she was listening to the news, just as Bex entered the room.

"I wondered…" she began.

Gill waved a hand at her. "Ssh, it's the news."

Three minutes later both women stared at each other.

Gill turned away and wrapped her arms around herself. "So, Lawrence is still alive. The reporter said the dead man is Nathan. She mentioned a woman lived with Lawrence. They'll soon discover and release my name. Oh, Bex, what shall I do? Lawrence will blame it all on me. I made one hell of a dent in his head with the frying pan." She suddenly stopped, turned and confronted Bex with a horror-stricken look. "He'll come after me. I just know it. I must get out of here. He'll come straight here ... oh god, what about you? He might take it out on you. He's vile enough."

Rebecca stepped forward and wrapped her arms around her. "Hush. If he does, I'll deny everything. Don't you think you should go to the police now? I'll come with you and help explain everything."

Gill shook her head. "I can't. Please, let me disappear just for a few weeks. I have to come to terms with Nathan's death. It was all so horrible watching him being beaten to death. The awful thing is, I'm sure Lawrence *meant* to kill him. He's been stewing over Nat for days. Nat was small compared to him—Lawrence is all muscle." She burst into tears, and Rebecca hugged her tightly while they shed tears for Nathan.

After a while, Rebecca drew back gently and locked eyes with Gill. "I'm still not sure this is the right thing to do, but listen. You remember me telling you about Phil? He has a motor boat down on the Hamble. I know he's going across the channel this weekend. What if I can get you on his boat? Say you're going to Europe for a bit of travelling. That way, you can travel freely from here and into Europe without showing your passport. If you flew or took the ferry from here, they'd be looking out for you…private yachts seldom get approached."

Gill gulped back her tears. "That might work. Thank you. I'll never forget this."

Chapter Three - Gillian A week later

The past week had been one of the worst of her life. Not only had Gill left her home and best friends, she knew she couldn't let her guard down. Her heart felt heavy when she thought about Nathan and how he'd gone to her aid and suffered the consequences so dreadfully. She'd never seen him again.

Rebecca had been true to her word. She contacted her friend, Phil, and persuaded him to let Gill travel on his yacht across to St Malo in France. Phil wasn't the type to ask questions; people's business was their own, and he knew if Bex needed to ask for a favour, she had a good reason. During the crossing, Gill had been as pleasant as she could be, considering everything that had happened. She helped with meals and drinks on board for the two of them and retired to her cabin when she felt the need for solitude and shed some tears.

In St Malo, she and Phil parted company on the quayside. He shook her hand and said he hoped she'd find what she was looking for. Gillian was startled by his choice of words, wondering what Bex had told him. But when he turned away and went below, she realised that for all her calm and quietness, he must have seen through her bravado and knew she was troubled.

Now she'd reached Portugal and guessed she needed to keep moving, even if her sense of loss outweighed everything else. She had to be strong and clear-minded, for once. She'd been downtrodden for too long. She had no one else to watch out for her.

She sat at the table nearest the main pontoon of the marina. She had no idea what to do next. Getting a job was out of the question; there were too many Brits there who followed the news back home. She needed to get far away. Europe, she considered, was out. Maybe the States or farther, South America? The Far East even. Surely, she could come up with *something*?

Sitting around doing nothing made her feel useless, but as she weighed and considered her options, she had an idea. It was tenuous but possible. She needed to get on a yacht that was sailing far south. She watched the comings and goings of each boat as it passed through Lagos marina. She noticed that some sailed with a full crew, often two couples or occasionally, a family. Sometimes, just two people or a lone sailor. How would she find out if anyone was looking for crew? She could hardly just go up and ask; it was looking for trouble. She decided to stop feeling miserable and get out and look. She read through the advertisements on the board inside the marina office, where she discovered a few yachts were heading south and their skippers were asking for crew volunteers.

She made a note of the boat names and set off down the pontoons to identify each yacht. She knew she looked presentable enough; her bruises and split lip were healing, and make-up camouflaged the worst of her injuries. She knew she was no stunning beauty but reckoned she was attractive enough. For once, age was in her favour: not too old, not too young and the right side of forty. Plus, as well as being fit and healthy, she knew a bit about boats and considered herself to be a quick learner. All it needed was the yacht and right crew.

It had been a relatively easy journey to the Algarve. She had travelled one leg by coach, followed by a train, which eventually took to her current location. She remembered Lagos from a previous visit, a few years earlier, when Lawrence and she had first got together. They spent two glorious weeks lazing in the sun, drinking cheap wine and having great sex. Everything seemed right at the time. For the first few months, Lawrence was easy-going, always happy to do what she suggested and rarely contradicted her. Gillian found it easy to live with him. Other pluses were his—apparent—attractive salary, and he never ever looked seriously at other women. They rarely discussed marriage or even love, but there was an unwritten, unspoken, lazy way between them. The only thing she found irritating was that he liked to vet everyone she met. Insidiously, it all seemed to change, the measure of control gaining momentum until Gill found she did everything he asked because if she didn't, she would soon receive the venom of his vile tongue or the back of his hand.

Thankfully, that now belonged to another time, another life. Gillian's new one was just beginning. She doubted she'd ever return to England. She sighed as she thought of Bex and Nathan and wiped away a threatening tear. It still hurt so much.

She noticed movement on the pontoon out of the corner of her eye. Without being too obvious by turning her head completely in his direction, she watched the skipper of the forty-foot sloop, *White Lady*, moor three boats down the trot and walk towards where she was sitting.

He was tall and slim, almost skinny, and strolled in her direction with a long loose stride along the wooden pontoon. Dressed in navy shorts and a white polo shirt, his blond-streaked sandy-coloured hair poked just below the rim of his cap. He was definitely older than Gillian; she'd already guessed him to be touching fifty. She'd been scrutinising him and the other two skippers looking for crew as much as possible since her arrival. The other two were a lot younger—nearer her age—and like Lawrence. She wished there was a nice family travelling south; in many ways it would have felt safer on a busy noise-filled boat. She could have joined in without giving away too much of herself. Anonymity was what she craved. She picked up her coffee cup and took a last mouthful as the skipper nodded at her before walking past and approaching the bar.

"Cerveja! Sagres, please."

He slid a note across the marble top before turning away to face the boats. With one hip leaning into the bar and ankles crossed, he picked up the bottle nonchalantly and took a pull of his beer. A satisfied sigh escaped him. The waiter wandered over to Gillian's table, and when he picked up her empty cup, she asked for a Cerveja, too. Ignoring her heart thundering in her chest, she casually removed her sunglasses and wiped the lenses with a clean tissue.

The waiter returned with her beer. As she took a sip, her eyes met those of the skipper. He raised his bottle in salute. "Cheers!"

"Cheers," she returned, her mind in a panic. She wanted to look away but knew that finding a skipper there was her only chance. She'd already seen a photograph of herself in the Daily Mail the day before. Thank god her red hair was long in the photograph, not short and dark like now.

"Nothing quite like it, is there? The first beer after a long hot day." He straightened up and ambled over towards her.

"I'm Harry, by the way. May I?" He thrust out a tanned hand in greeting and then surprised her by pulling out a chair from the next table and sitting down. His manner was self-assured and calm. She registered how rough his palm felt and how he sounded quite posh. "I've noticed you around. Are you working here or on holiday?"

It was now or never. Get a grip. She swallowed. "Gillian. A bit of both, really. I came away because I needed a long break…and as my time's my own, I thought I might look for some casual work. Sort of extend my time off before I think about my next career."

"Oh yeah? What sort of work? I know a few people here who might need some help. Bar work, waitressing or something else?"

She hesitated before wrinkling her nose. "No, not bar or waitressing work. What I'm actually looking for is to work my passage somewhere. I'm yearning to cross the Atlantic or maybe venture beyond, into the Pacific."

"Ah! As a cook or deckhand?"

"Well...both, really. I can cook and I know a bit about sailing."

Harry looked thoughtful for a moment and drank some more beer while taking the time to study her face and give her body a quick appraisal. Gillian wondered if he'd noticed the interest she had taken in his yacht, although she'd been very discreet. "There are always a few skippers with boats either with empty berths for sale or ones looking for working crew. I'm going back across the pond myself this week. You say your time is your own. Does that mean you want a long stint away or just a few weeks?"

Gillian examined the man before her. His expression was open, friendly but not too curious. She knew very little about this sailor, other than what she'd seen during the last few days and the answers to a few casual questions she'd asked the bartender. He was older, so he'd seen a bit of the world. She trusted what she'd learnt, but a single woman needed to be on her guard. She'd found that out the hard way. She decided to give him the benefit of the doubt.

"A few months would be good. I'm not married nor tied down to a permanent job."

Harry grinned. "Me neither. At the moment the sea is my mistress."

Gillian relaxed and returned his smile with the lines she'd rehearsed back in her hotel room. "Truthfully, I want to get away somewhere quiet and not stressful. I...I had a shock a short while back, and I'm trying to come to terms with it."

"I'm sorry. A loss is always hard to take."

She stared at his words and frowned; the back of her throat ached as she remembered Nathan. "I didn't say I'd suffered a loss...but yes, you could say I have. I just need peace and quiet for a while."

"Point taken. How much sailing experience have you actually had?"

"I sailed a bit when I was younger. My father taught me in a Wayfarer. Then later, I spent a couple of weekends on small yachts. Trips across the channel to Cherbourg and Guernsey—things like that."

"So, can I presume you don't suffer from seasickness? You can hop ashore with a rope in your hand to tie up?"

"God, yes." She laughed. Even if she felt miserable inside, she needed to give the impression she was at ease. Confident even. "*And* I can stand a night watch on my own."

He nodded, studying her closely. "Where are you staying?"

"In a small pension hotel off the main drag in town. I have a small room—a bit noisy from the restaurant below—but at least it's clean and cheap. It's called The Yellow Bird."

"I know it well. The food's good there, anyway. Tell you what, I'll have a think and ask around a few of my mates. I can meet you there later this evening. Perhaps we can have a drink or a meal together?"

She nodded and forced a smile. Was this wise? "I'd like that. Seven o'clock okay?"

As he agreed, Gillian realised the first hurdle had been crossed easily. One skipper down and two more to talk to. Harry was easy-going and likeable. He hadn't pressed her about her private life; she liked that. Plus, he was older. An older man would be more reliable, right?

Chapter Four - Harry

As Harry left the marina bar, his thoughts were still focused on the woman he'd been talking to. He'd first seen her around Lagos four or five days earlier and was struck by how her face instantly reminded him of long-departed Marlene: the woman with whom he'd had his first and only long-term relationship. He'd never got over her and hadn't found anyone to replace her.

But apart from that initial observation, he was right. She had been trolling around the boats soon after she'd arrived. There was something about Gillian that made him think she had a chequered past. Harry had seen all sorts of women pass through over the years: the young, the old, the fallen and those about to fall. This woman had a slightly detached air about her, which interested him; and he'd noticed her looks and slim body. She'd suffered in some way during her life; of that he was sure. She bore strange faint markings on her wrists—old wounds but just visible, nevertheless. And despite her apparent good health, she carried an air of frailty as well as sadness and mystery. He decided that despite what she'd said, she'd lost someone and more likely than not, very recently.

Apart from her resemblance to his old lover, her face was vaguely familiar. Maybe she'd visited Portugal before. Harry made up his mind to check up on Gill; he wondered if that was her real name. He came to a snap decision. Regardless of what he'd said, he wasn't going to ask around for work for her. Harry needed a cook and a good crew member was invaluable. She was moderately pretty, slim with short brown hair and an interesting face. Having female company across the Atlantic was usually eventful and helped pass the time.

***

Harry glanced down at his watch and saw that he was ten minutes early. It didn't matter, as he knew the owner of The Yellow Bird, and Bento might have had more to tell him about his house guest. Harry chuckled under his breath. Bento always had his ear to the ground, and if anyone knew anything, it would be him.

"Harry! Good to see you. Como vai? Cerveja or wine?" Bento said, clapping Harry on the back before disappearing behind the restaurant bar.

"You too, Bento, and thanks, I'm good. Sagres will be fine to start with. I'm meeting a guest of yours here for a drink."

Harry noticed how the bar owner's deep-brown eyes twinkled, and he nodded knowledgeably while flipping the cap off the beer bottle. "Ah, that would be a certain lady, eh?"

"Yeah. I've seen her around this last week and finally got chatting to her today."

"She has good figure. I know she looking for lift on boat as she ask me if I knew anyone. She say she not worried where it going."

"That's right. I thought about taking her with me to the Canaries when I leave in a day or so."

Bento shrugged. "She good crew. I speak to her every day, but she is, how do you say…private? She not say much about her life, where she coming from. That's okay. I respect people's private life. But she right for you, Harry? She seem sad and is long time at sea across ocean for you if she not want sex."

Harry grinned. Nothing changed. Bento enjoyed the ladies and no doubt would have fancied his own chances with Gill. "You're one huge step ahead, Bento. She tells me she's a good sailor, and I don't want a female who yaps all the friggin' time. She said she's looking for some long-term sailing. I thought about asking her to join me across to the Canaries. I can always decide once we're there if I want to take her further. A few days at sea alone soon sorts out personality clashes."

"You think good. Just you two?" His filthy grin said it all and Harry laughed.

"Probably. No more dirty thoughts. I just want a good crew member."

Their conversation came to a natural end, as Gill chose that moment to enter the restaurant. Harry noticed she'd changed out of her daytime attire of skimpy shorts and sun top into a white cotton dress, nipped in at the waist by a wide red belt. A waft of musky perfume caught his nostrils. He noted she was wearing some eye make-up and lipstick, and her short dark hair shone from a recent washing. She looked and smelt good, and both men stared appreciatively.

"I'm impressed. Most women I arrange to meet are usually late," Harry said as she walked over to the bar. The resemblance to Marlene was striking.

She returned his smile with a slight lift of her eyebrows and replied in a cool tone, "I didn't know this was a date." Her lips twitched, and he could see that she was teasing. He always liked a woman who could take a joke.

He returned her timid smile with a grin. "What can I get you? I'm enjoying a Sagres, but if you'd like to join me for dinner, perhaps you'd prefer wine?"

"Thank you, that's very kind and I'd love to. A glass of red, please."

Harry ordered a bottle of red wine which Bento praised above all else. The Quinta Reserva came from an inland estate, and Bento explained his family connections to it. Bento declared it went well with roast meat, and Harry trusted his judgement. With a bit of a theatrical flourish, Bento showed them to a table away from the pedestrian walkway. Early evenings were always busy with tourists and locals promenading before entering their chosen restaurant, and as they sat down away from the crowds, it meant they received a good view of everything going on around them.

"How's your day been? Do you know many people here?" Harry asked after they'd ordered and were savouring their first glass of wine.

"Fine, thanks. But no, I don't know anyone. It's…my first time in Portugal." She took her time glancing around the restaurant. There were a few other diners who gave the newcomers a quick appraisal.

"Right. First time, eh? Well, I always enjoy my trips here. It's a natural stopping-off place after coming across the Atlantic, going eastwards. I head for the Azores and then here for a stay or go into the Med." Harry noted her slight hesitation, and wondered if she'd just told him a downright lie. Fine. He enjoyed a bit of mystery.

"That's in the spring, right?" Gillian switched her attention back to him.

Harry nodded. "Yeah, unless I get out of the hurricane area, I need to have the yacht lifted and stored on land for safety. Sometimes I come back across the ocean, or I sail down towards Panama and out into the Pacific."

"It sounds lovely…the Pacific, I mean." The waiter arrived with their meal at that moment, and Harry waited until he'd left before continuing. "It is. Look, I may as well tell you now. I didn't find anyone looking for crew on a Caribbean crossing today, and there aren't many yachts entering the Med now, either—it's not the season. Did I mention earlier I was looking for crew myself? To be honest, I usually prefer someone with strong sailing skills, but as you have some experience and say you can cook at sea, maybe we could give it a try if you're willing? I presume you know which one is my yacht?" Harry was convinced he'd seen her, despite the huge floppy hat and sunglasses, strolling along the pontoons and taking everything in. He thought it a good idea to let her know he wasn't a complete pushover. If she accepted and they were to spend up to three weeks together in a confined space, she had to know who was the skipper.

He noticed with satisfaction how her cheeks flushed a faint pink as she picked at the plate of grilled sardines in front of her. "Yes, I think so. The sloop on the left-hand side of the pontoon. White Lady…is that right?"

"Yep. So are you still interested?"

"She looks lovely, and yes, I am. Which island are you heading for and when are you leaving?"

"Great. I aim to leave for Antigua via the Canaries the day after tomorrow, once I've finished all my business here. Most of the supplies are already on board, but you can check them over and see if there's anything I've missed, as you'll be doing most of the cooking. Just a few house rules. I'm the skipper, and my word is final when it comes to running the ship. No drugs are allowed on board, and I keep your passport until we reach your destination—the Canaries or Antigua. Don't look so worried…that's fairly standard. Holding a crew's passport is a sort of insurance for the skipper in case you decide to jump ship as soon as we arrive and run off with all my money. It'll be locked up in my safe until we reach land. Oh, and no smoking. Is that okay?" He grinned and speared another sardine. Better to let her know his rules there and then and who was boss, woman or no woman.

Harry noticed she hesitated a fraction before replying and guessed it was because he mentioned hanging onto her passport. People often hated handing it over.

28

"That's fine by me. I don't do drugs or smoke, and as I've never been to the Canaries or the Caribbean before, Antigua will do nicely." She smiled and looked down at her food.

"You'll like both places. Just one more thing…mobile phones don't work at sea, so you won't be able to ring home for a few weeks at least."

"That's all right. I have no family."

Harry nodded, faintly puzzled by her compliant attitude. Apart from her slight pauses, she hadn't batted an eyelid. Was her bravado all show? Most people usually had more to say about relinquishing their passports to a comparative stranger, skipper or not. Neither did she seem very interested in where they were sailing. Was he making a mistake? He'd asked around earlier, but no one could tell him more about her. He gave a mental shrug. He needed to chill. He was in charge here and she'd do nicely.

She had all the necessary criteria for his needs. Youngish, apparently unattached and as she'd just said, no family. That last item was particularly beneficial. No one would come looking for her.

Hopefully, they'd get on well. He raised his glass in a toast. "To Antigua it is."

Chapter Five - Gillian

Well, that had been easier than she'd anticipated, Gillian thought as she undressed that night. There had been one uncomfortable moment when Harry explained about holding on to her passport. She'd have to find a way of putting him off until they were well away from land. The photograph inside her passport clearly showed off her long red hair, and if he'd been following the international press, there was a risk he'd recognise her. She'd think of something.

After sliding between the sheets, she reached for her handbag and withdrew her passport. She flicked to the back of her British-registered passport and stared at the details. Priscilla Gillian Hodges. The next-of-kin page was blank. She gazed at the photograph. It showed a woman with shoulder-length red hair. Now, her hair was short and dark. So what? Nearly all women experimented with hair colour and style. Who was to say which colour was real? She tilted the booklet to study the photograph more closely. Unfortunately, it still bore a good resemblance to her. Hopefully, Harry wouldn't even glance at it.

She tucked it back into the zippered compartment of her handbag and placed it under her pillow, before shuffling down the bed. She felt more edgy than tired and wondered whether sleep would evade her again.

The bedside lamp on the small table beside her gave out a bright light, but she didn't notice. Instead she drew comfort from its harshness. It had been years since she'd slept with the lights completely off. Even now, she still experienced recurring nightmares.

She turned onto her side restlessly and stared at the wall opposite. She had some money…almost ten thousand pounds, but it wouldn't last forever. She'd emptied Lawrence's hidden stash before leaving but was disappointed with the amount. She'd been taken in by his lies. She clearly remembered him saying he'd buy a house for them once he'd saved enough for a deposit. How could she have been so stupid? After only a few months, he'd demonstrated how manipulative and controlling he was. Then the abuse began. If only she'd found some way of escaping him, none of this would have happened. Thoughts of Nathan crept into her mind, and she felt fresh tears slide down her cheeks, soaking into her pillow.

Her eyes closed gradually as she felt lassitude envelop her and her body became heavy. Old scenes drifted into her mind: a tall, stern, upright man—her father. She could still hear his harsh, unrelenting voice as he dictated his decision. She had no say in the matter. Her mother was as severe with her own rules and beliefs as he: unyielding and unsympathetic. And perhaps because she was her mother, her forbidding attitude seemed twice as hard for Gillian to bear. Where had the feminine softness and understanding been when she needed it most?

She felt her body stiffen and her heart pound as she remembered what they'd done—and she so young. She'd hardly had any say in the matter. In the long days that followed, suffering with such confusion and misery, she withdrew into a shell of herself; then later, after being discharged from that abysmal hospital, she struggled to live a normal life. All she'd ever wanted was love.

Gillian grimaced as the scenes played out beneath the pale shutters of her eyelids. She sighed as a tremble passed through her body, betraying her self-confidence. *Be strong.*

Harry had suggested meeting in the hotel lobby after breakfast and he'd help carry her luggage over to the marina. The day after that, they'd leave Portugal and enter the Atlantic Ocean. Once they were well clear of land and people, Gillian was confident her self-assurance would grow. It had to. She prayed it would, as she knew there was no going back. Was Harry trustworthy? On the surface, he seemed to be. The only thing which made her hesitate was how he'd first stared at her at the marina bar. It hadn't happened later. He must have been assessing her credibility and working out whether to take her on or not, she decided sleepily.

Chapter Six - Harry

"Shore-side shoes can be left in the basket on deck. I'm sure you know the importance of not wearing them below," Harry said as he slipped his deck shoes off before climbing onto the passerelle.

Gillian surveyed the slim boarding ladder swaying slightly beneath Harry's weight. "Sure. Grit and other dirt. I'm fine with that. I like going barefoot, anyway."

He glanced down at her feet: neat with well-trimmed and unpolished nails. "Yes, plus roaches, cockroaches. Shoes have a nasty habit of picking up their eggs in the soles. Cockroaches mate once only and go on laying eggs for life. If you get an infestation below, it's almost impossible to get rid of the little buggers." He grinned as she shuddered.

"I never knew that. Definitely no shoes, then." Gillian handed her soft cases across to Harry, who swung them down onto the deck he was standing on. She removed her shoes and followed him across the passerelle.

"Welcome aboard White Lady. Have a look round the deck while I stow your luggage, and then I'll show you below."

While Gillian went forward along the outside deck, Harry climbed down the companionway ladder into the saloon below. The forty-foot boat was roomy inside. As well as the saloon and side galley, White Lady boasted two cabins for sleeping. Harry liked to occupy the aft cabin with the double bunk and allocated the forward cabin containing twin bunks for crew members. He placed Gillian's soft bags on the cabin sole and gave them a quick glance of interest. They weren't particularly heavy, which surprised him, as most women he knew usually carried far too much luggage. She was either frugal with her packing, or she disliked being encumbered by personal belongings. He guessed she'd left home in a hurry, as she'd intimated a stress of some kind or other. Man trouble, no doubt. He heard footsteps on the deck above him heading forward, and knowing he had a minute or two, swiftly unzipped the largest case. Slipping his hand inside, he parted the layers of folded clothing and searched through her belongings. Nothing of interest came to light, and satisfied she wasn't carrying drugs or weapons, he smoothed the contents back in place and refastened the bags. He realised she also had a small handbag looped across her shoulder but doubted she'd be stupid enough to conceal anything there. He felt no guilt about checking her luggage. He'd been caught out before, so he knew only too well that travelling alone with a stranger could have unexpected repercussions. As skipper, the buck passed to him. Plus, he had his own agenda and wasn't taking any chances.

He left the cabin and returned to Gillian up top. "What do you think, Gill? She's no spring chicken, but I'm very attached to White Lady."

"I think she's lovely, and I'm glad she's not a new yacht. I prefer older boats. Does she handle well in rough

34

weather?" she said, walking back towards the cockpit and climbing down to join him.

"Yes. Because she's a tad beamy, she's very stable, and so long as she's not carrying too much canvas at the time, she can cope with most weather conditions. I can usually sail her single-handedly, and it's only in extreme rough conditions that two people are needed. Shall we go below? You can explore while I fix us a drink. Sagres okay?"

"Sounds great."

Harry led the way down the ladder and Gill followed. He watched as she cast her gaze around the saloon and galley area with apparent interest.

"Your quarters are forward. There are twin bunks on the port side and heads including a shower on the other. Usual rules apply—short showers to conserve water and minimal amounts of paper down the loo."

Gillian nodded as she walked forward and peeked into both cabins. She looked back over her shoulder at Harry and smiled shyly. "Of course. I'm sure I'll be very comfortable." She turned back to the bunk room and took a longer look at the area. Harry had placed her bags on the cabin sole.

"I sleep aft. Have a look if you like, then when you're ready, come and have a beer. Here's to blue skies and calm seas."

After taking a quick glance at Harry's cabin, she walked the few paces back into the saloon and took the proffered bottle. Matching his beam, she joined him in a toast to their forthcoming trip. "Blue skies and safe sailing."

Chapter Seven - Gillian

She noticed at once that the zip on the larger bag wasn't quite closed. She guessed he'd taken the opportunity to take a sneak peek when she was on deck. At first, she deemed his action underhand and wondered if Harry wasn't all he appeared to be. After some thought, she changed her mind. Yes, it was a bit cheeky, but there was nothing incriminating in her bags, so she didn't mind. She'd have done the same in his position, for certain, and checked out her travelling companion. Harry was the skipper and had certain responsibilities. Besides, she had to keep reminding herself that not everyone was like Lawrence. Thank god.

"Make yourself at home as soon as you like. Check out the galley. You'll find the fridge and small freezer are stocked up, and we just have to take on the perishables like fruit and veg tomorrow. If you can take that small job on, I'd be grateful," Harry said as he opened a locker near the chart table and took out a life jacket and full set of waterproof trousers and jacket. She noticed he gave her body a cursory glance before holding them out to her. "These should fit, but make sure you try them on for size. I'm sure I don't need to tell you to adjust them as necessary. Ship's rules mean we wear a life jacket whenever we're on watch during the night. If either of us has to go out of the cockpit during a night watch, then we must be clipped on. If you or I fell overboard, I doubt we'd ever be found."

Gillian thought about her previous experiences of sailing at night: the boat silently slipping through the waves, an almost black sky enveloping them while a cold silvery moon hung suspended above the tall mast. At times, it felt almost eerie. If she hadn't been quite so desperate to get away, she wondered whether she'd have had the nerve to go at all. She enjoyed sailing in fine weather but knew how hazardous stormy weather could be. Night-time sailing also had its pros and cons. The time spent alone could be balm to the soul, but accidents and mishaps occurred at night all too often. Plus, small problems got out of perspective if you let them. Thoughts at night often played tricks on the mind.

She eyed the foul-weather gear and after putting her drink down on the saloon table, took the garments from his hands. "I'll try everything on before we leave," she said.

"Right then. I'll leave you to get acquainted with the boat. As I said before, if you think of anything we might need, let me know and I can pick it up before we sail. I'm off ashore as there are a few things I must do. I'll see you later. If you get off the boat, make sure you lock up and all the open hatches are locked on vent. This marina's pretty secure, but I prefer to be safe than sorry. Here's a key for you." He threw a cork keyring her way.

***

Gill unpacked her bags and placed her belongings into a couple of lockers in her cabin. She kept her passport and wallet in a body-pouch clipped around her waist, along with the rest of her cash. She glanced round the cabin. She wanted to hide her valuables, but guessed Harry would know his yacht inside out. She just had to take a chance he wasn't some kind of crook. She doubted it. He was obviously known around Lagos and no doubt in other ports of call both sides of the Atlantic. If he was a rogue, people wouldn't have been quite so relaxed and friendly round him, surely? She sighed as she closed the locker door. She was just naturally suspicious. Harry had treated her well, and seemed kind and reassuring. A little older and he could just about have been her father.

She wandered into the saloon and cast a critical eye over the upholstery around the cabin. White Lady wasn't a new yacht by any means. Harry seemed to keep a tidy ship even if it did need some tender loving care. The floor—or sole as she remembered its proper name—was scratched and worn in places. It needed a light sanding and varnish. She stole aft and again peeked inside the main sleeping cabin. She spied one large double bunk with lockers down either side. A door on the left proved to lead into a head, complete with shower. It all looked clean and shipshape but rather outdated. But there was one good thing. Having two loos and showers on board meant she didn't have to share the facilities with a stranger. There was something in small mercies.

She left the cabin and explored the galley. Like the rest of what she'd seen, everything appeared to function; the fridge and small freezer contained chilled and frozen foods, the water pumps sprang into life as soon as she turned on the taps. So Harry kept a serviceable, well-maintained ship, albeit not as luxurious as some floating palaces. White Lady was classy if a little travel-worn. She wondered whether Harry had money. He hadn't mentioned a house, but no doubt, once they got to know one another on the journey, he'd tell her more about himself.

But what about her? Her body trembled. She didn't want to disclose anything about her past if she could help it. A sudden ache filled her throat, which she thrust aside. How long ago was it that she thought everything was going to be all right? She liked Lawrence at first and enjoyed his company—before he turned into some ghastly control freak. She turned away from the galley area and strode back into the saloon. She wouldn't succumb to depression; she'd been down that route, and she remembered how painful it was to drag herself from the bowels of despair.

But she had to keep reminding herself that she wasn't just on the run from the law; she had to set herself free, too. To anyone else, this escape would have seemed like an adventure. Her stomach was churning as much from the stress of leaving as from the thought of what she'd done. It was too late now, though. There was no turning back.

Chapter Eight - Harry

Harry squinted up at the sky. It was the hottest day they'd had since leaving Portugal. The weather between Portugal and the Canaries during the winter months was generally balmy, and rain wasn't unknown. This time, instead of being around twenty odd degrees, temperatures were touching the low thirties. The wind had died during the last hour, and the lull which accompanied it had the additional unpleasantness of sticky humidity.

His attention was diverted by Gill climbing into the cockpit and handing him a cool beer. She sat down on the teak cockpit bench and sipped at her own drink, beads of condensation falling from the chilled bottle onto her shorts and tanned bare legs. Harry studied her covertly behind his sunglasses.

During the last few days, he sensed that a mutual respect had grown between them. It was too soon to call it friendship. Although she hardly said a word, preferring to read instead of talking, he realised he knew little more about her than when they'd first met. Apart from keeping herself to herself, he found her to be a good crew member. Gill stood her watches without complaint and didn't make a fuss when he roused her early in the morning to help him pole out the mainsail and gennaker. He knew that with a push, he could have done the job on his own, but because of the wallowing and roll of the yacht in the sluggish swell, it was easier and safer with two pairs of hands. She'd woken immediately with a light touch to her arm and joined him on deck, fully dressed and life-jacketed within a couple of minutes. Harry also appreciated that true to her word, she could cook and didn't seem to mind any task he gave her.

"Thanks. We might have to break the ship's rule and have an extra beer today. I can't remember it ever being this hot at this time of year."

Gill removed her sunglasses and dabbed at her face with a tissue. He noticed that her cheeks were flushed and watched with interest as a fine line of sweat ran down her neck towards her covered breasts. She wasn't his usual type; he preferred voluptuous blondes who enjoyed the idea of being on a yacht and didn't ask too many awkward questions. He'd never had the inclination to form a lasting relationship other than with Marlene. Women to Harry were merely part of life. He didn't treat them particularly well or badly and usually spelt out exactly what he expected of them. Gillian, however, had piqued his interest in an unusual way. It wasn't what she did or said…more like what she didn't say. Apart from his assumption during one of their first meetings that she had suffered a loss, he knew no more than that, and so far, she'd skilfully avoided any more personal talk. He decided if he wanted to make any headway with her, it would be up to him to make the first move.

"Will the weather last?" she asked eventually.

"According to the latest info on the radio, no. In a couple of days, things will be back to normal." Harry stood up and moved towards the front of the cockpit where the yacht's instruments were housed. As well as the usual depth gauge, speed and wind direction, the equipment included the latest radar and computer chart plotter. He played with the plotter for a minute. "At this speed of three and a half knots, we'll get into Tenerife just after dark. I think we'll take in some of the canvas and motor-sail the rest of the way. It would be nicer to arrive in daylight. Agree?"

Gillian nodded eagerly. "It would be nice to pick up some speed and at least have a breeze."

Harry started the engine and left it running in neutral while they brought in the headsail. The lightweight canvas was doing nothing useful except provide some meagre shade by hanging limply in the still air. Once safely stowed away in a forward deck locker, Harry turned up the revs and the boat responded; the bows slid through the glassy surface of the sea at a comfortable six knots. With a satisfied nod, he sat back down in the cockpit after fetching them both another beer from the galley. The boat was running happily under automatic pilot. He decided to stop shilly-shallying around. It was time to get to know Gillian better.

"So, Gill. You said you're from Surrey. Which part? Have you lived there all your life?"

He watched as she paused before answering, her mouth hardening at the corners. Was she preparing to prevaricate again? She shook her head. "No, Devon, but only for a short time. Before that I lived in Gloucestershire, when I was a child. We…moved around a bit."

He nodded as if believing her but sensed she was lying. She had a faint accent which sounded more like a Hampshire one. Portsmouth or Southampton, he guessed. Before he had time to frame another question, she beat him to it. "What about you? Have you always sailed?"

Harry shook his head. "No. I started in my late thirties. My father decided to buy a sailing boat, and we learnt together. He always owned motor yachts before that. He passed away, unfortunately, but he did leave me White Lady and his business."

"Oh? What type of business?"

"He owned quite a lot of land on some of the Caribbean islands. He was a good businessman, invested well. I prefer to sail."

"So who looks after the business for you while you're sailing?"

"I have a manager."

"Do any of your sailing trips involve business?"

Harry thought about her question for a few seconds before replying. He weighed up the consequences of how much to tell her. "Some, but I do the long runs because I enjoy them. No two trips are ever the same and never without some excitement. It's good to live on the edge sometimes."

"It sounds a good life. I...I envy you."

He grinned, realising that for once, he'd caught her interest. He wondered how much more alcohol it would take to loosen *her* tongue. "I fancy a glass of wine. Care for one?"

"Just a small glass…we've already had a couple of beers."

"Yeah, I know. Just this once." He slipped below and lifting the sole in the galley picked up a bottle of red from the Douro valley. He considered adding a crushed Rohypnol tablet but dismissed the idea. Although he wanted her compliant, he didn't want her helpless. Better if his seduction was subtle. When he returned on deck, Gillian was sitting on one of the cockpit cushions with her feet tucked under her bottom. He sat down next to her. "Cheers!"

"This looks interesting." She took a sip from the glass, her gaze resting on him timidly. "Wow! That's delicious. I think you're spoiling me."

Harry chuckled. "Maybe someone needs to. You seem distant and lonely at times. Are you going to tell me why you're really here? Travelling on your own…seemingly lost and sad."

She took a huge gulp of her wine. "I am alone. Completely alone. Both my parents are dead."

"I'm sorry. What happened? Or is it too painful to talk about?" He leant over and refilled her glass; she was almost pouring it down her throat. This was one miserable woman.

She shook her head. "No. They were middle-aged when they had me, so they were elderly when they died."

Harry watched her for a few minutes. She now seemed perfectly calm and in control. Even so, it didn't explain her distracted air when she thought no one was watching. "No partner of your own?"

Again, she shook her head, only this time, she turned to face him. He couldn't quite fathom the expression which flitted across her features, but he swore she looked despondent. "No. I've never had a serious partner. I lost a very good friend, who…he…he passed away."

"I'm very sorry to hear that. That's sad. You have my sympathies. Has it been long?"

In answer, she drained her glass in one go. He watched as she clutched the stem between her fingers. He noticed tears gathering in her eyes. Perhaps she wasn't so indifferent and poised, after all. He liked a woman who showed a degree of vulnerability. It helped things along. "Six months."

He reached out and placed his hand on hers. It felt cold despite the heat of the day. He decided to fetch another bottle of wine. "Stay there. I think you need another drink."

Chapter Nine - Gillian

She knew Harry had used the excuse to go below so that she could compose herself. She took in enormous gulps of air as she fought to calm down. She then sat upright, gave a loud sniff and stared across the cockpit to the horizon beyond. She had willed herself over the days to replace her earlier feelings of panic and worry into something more cold and detached. It was the only way she could cope with Nathan's death. She had no one to confide in. On hearing Harry's foot on the steps, she turned towards him, a tenuous smile in place across her face. She knew he was being kind and treading carefully around her, as if guessing how she felt. For the first time, she considered how nice he was. Far more considerate than that pig, Lawrence.

"Here. I know what I said about one drink only when sailing, but I really think you need this." He passed Gillian a full glass as he sat down next to her and placed the wine bottle in a handy fiddle on the binnacle.

"Thanks," she whispered and took a sip.

"May I ask what happened? Do you feel able to tell me?" His voice was low and calm, tender, as if caressing her.

She flicked a look his way and lifted her shoulders slightly. "Of course. He was killed when a burglar broke in. He was beaten up and died."

"That's awful. I'm sorry." Harry touched her hand again and rubbed her wrist gently beneath his thumb. Gillian glanced down, thinking with surprise how welcoming and comforting his touch was. She was right. Harry was friendly and kind. His eyes were warm and almost inviting. Surprised by her thoughts, she decided it was time to change the subject and show some interest in the port they were sailing to. She'd never been to the Canary Islands.

"Tell me about Tenerife. I've never been to the Canaries. Is there much to see? I feel quite excited about sailing into a new place. Is it all Spanish-speaking there? I don't know a word."

He laughed and Gillian frowned. Was he mocking her? "What? Have I said something daft?"

"No, not at all. I'm glad you're excited, really I am. You'll find the island quite touristy, and most people around the marina area speak English. There are fewer tourist traps off the beaten track, and Santa Cruz is nice. We'll only be there a day or so to take on water and a bit of diesel. You can have a few hours wandering around town. If it's scenery and nice quiet beaches you're after, then you're better waiting for the Caribbean…Tenerife's beaches can be busy. The island is volcanic in origin, and Mount Teide is worth a visit if we've time. They even get snow up there during winter." He poured a little more wine into her glass.

"Sounds good, interesting. I might just do that."

"Unfortunately, I don't have time to come with you, as I have things to do, but you can hire a car easily. That reminds me. I forgot to get your passport off you to put into the safe, but you'll need it when we check in, so you may as well hang onto it for now. And you'll need it if you want to hire a car—the hire-car companies will want to see it. They generally need some form of ID."

Maybe he wouldn't take her passport off her at all. She'd feel better knowing it was hidden away and in her safe-keeping. Anything could happen. As they say, *worse things happen at sea*. Besides, she might need it in an emergency. "That's true, they will. But it's a shame you can't come with me. It's always nice to have company."

Harry looked surprised and pleased at her comment. She noticed how his eyes sparkled as he took a sip of his wine. Perhaps she shouldn't have said that; it might have given him the wrong idea. How stupid she was at times. Perhaps it was best not to drink anything else—keep her wits about her. Not that he wasn't attractive for his age.

"There'll be plenty of time in each other's company. An Atlantic crossing takes anything up to three weeks. You might be fed up with me by then."

She laughed. "And you me. I take it I'm okay to stay on board all the way to Antigua, then?"

Harry studied her face, his gaze slipping down her throat and lingering for a few seconds on her breasts before travelling the full length of her body to her toes. "Aha. I have a feeling you and I will get along just fine."

49

Gillian sat back; her head was spinning a little from the alcohol. *Take it easy, girl, and think what you're doing. This is an older man you're talking to. He's been around, seen life, and he'll definitely get the wrong idea.* "I think so, too, and three weeks is a good time for restorative healing."

"It'll be a good start. I have a suggestion for when we reach Antigua, something that might help by extending your recuperation. A few more weeks will work wonders for you." He reached for the wine bottle and topped up her glass.

"Oh? I'm intrigued. Can't I know now?" She tilted her head. From the expression on his face, she guessed his proposal would be unusual.

He hesitated. "I have a house which needs looking after while I go away on business. You'd be completely alone but quite safe."

She sat forward, her face alive with interest. Safe and alone? It sounded like the perfect hiding place. Hang on, though…surely a little too good to be true. There had to be a catch. She frowned. "You'd take me there? Let me stay there for free?"

"Of course. As I said, it needs looking after…just a spot of cleaning and tending the, er, garden."

"A garden? Is it on Antigua? What is it? A villa or something?"

The skin around Harry's eyes crinkled as his smile deepened. "Not exactly. Somewhere much nicer than Antigua, and it's not a villa but a traditional house on a private beach. Trust me, you'll like it. You can visit Antigua before we sail to this place."

Was he having her on? So far, he'd been nothing but proper, but so had Lawrence at first. "It all sounds wonderful. I can't wait to see the islands and your house. Let me have a good look when we arrive, and then maybe, if it feels right, I'll help you out. You understand I have to be sure?"

"Of course. Look, believe me, if you don't feel comfortable, we'll forget about it. I won't be offended. But I bet you'll love it once we get there. Good, that's settled then." He raised his glass and chinked it against hers. "To our Atlantic crossing and possibly, your therapeutic new home. Another drink?"

Gillian grinned, hardly registering what he'd said as he went below decks. "Yes, please." She couldn't believe her luck. Not only was she getting a free ride across the Atlantic, away from everything she'd left behind and didn't want to hear about *ever* again, but she was going to stay on a beautiful Caribbean island for free *and* have unrestricted use of a luxurious house with its own private beach! Oh my god! Had she landed on her feet or what? Who was this man? Her saviour?

While Harry clattered around below, Gillian looked around at the wide empty expanse of ocean and then lay back in the cockpit. Through a woozy alcoholic haze, she gazed at the tall mast stretching up into the blue sky above. Harry must have been rich. His father had left him his business, his yacht, and now she'd just learnt he possessed a Caribbean house with its own beach. She wondered about that. Heavens, what if he was another Richard Branson and owned his own Necker Island? That would have been just too amazing for words. She stretched like a cat along the sun-drenched teak. Surely it was time for her to have a bit of cheer in her life for once? So far she'd had nothing but misery.

A footstep sounded on the stairs into the cockpit and turning her head, she saw Harry had returned with another bottle of wine. His other hand was empty, and she realised she'd drunk more than him but didn't care. The alcohol had rubbed off the edge of her fears and doubts. He placed the bottle into the safety fiddle, and before she knew what was happening, he leant forward and kissed her gently. Too surprised to do anything, she lay perfectly still. The kiss lingered on, and when she didn't move or resist, he pressed his body against hers.

One thought went through her mind, triggering an alarm bell. Is this what I want? Then, almost against her will, she was reminded of how she'd been starved of any loving or sexual contact for ages. And despite the difference in their years, his lips felt enticing and sexy. When his hands moved tenderly across her breasts, releasing the catch of her bikini top, she discovered she ached for more. Surely, just once wouldn't hurt?

Harry grabbed both her wrists in one hand and pushed himself up, his legs straddled across her waist. Fighting against the debilitating effect of alcohol, Gillian caught her breath in a rush of excitement as he slaked his gaze down her body before ripping off her bikini. His grip was tight, but the delicate kisses on her jaw and down her throat were as light as butterfly wings. She felt a sudden wetness between her thighs and ground her groin roughly into his.

Without realising, she moaned helplessly. "Yes, oh yes."

Chapter Ten - Harry

On reaching Tenerife and safely docked in the marina, Harry became more business-like. He wrote out a short list of groceries and handed Gill a hundred-euro note. "I'm not expecting the fruit and vegetables to cost anything like that, but I don't have anything smaller. Make sure the bananas are hard and green and get a large bunch. We'll have to split them, or they'll ripen all at once with this weather. All being well, you can go ashore and do your touristy bit tomorrow. We'll leave here the day after."

"Okay, that's great. Shall I get everything on the list in the market?" She scanned the sheet of paper.

"Yes, it's not a bad place to shop, and the prices are as good as any in town. I'll see you later. Maybe we can eat ashore tonight."

"That would be nice...our last meal on land before the Caribbean. It sounds almost romantic. Oh!" She laughed, and Harry realised she felt embarrassed by what she'd said. Since that first time in the cockpit, they'd had sex twice more, but he assumed they both knew it was nothing more than just that: lust, pure and simple. She grimaced at the amused look on his face. "Sorry, that sounds bloody corny. I didn't mean it to come out like that. But the...the Caribbean does hold enormous appeal."

Harry shrugged and laughed it off. "I'm sure you'll love it. Most people do. As I said, I'll be back later. Make sure you lock up properly when you go ashore. There have been thefts in this marina from time to time, and there's always someone looking for the main chance."

With an easy grace, Harry stepped from the cockpit, blew her an exaggerated kiss and left the yacht by means of the passerelle. He then gave Gillian a brief wave and set off down the pontoon. He teased her remark around in his head for a moment, wondering if she'd meant to let it slip out as a provocation, or if she'd spoken without much thought. The first-time sex with her had been surprisingly good and gone exactly as he'd planned. He'd maintained his own alcohol level lower than hers to keep ahead of the game, and he'd guessed right: she was vulnerable and pliable to sympathy. So much the better. He had such plans for Gillian.

***

Much later, after Harry had finished his spot of business in town, he headed back towards the marina. Everything had taken much longer than he'd anticipated. He glanced at the clock tower in the square and realised it was nearly ten o'clock. He assumed Gillian would have been hungry and would make some supper for herself; his own stomach was grumbling from hunger and one-too-many beers. Perhaps some toast and soup and off to bed.

"Harry! I hoped it was you!" He turned around at the slap on his shoulder.

"Theo. What are you doing in Tenerife? Last I heard you were in one of the old Soviet states, the Ukraine or Lithuania."

"Harry, old son, good to see you. Just the man. And no, not the Ukraine, Latvia."

"Right. Not too far off the mark then."

"Far enough. Anyway, I've finished my stint there." He thrust a hand in Harry's direction.

"So what are you up to now? A holiday?" Harry looked Theodore Jerome up and down. The man was his age. Unlike Harry, who was tall and slim, Theo was short and stocky. They were at public school together, but never real friends. Harry preferred sports and drama. Theo liked politics and debating, but Harry remembered he'd been a top shot in the school gun club.

"No, well…sort of. I was kind of half hoping I might run into you. Look, how about a drink? I'm parched. I've got an idea I'd like to run by you." He hitched his rucksack further up on his shoulder and glanced around for a likely bar.

***

Harry sat back, his legs thrust out in front of him. He knew he owed Theo a favour, but his timing was appalling.

"Just the trip over. It won't take more than, what? Two, three weeks?" Theo drained his glass and beckoned the waiter over. "Same again, plus more tapas, por favor," he said indicating the empty glasses on the tile-covered table. "I'll be no trouble, and besides, you owe me big time."

Harry glanced away, thinking about how this might pan out. He was making headway with Gill and his plans. He'd hate a cuckoo to fly into the nest. He turned his head Theo's way. "Sorry. Any other time, mate. Thing is, I've got someone with me already."

Theo chortled. "What's her name, you dirty bugger?" He leant his elbows on the table and stared unblinking into Harry's eyes. The alcohol didn't seem to have affected him. "Look, it'll make no difference. You won't know I'm around. I'll do my share of watches, cook as well, although my repertoire is sadly limited. When I'm off watch, I'll even stay below in my cabin if you prefer. I have weeks of sleep to catch up on after my last foray into the old European Baltic states. I need some rest. I swear you won't know I'm there. I'm a great sailor, by the way."

Harry remained unconvinced. Theo was unpredictable. At school, Theo would argue with some of the masters; he always enjoyed having the last word. Convincing, cajoling, insistent. He should have followed a career in politics— he was wasted in journalism, no matter how great the story he covered. Besides, Harry couldn't help feeling their coincidental meeting was no accident. Theo was as slippery as an eel and always had a hidden agenda. He guessed Theo had already spied White Lady in dock before their chance meeting.

"It's not that, I'm sure you are. It's more because of Gill."

"Aha! So that's her name. I'm sure I can persuade her I'll be invaluable as crew. I can even stand her watches as well as mine."

"No. I have to say no. You don't understand. She's not a people's person, likes her space. There could be trouble with three on board."

Theo's eyes narrowed, and he leant even nearer towards Harry across the beer-smeared table. His eyes were more bloodshot than when they'd first met that evening. "I'm not making myself understood here, am I? Harry, do I need to spell this out? I know what you get up to mid-channel. I'm not blind. Christ knows why you do it. It's not as if you need the money. Mexico, Colombia, the whole bloody Caribbean island chain. I'm just after a goddam lift away from here, for fuck's sake. I've had enough of flying to last me a lifetime, and between you and me, I want anonymity when I leave here."

Harry felt his face pale. He should never have underestimated Theo. He knew everything that went on over on the dark side. Friend or no friend, he wasn't worth crossing. Shit!

Theo sat back with a smirk and slapped his hand down upon the table. "So. Where's White Lady? I could do with a refreshing shower."

Harry set his mouth in a grim line. *As if you didn't already know, Theo.*

Chapter Eleven - Gillian

Gill listened without saying a word. It was Harry's yacht to do with as he liked. There was nothing she could do. She was perturbed about the sleeping arrangements, though. On small yachts, it was common for mixed crew to share cabins. They had some private time when their companion was on watch and vice versa. Even so, she disliked the idea of being in close proximity with someone she'd never met until just an hour before. There was also the chance he would ask awkward questions, too.

She and Harry were down below in his cabin while Theo was hogging the forward heads under the shower. His rich baritone could be heard while they talked. Harry must have been reading her mind as he reached for her wrist and gently pulled her towards him. He tilted her face with one finger beneath her chin and Gill let him. His smile was gentle and flattering.

"I understand you're a bit narked and upset, but I don't want you to be. There are two things we could do. You can either have my cabin to yourself and I'll sleep in the saloon, or we can…" He paused before murmuring. "I'd like it if we slept together. Don't worry. There are no strings attached to this suggestion. It's purely a solution to a situation I can't get out of, but it does have its own compensations, if you agree."

Gillian locked her grey-blue eyes onto his. Should she go along with this suggestion? She enjoyed sex for what it was—not that she wanted to give him the idea she was usually promiscuous. Although she realised there was little real sexual chemistry between them, just being held and caressed was enjoyable and comforting. It was only for a while, anyway. Harry had insisted there were no strings attached. "Maybe we could give it a try. It doesn't seem fair to turf you out of your cabin. There is one condition, though. I don't want to get pregnant, so we must use contraception."

Harry laughed. "No one's ever accused me of slipping up, but yes, that's okay by me."

***

As she packed up her things to take through to Harry's cabin, it crossed her mind, why couldn't Theo sleep in the saloon himself? After all, he *was* the last one to join the boat. His presence made her feel edgy. She resolved to keep a close eye on him at all times. Harry hadn't fully explained how he came to be there or why he felt obliged to give Theo a lift. But underneath Theo's warm grin and chumminess, she sensed an interest in her, which made her uncomfortable. She wondered what his real business out there was and realised she had to be on her guard. She couldn't let anything slip out about her other life.

She threw the remaining items into her bag and took a last look around the cabin. Apart from her scent, there was no trace of her ever being in the compartment. Theo's own belongings were strewn across the top bunk. She peeked into his half-unpacked rucksack and noted a few items of clothing and a small tablet. There was no sign of his mobile phone or wallet and passport, and she guessed he had them with him in the heads. She grimaced and almost laughed. All three people on the yacht seemed to have their own secrets…or was she imagining it?

Chapter Twelve - Theo

Despite his cheery voice bellowing under the shower, Theo was feeling anything but jovial. His sudden frantic dash and near-death escape from Algeria had left him more shaken than ever before in his life. He threw back his head, closed his eyes and let the water cascade over his chest and torso. He was getting too old for this life.

After leaving university, he decided he wanted to be a journalist. Over the years, he'd developed an interest in investigative journalism and the thrill and dangers that sometimes came with the undercover fact-finding. His expertise attracted the attention of others, in particular an intelligence officer within MI6, who was an agent runner. This agent runner at the sharp end of intelligence gathering saw potential in Theo and recruited him to willingly pass intelligence back to the UK government. Theo's intelligence work took him through many parts of Europe, the Middle East and latterly, Algeria, Tunisia and Morocco. The secrets he uncovered were passed on to a reports officer, who in turn passed the information on to the individual in Whitehall, who'd instigated the investigation in the first place.

This last intelligence cycle nearly ended in failure, and Theo escaped with his life only by buying his way onto a private yacht leaving the Spanish enclave of Ceuta in Morocco. He then travelled on various means of transport until he eventually arrived in the Spanish Canary

Islands. Theo had come to know Harry's irregular pattern across the Atlantic in both directions, and with luck and more than a bit of discreet networking, managed to dovetail his arrival on Tenerife to coincide with Harry and White Lady.

Feeling refreshed and cleansed of miles of dust and sweat, Theo turned off the jet and towelled himself dry. He'd offloaded his information back onto his agent runner before hopping aboard the yacht, and it was as if a huge weight had been lifted from his shoulders. He now needed to get some miles under his belt and drop off the map while he thought about which course he wanted to take. He wondered what his options were, as he was serious about a change in direction. Theo had saved enough money to retire on comfortably, plus what he'd inherited from his father—or the 'old man' as he still called him. The thought of a place in the remote Scottish islands, miles from the stench of humanity, appealed. His only regret was that he hadn't met a woman with whom he wanted to spend the rest of his life. He'd had a few women, but not one had captured his interest and heart completely. Maybe if he stayed long enough in one place, he might meet someone.

He grinned as he thought of Harry and his own life— similar in some ways, although Theo considered his was more legal, if not as lethal. So where did Gill fit in? It was obvious Harry was shagging her, even if she had kept the bulk of her belongings in the twin-berth forward cabin until now. How long had he known her? Did she understand exactly how Harry conducted his life? Her face had immediately caught his attention as soon as he set eyes on her. Not for her looks, which were interesting enough if not outstanding. He thought he'd seen her before, which was crazy, as he'd been incarcerated along the north coast of Africa for a few weeks. He'd kept up to date with world and UK news as much as could, though. Maybe something would trigger his memory and he'd remember.

Theo poked his head out from behind the door of the shower compartment, and as his cabin opposite was empty, moved across the passageway. He guessed the woman had taken the opportunity to move her luggage. Theo had a sudden flash as he recalled the look in her eyes when they were introduced; Harry had explained he was a journalist. Wary, he remembered. She'd been cautious and prickly when they shook hands. Now, what was that all about? He'd been around too long to have imagined it. The next three weeks might prove to be very interesting, and he'd enjoy seducing her secrets from her. Theo prided himself on his talents. He might not have been a secret agent in the Bond way, but he had his own charm and methods.

Chapter Thirteen - Harry

"I can't believe he's forgotten the time and that we're leaving in under ten minutes. He's a bloody menace." Harry paced the deck as he loosened the yacht's mooring lines ready to slip once they were under engine.

"Does it matter if we leave late? I mean, it isn't as if we have an appointment to keep or anything." Gillian asked. "Perhaps you're worrying unnecessarily. You need to chill a bit more." Harry glanced across the foredeck. She was sitting with her back against the mast, barefoot and nibbling an apple.

Surprised at her sudden and atypical forwardness, he was about to rebuke her when he noticed Theo walking along the dock towards them. He was carrying two fresh loaves of bread and a box which chinked. A newspaper was tucked under his arm. Theo tossed his shoes aboard before following them.

"Sorry if I'm a bit late, but I had to buy some of my favourite Rioja. Glad to add it to the store, Harry," he said with a grin as Harry stalked onto the aft deck.

"Thanks. That's all very well, but you're cutting it a bit fine. We're leaving any minute," Harry's voice held more than a hint of irritation, and he knew he was being unreasonable, but Theo's attitude was aggravating him. He felt even more annoyed when he noticed the look

Theo and Gill exchanged. "Come on. Get those bottles stowed below and prepare to slip the dock."

Theo looked round in surprise. "What, no time for a brew before we go?"

"No, we can bloody well have one once we're on our way." Harry leaned over and started the diesel marine engine.

"Righto, old son. Keep your hair on. Be back in a jiffy once I've put this lot away. I bought a paper. Interesting what I've been reading. I simply lost track of time." Theo crossed over to the steps but not before throwing Gillian a leer.

Harry turned to her. "Okay, you know what to do. Remove the springs, and then I'll let you know when to slip the bow and stern free. The fenders can come in once we're on the move." He indicated the ropes fore and aft. "I haven't got time to wait for him to get his arse in gear. Wasting time reading newspapers. That's what you get for having a journalist on board."

Gill was quiet as she went about her business, silently removing the ropes and coiling them, ready to be stowed away in lockers once they put out to sea. Once Harry had eased the yacht from her mooring and was happy with her progress across to the harbour exit, he glanced across to Gill. "Are you okay? You're not worried about being at sea for a few weeks, are you?"

She smiled, but he noticed how pale her face had become. "No, of course not. I'm fine, just a slight headache. I must have been sitting in the sun for too long."

Harry nodded, not entirely convinced. She'd been perky enough earlier. He recalled the early hours of that morning when he was feeling particularly horny. She hadn't been complaining of a headache then. He wondered if it was anything to do with Theo. He was an expert at causing mischief if he felt like it. He remembered the looks he'd thrown at her along with some needling. He overheard him asking her some personal questions too. She hadn't answered them properly and sidestepped the mild interrogation. "There are some paracetamol in the first-aid box. Take some before it gets worse."

Theo joined them on deck and helped Gill bring in the last few fenders, shoving them away in the deck lockers. "We won't be needing them for a few weeks," he said with a laugh. "Shall I brew up now? Or does anyone want something stronger?"

"You know the rules, Theo." Harry scowled. "Only one alcoholic drink while at sea and preferably with dinner. Tea will be fine."

Chapter Fourteen - Harry

Harry finished writing his entry in the ship's log for that day and put the book back on the shelf above the chart table. Since leaving Tenerife, they'd sailed a good distance towards their next port of call, Antigua. During their first few days at sea, the crew of White Lady experienced light winds and calm seas. They sighted many dolphins and the odd whale or two as well as sharks patrolling around the boat. Despite being an experienced diver, sharks always gave Harry the shivers. As they entered their second week, the winds picked up to a more exhilarating fourteen knots, and the yacht sped along, averaging a good five and a half to six knots. Harry was happy with his vessel; she favoured these conditions, gently listing onto her port side as the north-easterly, Beaufort force-four wind filled her sails. The sea was slight-to-moderate with waves no more than one or two metres at most. He sighed. If only every crossing were like this. He had the engine running to charge the batteries and make fresh water. Another twenty minutes and he'd switch it off. A slight noise on the deck above reminded him that Theo was on watch while Gillian was sleeping in the aft cabin. He knew he really should take advantage and turn in for his own six hours of off-duty. Not feeling particularly sleepy, he made some tea and carried two cups up into the cockpit. Ten minutes more wouldn't hurt.

The sky looked spectacular that night. A bold moon was rising aft of the stern, while above, the Milky Way stretched as wide and as far as the horizon allowed. Harry had read somewhere that the galaxy contained somewhere between one and four hundred billion stars but that the most you could see from any given point was two thousand at most. Even so, this ancient and beautiful warped spiral in the heavens never failed to impress him. He passed a mug across to Theo, who was standing and gazing across the cockpit sprayhood.

"Thanks, I was just thinking of making a brew myself." He sat down and took a swig.

Harry grunted and took a seat on the opposite side of the cockpit. So far, the journey had passed without any major arguments. At times, there had been a bit of minor bickering between Theo and Gill over whose turn it was to wash up or who'd left a glass to roll along the galley worktop and break when it fell in the sink. But Harry was no fool. As well as the niggling, he recognised a thread of antagonism running between his two crew, and he wondered why.

Off watch, Theo spent a lot of his time on his laptop. When Harry asked what he was working on, Theo told him he was writing up a series on the old Baltic States and intimated that one of the top geographical magazines was paying him a handsome figure on completion. Harry had often speculated whether Theo was playing some underhand game, masked by his journalist credentials. He knew he was clever and articulate, and it would have answered a lot of unasked questions—like his turning up on Tenerife, for example. Harry also knew he'd never get a straight answer. Theo always had some roundabout, yet plausible, reply.

"Gill asleep?" Theo asked with a nod in the direction of below decks.

"As far as I know."

"I guess you think you fell on your feet finding her as crew. She's a great cook."

"I did. It makes a change from living out of tins."

"So what happens once we reach Antigua? Has she somewhere or something else planned? I asked, but she's somewhat difficult to engage in conversation." His voice was level, clear and distinct.

"I don't know. She mentioned going through to Panama and then travelling overland, but as she hasn't mentioned it recently, she may have changed her mind."

"So, there's nothing between you two then? No romantic spark?"

"Good god, no! Once we reach land, I suspect she'll soon disappear onto some other boat. I have no plans to keep her around me or getting involved."

"Right."

Harry turned his head and stared at Theo through the moonlight. "Why do you ask? You don't sound as if you believe me." Harry felt a tingle of apprehension as he wondered where this was leading.

"Oh I do, old boy. I think she's a sea tramp looking for another free ride, but also ... "

"But?" There it was again.

Theo paused, and when he took time to raise his mug for a gulp of tea, Harry guessed Theo was about to disclose something he wasn't going to like.

"Tell me, what do you actually *know* about the woman?"

Harry shrugged. "Not a lot. You know the circumstances and where we met. Nothing more. As you've just said, she's not very talkative."

"I would suggest her past is more dubious than yours. What if I told you she was on the run…wanted by the law?"

It was Harry's turn to pause. He felt his pulse quicken with excitement. "To tell you the truth, I wouldn't be surprised. Everyone does something stupid in his or her life at least once. I do what I do because I get a kick out of it. It's what makes us human."

Theo shook his head. "I'm not talking about something like a parking fine. Have you considered she might be dangerous?"

This time, Harry laughed. "Have you really looked at her? Slim as a whippet and not exactly built like a female wrestler. No, I don't. Yes, she has secrets, but don't we all? You may be right about the law, but dangerous? No, I can look after myself."

"Have you checked her ID?"

Harry shrugged. "I've seen Gill's passport and it's her photo inside. Longer hair, but I reckon it's accurate and valid. What else should I have done?"

"Did you check the name inside?"

"Yes. She prefers using her middle name. Lots of people do, so what?"

"Did the name Priscilla Hodges mean anything to you?"

"Nope."

Theo shook his head. "You really should pay attention to the news more. Priscilla *Gillian* Hodges is wanted in connection with the death of a friend."

Harry nodded slowly. "I knew one died about six months ago. She told me all about it. He fell victim to an assault by a burglar. Gill said that's why she left England. She'd had enough and wanted to get away and come to terms with his death, as it was difficult back home. There's nothing wrong with that, surely? His death has been so painful for her."

Theo leant closer, and Harry could clearly see the whites of his eyes in the bright moonlight as he emphasised his words. "He died *less* than a month ago. And it was no burglary. She was there in the house. She killed him and then turned on her boyfriend. Left him with a huge laceration to the head, and he might never live a normal life. As soon as I saw her, I was sure I'd seen her face somewhere. It's been weighing on my mind, and then it all clicked into place this afternoon. I was going through some research notes about violent crime in Estonia and I came across a piece I'd downloaded earlier. The link just jogged my memory. I bet you a tenner she killed him. You could well be shagging a murderess! I think that challenges your own violations of the law, don't you?"

Harry expelled air through his mouth. "Bloody hell, you can't be serious?" He glanced in the direction of the aft cabin hatch which he noticed was open a few inches for ventilation.

Theo continued. "That's not all, as I recall—"

He was interrupted by a sudden thud against the hull and both men shot up out of their seats. "What was that?"

Harry hurried from the cockpit after ensuring his safety line was hooked on and leant over the guardrail. He fished a torch out of his pocket and peering down into the water, saw they'd hit something floating. He shone the torch down onto the flotsam. "It's a wooden pallet, and it's entangled in netting. If I cut some of the loose netting off, can you bear away? We can't drag the thing on board and we don't want to have any nylon rope around our prop."

Theo leapt towards the wheel and flicked a switch on the console to turn the autopilot to manual. Once Harry had given the order, by turning the wheel, Theo steered the craft away from the floating driftwood. Once satisfied they were clear of the debris, Harry climbed back into the cockpit, dragging a bundle of wet netting with him. "That should do it. Floating junk on the seas causes no end of trouble. We'll dump this when we reach Antigua." As he was speaking, the engine's gentle throb changed to a sudden knocking noise.

"Bugger. That doesn't sound too promising. I'd better go below and take a look. Look, we'll talk again tomorrow. I want to have a think before we go accusing anyone," he said. He turned the engine off and left Theo alone in the cockpit while he went below to investigate.

***

An hour or so later, Harry emerged from the engine compartment. He'd finally sorted the problem and was desperate for some sleep. Sweating profusely after being confined in the small engine space, he stepped out of his oily shorts and T-shirt and left them lying on the floor. Clouds had drifted over the moon, but he could make out a pair of legs standing in the cockpit and glancing at his watch, saw that Theo still had an hour and a half of watch to complete before Gill took over. He decided not to talk to him, as he'd lost precious hours of his off-watch time and needed to crash. Harry blinked the sweat from his eyes and dried his face with the galley hand towel. He didn't want to disturb Gill in the aft cabin, so he made himself comfortable on the saloon sea berth. He knew he'd be asleep in seconds.

Chapter Fifteen - Harry

Harry yawned and stretched. His mouth tasted rancid and his throat as parched as a desert.

Glancing at his wristwatch, he saw he was due to take over on watch within half an hour. First, he needed a hot shower and a mug or two of tea. He sat up on the bunk and swung his legs down onto the teak-and-holly wooden sole. His head felt pretty muzzy, and he remembered that due to that night's activities, he hadn't got his full quota of six hours' sleep. Perhaps he could catch up later if they had an uneventful day at sea.

Eventually, he was awake enough to stand and wander over towards the galley. Passing the steps and glancing up towards the cockpit, he saw Gill sitting on the bench, book in hand and reading with the aid of a tiny torchlight. The events of the night before flooded back to him, including Theo's outrageous accusations. He frowned. He knew he should never have agreed to Theo joining them on this crossing to the Caribbean. He should have done something about him. Theo had intimated back in Tenerife that he knew all about his misdoings, and one word could have brought the whole of Harry's world down. And if he was right about Gill, he had them both by the short and curlies. As for Gill's crimes, he couldn't say he was taken aback; apart from her grief, he'd always felt she was keeping some dark secret. Then there was that remoteness about her, which intrigued him. But murder? It could explain her reticence to talk about her life or fill him in with anything other than the bare bones. Harry stood where he was and scrutinised her face for a minute before silently moving into the galley and picking up the kettle. Once filled and the gas lit, Harry stalked through to his cabin. He stripped off his boxer shorts and stepped into the shower, the warm water hitting his sweaty skin and reviving him instantly.

As he lathered the soap, he asked himself whether his crew and temporary bed mate really was a murderess and whether it bothered him. He wasn't surprised to discover that it didn't. In fact, as he ran his soapy hands over his torso and thought more about Theo's words, the idea was turning him on. Instead, he fantasied about having sex with someone who would stop at nothing—and that included murder.

***

"Quiet watch?" Harry asked as he climbed up into the cockpit, two mugs of tea in one hand. He handed one to Gill and leant against the binnacle while scanning a full three hundred and sixty degrees across the sea. The wind had freshened by a couple of knots, and the yacht slid easily through the water. "Looks like we might have a spot of rain before too long." He indicated ahead; a sullen patch of cloud sat squarely between clearer air. Behind, in the east, the sun was just breaking above the horizon.

"Very quiet. I'm afraid I completely nodded off at one point. I was lying in the cockpit on my back, counting shooting stars one minute and dreaming the next. We had a few spots of rain an hour ago but nothing much."

Harry sat down and drank some of the tea. He looked at her over the rim of his mug. He imagined her killing her friend and wondered if the crime fitted her personality. She didn't have a strong body, so anything physical seemed unlikely. Could he imagine her wielding a weapon? Maybe she preferred the more devious methods for murder: poison, asphyxiation, drowning or pushing someone out of an open window.

"Shall I get breakfast? I thought bacon butties this morning would be good," she said, standing up and glancing down at him. She moved towards the steps and unzipped her life jacket before tossing it down onto the cockpit bench.

"Sounds good to me. We'll have ours and then wake Theo. He had a bit of a scare on his watch. We ran into a pallet and I had to cut it free. I'm surprised the bump didn't wake you."

"Really? I didn't hear a thing." Her eyes were wide on hearing his words. "I slept so heavily. It's funny, but I'm sleeping better on board than I have for years. Once my head hits the pillow, that's it. Out like a light until it's my turn for watch."

"Lucky you. I spent another hour or so in the engine compartment. It was bloody hot, I can tell you. That's why I didn't disturb you by coming into the cabin. I thought crashing out on the saloon bunk the sensible thing to do."

She smiled. "That's thoughtful. Thank you. I'll get on, then. Theo can have his breakfast when he wakes."

Harry leant back, his hands locked behind his neck. Squinting, he cast his skipper's eye up at the rigging, down the mast and along the spars. Everything looked shipshape. The mast creaked as the yacht rode up one side of a wave and slid down the other side. The side decks were clear, apart from a few flying fish, which had no doubt jumped out of the water during the night. They'd make a tasty breakfast; maybe he should add them to the frying pan. He glanced behind on the aft deck and noticed that one of the stanchion guard-wire safety lines around the deck had come undone. He got up immediately to close the pelican hook and so complete the safety guard. He squeezed it shut and found it responded with little effort; he wondered why it was open. Stupid to have missed that…and dangerous. Maybe it had just worked loose and he needed to service the gate eyes and pelican hooks; it wasn't a difficult job, and he could do it once the light was better.

Within minutes, Gill reappeared with two plates. The smell of fried bacon filled Harry's nostrils, making his mouth water, and he bit into a sandwich with gusto. "Delicious," he mumbled between mouthfuls. "There's nothing like a bacon sarnie at sea. Did you save enough for Theo?"

Gill nodded as she tucked into her own breakfast. "I've left the bacon warming in the pan, but knowing Theo, he'll more than likely smell it in his sleep and be up before we've finished."

"He does like his food. I'll put the kettle back on for more tea and then go and get him. You stay there and finish your sandwich." He picked up their two empty mugs and stood up.

"There's plenty more if you want another," she said moving her legs aside to let Harry pass as he clambered down into the galley.

"Great. I'm bloody starving this morning."

Harry put another sandwich together and filled the kettle for tea. He grabbed a third mug from the cupboard and then walked forward through the saloon to Theo's cabin. The door was shut and he gave it a knock. As there was no answer, he knocked again before glancing in the heads opposite. Nothing. "Theo?" Harry called, at the same time as he pushed the cabin door open.

The cabin was empty.

Chapter Sixteen - Harry

Harry strode back along the saloon floor until he was standing at the bottom of the steps. Gillian eyed him with a frown.

"What's up?"

"He's not there!"

"What do you mean, not there?"

"What I just said. His cabin's empty."

"Have you checked the loo? Or the forward sail locker?"

"Yes. I tell you he's gone."

Gill gave a short laugh. "Don't be daft. What about your cabin? Maybe he's playing tricks on us. What a childish thing to do."

Harry spun around on his heel and stalked into the aft cabin. The cover on the bunk lay in disarray, and Harry twitched it aside. The double berth lay empty, except for a sarong Gill used as night attire. He threw back the door to the heads and peered inside. He marched back to stand at the foot of the steps and glared at Gill.

"What?"

"What have you done?" Harry shouted.

"Done? Me? I don't understand." Gill stood up.

Harry ran up the steps and grabbing her arm gave it a violent shake. "He's nowhere below and there are fuck-all places up here to hide. He must have handed his watch over to you. What happened during your watch?"

Gill shrank before his glare and pulled her arm back. "Ow, get off! What are you on about? Yes, he woke me at two, and I dressed immediately and went up on deck."

"Did he stay on deck or go below."

She paused in rubbing her arm and frowned. "I think he went straight to bed. I didn't see him again."

"So he didn't come up here again?"

"No. Haven't I just explained?"

"So where is he?" Harry clapped a hand to his head and looked out to sea, far behind from where they'd sailed.

"I did go to the loo not long after I took over," she said in a quiet voice. "I had a bit of a stomach ache. Must have been the fish curry I made. I suppose I was down in the heads for at least five minutes or more."

"Jesus, he must have come back up on deck for some reason and gone overboard."

Gillian gasped and joined Harry in gazing back at their wake churning behind the stern. Eventually, it was she who spoke first and she half turned her body towards his. "What shall we do?"

Harry's gaze flickered down to Gill. "We should go back. Do a figure of eight search."

"But it's been almost five hours since I last saw him. What are the chances of finding him?"

Harry's stare was bleak as he studied the woman in front of him. "I know. Five hours is a bloody long time. He must have been wearing his life jacket, as there's no sign of it on board. Even so, there are plenty of sharks in the ocean. You've seen them snapping at the food scraps we throw overboard. No one can survive in the sea too long. Plus, hypothermia sets in pretty quickly."

Gillian turned back towards the churning sea behind the yacht's stern. "So we'll never find him," she murmured. She turned her head a fraction and she held his gaze. "How awful. Poor Theo."

"You heard what we were talking about last night."

"I heard what he said about you," she countered, sticking her chin up slightly in defence. "Even so, we should—"

"We'll not talk about this again. Understand?"

There was a palpable pause between them, before she answered. She shuddered, and then, it was as if she hadn't heard the previous conversation.

"Some more breakfast, Harry?"

In answer, he pushed her up against the binnacle and kissed her roughly.

Chapter Seventeen - Gillian

At first, Harry's behaviour shocked Gillian. Guilty or not, ninety-nine per cent of people would have turned the boat around and spent the daylight hours criss-crossing the track from which they'd just sailed in search of the missing crew member. But as she thought more about it, she realised that with Theo's disappearance and certain death, it would solve Harry's own problem, as well as her own.

Yes, she'd heard everything Theo had said via the open hatch, and at first, she'd lain there in a cold, terrified sweat. If Harry believed Theo, then he'd hand her over to the authorities as soon as her feet touched the Caribbean sands. But as she listened, willing her racing heart to slow down and for the pounding in her ears to cease, she heard, crystal clear, the rest of Theo's statement. Harry was up to his neck in something criminal, and it didn't take much to put two and two together. A fast yacht with plenty of hold space, regular trips across the Atlantic, a locked cupboard surely containing firearms and then there were Harry's 'business dealings' on both sides of the ocean. Oh yeah. She was sure Harry wasn't simply buying and selling trinkets and beads from and to the locals. All in all, maybe Theo's disappearance couldn't have come at a better time.

She removed the rest of her clothes and stepped under the shower head. As water cascaded over her head and body, she trembled. She felt an ache between her legs; Harry had been rough and used her quite brutally the last time. The bruises on her upper thighs were coming out, and no doubt, she'd have duplicates on her back where he'd crushed her against the yacht's metal binnacle. And he didn't use contraception despite her protests. Men were such disgusting pigs at times…and liars. She decided that as soon as they reached the Caribbean, she'd stop sleeping with him. She was also having second thoughts about visiting his 'island'. What on earth had she got into this time? Why did she make such a mess of her life over and over again?

Should she find out for herself just what Harry did? She thought back to when she'd first shared Harry's cabin. He was on watch and Theo was quietly tapping away on his laptop in the saloon. She knew Harry kept his personal items in the deep locker on his side of the double bunk and decided she'd have a quick look while he was engaged.

The previous day, she'd entered their sleeping quarters and found him with his back to her, staring at a photograph in his wallet. As Gillian wore no shoes, he wasn't aware of her presence at first, and it enabled her to catch a glimpse of the woman in the photo as she looked over Harry's shoulder. Within seconds, he'd snapped the wallet shut and whirled round. Gillian instantly dropped her stare from the wallet to the cabin floor. "Have you seen my deck shoes. Oh, there they are." She promptly snatched them up and left the cabin. As she left, she thought she could feel Harry's eyes boring into her back, but she acted as if she hadn't seen anything and certainly didn't mention the photograph. But, who was she? She recalled a woman in her thirties, with short dark hair, rather like her own, now that she'd dyed and cut it. Was it an old flame? A sister?

Back to the present, once she'd showered and dressed, Gillian lifted the lid to the locker and after sifting through Harry's effects—a paperback, torch, small camera, odd shackles and various bits of string—found what she was looking for. She flipped the wallet open and there was the woman, her serene gaze staring at the owner of the camera. Her mouth was upturned at the corners in a small smile, faint lines around her mouth and on her brow. Despite the softness of her face, Gillian thought she looked preoccupied. Again, Gill found herself puzzling over her identity. Could she have been Harry's wife, even though he'd said he never married?

More secrets and she wondered for the umpteenth time how much she could trust him. But looking on the bright side, because each knew the other held secrets, neither could tell on the other. Once in the Caribbean, she felt sure he would let his guard down and she could slip off when the time felt right. In the meantime, she would make out she was enjoying his company and that everything was fine.

***

"We'll have to rearrange our watches. You'll have to cope with less sleep."

"I'm sure I'll manage."

"The trade winds have been more fickle in the last few years due to climate change. Let's hope we've really caught the trades now and can keep up this speed. Stronger winds will easily shave a few days of our journey."

"That's good. We'll get to Antigua sooner. I'm looking forward to seeing the island."

Harry didn't answer. Instead, he climbed from the cockpit out onto the deck. He took his time, checking lines and rigging. Gillian watched him from her seat, her eyes half closed against the glare from the sun overhead. She felt a subtle change had come over Harry ever since Theo had disappeared. They no longer shared the double berth in the aft cabin, as someone had to be up on watch every hour of the day. He still demanded sex, and usually, this took place on deck, or it was a quickie on the saloon berth. Gillian tried not to care about his use of her body, shutting her mind to his rough embraces. As far as she was concerned it was a means to an end. She'd give him the slip as soon as they reached land. As they neared the island chain, she realised her period hadn't appeared. She always insisted they were careful, but for the first few times, they'd had unprotected sex. She pushed any unwelcome thoughts out of her head. A lack of periods meant any number of things. Besides, she'd been through a lot of emotional distress—no wonder her cycle was erratic.

Chapter Eighteen - Gillian A week later

"That's the island we're heading for…Isla de Cabra," Harry cried, pointing to a speck in the distance just visible on their port bow.

Gillian squinted until she could just make out something resembling a dot jutting from the sea. She knew the mainland of Colombia was further off to their left, but she couldn't make out any reassuring smudges of land on the horizon at all. She stifled a sigh. Harry had explained only two days earlier that they were bypassing the Caribbean island chain and instead heading straight towards Colombia.

"Why?" Gill asked with a puzzled frown and a feeling of unease running through her.

Harry shrugged. "Just because. I thought it prudent not to call into Antigua just in case Theo sent a message to someone there. You never knew with him. This way, we can rest assured no one will think of looking for us here if…and it's only an if…he sent word."

Gill wasn't sure she agreed or believed Harry, but she nodded reluctantly. She wasn't happy to miss out on Antigua, but guessed that Harry was thinking of them both. "Okay, I suppose. But what is this Isla de Cabra? What does that mean, anyway?"

"Simply, goat island. Don't worry, you'll enjoy it there. It has the most beautiful beaches, and the fishing over on the east side is good enough all year round to be self-sufficient. It's still part of the Caribbean, and it's where I planned on taking you later, anyway. We're just not going to Antigua first. We can later…after your stay on Cabra."

Gill blinked and pulled a face. "I've never fished before. You'll have to show me." She gazed up overhead at a pair of large sea birds and recognised them from the day before as being the magnificent frigate bird. These huge black birds with white chest plumage had kept them company ever since the yacht had entered Caribbean waters. They swooped lower, and she watched in silence as they played on the gusting wind. Harry had already turned away and gone down below.

As the hours passed and the island loomed closer, the waves grew bigger. Gill looked at the white caps turning the sea into a heaving frothy mass. The boat responded and drove through the waves faster and faster. The island appeared to rise from the sea, and by now, Gillian could make out a small hill, dotted with vegetation that looked like palm trees. Harry appeared back on deck and grinned at the sight of the approaching island.

"Not long to go now." His hair had grown longer during the past weeks and the wind caught it, blowing dirty-blond locks around his lean sun-tanned face. "We'll lose some sail soon and slow the boat down. There's only one place to anchor and it's on the leeward side. Every other place on the island is just too damn rocky."

True to his word, about a mile out, Harry lowered the mainsail, and White Lady continued under headsail only, the wind still pushing them strongly from behind. By now, Gillian could smell the land, earthy and humid, as well as making out what looked like a tiny inlet between the island's outer rocks.

"Surely we're not going in there? It looks far too small. What about rocks and coral beneath the boat's hull?"

"Just you leave the navigating to me. I've done this many times, and if you know where to look, there's a small passage just wide and deep enough for a single boat to get through." He switched on the engine and took in the headsail by using the winch.

Gillian stayed silent, watching the recording of the ever-decreasing depth below them on the instruments, her stomach churning at the thought of running aground or being speared by a jagged tooth of rock beneath them. As they motored slowly into the tiny channel, Harry pointed to the small hill in the distance.

"Behind that hill is your home for the next few weeks. You'll love it," he said with a grin and suddenly put the engine into neutral. "Just make sure we stay in this position while I run out the anchor." Harry ran along the deck and opened the anchor locker. Within seconds, Gillian heard the whine of the motor up front as the anchor paid out. Harry returned to the cockpit and after letting the boat settle in the now-gentler breeze, put the engine in reverse to dig the anchor in. After a minute or two, he seemed satisfied. "Well? What do you think? Your own Caribbean island."

Gill looked round the tiny anchorage. They were almost enclosed, apart from the narrow entrance channel, by huge granite rocks. Ahead of them stood the hill and below it a glistening, white, sandy beach, about one hundred metres wide and fifty metres deep. It was stunning.

"It's gorgeous. Nothing like what I was expecting. I thought there'd be a jetty at least."

Harry laughed. "Why? No one comes here. I run the dinghy straight onto the beach. Come on, let's get ready to go ashore."

They'd already packed up the stores of food to take onto the island, and Gill had thrown her belongings into her two bags. Harry lowered the dinghy from its supporting davits and secured it to the stern of the yacht. "We'll need to make two trips. I suggest we take your things ashore first, and then I'll come back for the remainder of the stores once you're safely on dry land. You can explore the house while I make the second trip."

Gillian sat in the front of the dinghy, her luggage and a few bags of stores lay between her and Harry who steered the boat towards the shore. As they touched the sandy bottom, Gill scrambled out and guided the 'rubber duck' up onto the beach. Beneath her bare feet, she felt the sand scrunch up between her toes.

"Oh wow! This sand feels like talcum powder."

Harry indulged her with a grin as he hopped out to stand beside her. He immediately began removing the rest of the items from the dinghy. "Welcome to your new home for the next few weeks. You go on up while I get the rest of the things. Just follow the contour round the hill, and you'll soon see the house."

"Won't I need a key?"

Harry had already pushed the boat back into the shallows and climbed back in. "What for? As I said before, no one comes here, and the only locals around are miles away. They know this island belongs to me, anyway, and know to keep away, as it's private. Smugglers used it in the past but not nowadays."

Once he'd started back across the tiny bay to White Lady, Gillian picked up her bags and began the climb up and around the hill. Away from the open seas, Gill discovered they'd lost the strong wind which had accompanied them for so many days. The heat was oppressive after the cooling breezes, and soon she was sweating as she toiled up the slope. She also realised after missing her footing twice that she'd acquired a rolling gait after being at sea for so long. 'What shall we do with the drunken sailor' entered her thoughts.

Rounding the corner, she was met with a huge surprise. She'd imagined a large Caribbean-style house with a wrap-around veranda and lush plantation gardens; this was nothing of the sort. Instead, she was confronted by a small wooden building. Thinking she'd made a mistake, she stumbled over the sand, wondering if the main house was further on. But no, a quick scout around showed that this was the only building on the island. What the...?

Feeling her temper rise, she dropped her bags and marched up to the front door. Maybe she'd misheard Harry when he was describing the place. Had he said she was to expect something resembling a palace? If it was ghastly inside, she wouldn't stay. No way. She'd insist he take her off.

The door opened to her touch immediately, and inside, she found it remarkably cool and fairly dark. The bottom three feet of the walls were made of stone, and the higher parts of the walls and ceiling were wooden. Gill walked over to the two windows and pushed the shutters open to let the light stream in. She could see the sea in the distance and wondered why she hadn't seen the house when they were sailing far off. She assumed it was because of the surrounding trees. Glancing round she saw that everything looked clean and tidy, if a little spartan.

The main room was obviously used as a sitting-room and kitchen. She eyed the sofa, which was made of stout rattan and covered with pale-coloured cushions. Another fabric-covered rattan chair stood nearby. A small table and two chairs were placed beneath one of the windows. Beneath the other window, she found a small ancient-looking stove next to a floor cupboard and tiny area of worktop for preparing meals. There was a small door to the left of this, which she opened, and on peering inside, assumed it to be a small larder. On the adjacent wall were a number of shelves plus a further cupboard and a door leading to the one bedroom.

This room contained a small double bed and a chest of drawers with a lamp on it. The window looked out onto a patch of land, which could have once resembled a vegetable garden, as she recognised certain plants. She inspected the inside of the chest of drawers and discovered a few sheets and pillowcases for the bed. Gill walked back into the main room. Where was the bathroom?

She explored the immediate surroundings outside and discovered a tiny shack behind a row of trees. She discovered a loo inside, which after inspection, she guessed was probably one of those eco-friendly composting ones. She pulled a face but on lifting the lid, realised thankfully there was no awful smell. But where was the shower?

"Here you are. I've brought everything up," a voice said behind her, making her jump. "Sorry, I thought you'd seen me."

Gillian spun around. "Oh, you gave me a fright. Where's the shower?"

"There isn't one."

"So how do you expect me—"

"Follow me." Harry took her arm and led her a short way beyond the glade of trees and up a small path between a group of granite rocks. Gillian gasped.

"Is that fresh water?"

"It is. In fact, it has more than a fair share of natural salts, so I suppose you could call it a natural spa."

Gillian moved nearer to the rock pool, which resembled a small almost square bath and dangled her hand in the water. "It's warm! How lovely."

"Have you seen the rest of the house?"

She nodded. "Yes. I have to admit it's nothing like I expected but…"

Harry immediately looked disappointed. "But, don't you like it?"

Gill smiled reassuringly. "Despite what I originally thought, I do. It's unpretentious and simple. I like it. But what about cooking? How does the stove work?"

"Ah, that's easy. Gas. Just your ordinary liquid petroleum gas. You'll find a cylinder in a small cupboard outside the kitchen window. I have a spare with me, so you won't run out."

"What about electricity? Does that come from the solar panels on the roof?"

"Yes, but although we get plenty of sun, when it's raining, the electricity produced drops off a bit, so you have to watch that. There should be enough for your needs in the evening, and there are plenty of candles in the cupboards."

"And food? I see there's no fridge."

"No, a fridge would soon drain the solar power." He took her hand and led her back towards the house and into the main room. "The larder is okay for most things, but you'll have to eat the fresh things first as they'll go off. Make sure you keep the perishable items on the granite shelf, as it's cooler than the wooden ones."

"Okay. I noticed there's a key hanging on a hook just inside the larder. What's it for?"

"Ah! I nearly forgot. It's for the 'safe room'."

"Safe room? What's that?"

Harry crossed his arms and leant back against the wall. "It's something I built some time back. It's a hidden room that's lockable. I thought it might be prudent to have one in case of any drug smugglers in the area. But before you object, I've never had to use it. Look, it's here, under the rug."

He kicked a cotton rug to one side, exposing a square of wood. There was a lock one end and a small handle to lift the trapdoor. He lifted it for her to see. "There's nothing down there except for a camp bed and an oil lamp, if I remember. It smells dank, as it's never been used—I tend to forget it's even here. The steps are a bit crumbly in places, so I wouldn't go down if I were you." He dropped the cover and pushed the rug back in place. "So, what do you think?"

As Gill stared down into the dark cavernous hole, old memories flew into her mind. A feeling of nausea flooded into her stomach, and it was all she could do to stop herself gagging. She took two steps back and shuddered. After counting to five, she raised her head and managed a small smile. Get a grip, she told herself sternly. It's only a small cellar and it's safely hidden beneath the rug. She'd never need to venture down there. She took another slow turn around the house, taking everything in, willing her heart to steady itself. Could she stay here? It felt more inviting than she first thought. Quiet, with no sound other than the gentle rustling in the nearby trees and birdsong. It had a calming, tranquil effect on her. She turned to the view from the windows. She could make out the white tops off the waves and the deep blue of the sky. It was a far cry from the wet and dismal England she'd left far behind…and all its menaces. But, it was *only* for two weeks. Coming to a decision, she turned back to Harry with a big smile on her face. He was right. It was the perfect place to hide for a while.

"I think I'll learn to love it here. Yes, I'll give it a go for a few weeks."

"Good girl, I knew you would. The perfect place to come to terms with your…loss."

Gill locked eyes with him for a moment before his gaze flicked to one side. She wondered why he looked away. What was he thinking? Despite the heat of the day, a shiver ran through her, and for one split second she wondered whether she was making a mistake. It was remote. No TV, no telephone. No other visitors. But she remembered Lawrence and Nathan…all the things she'd done and left behind. And then there was Theo…would Harry report his accident overboard once he reached Antigua? No. There was definitely no going back.

Chapter Nineteen - Harry

"So, shall we have lunch and then explore?" Harry said once all the provisions had been put away in the larder and cupboards. "Sandwiches okay?"

"Fine. Yes, lunch and then I'd love to look around. Maybe take my first Caribbean swim."

"Oh yes. We'll have to make sure you try out the lagoon."

Harry unpacked a wad of cheese he'd taken from the yacht's fridge and after cutting thick slices of bread, added a spread of butter and cheese. "Pickle?"

Gill nodded and wandered over to pick up the two plates. They'd moved the table and chairs outside earlier, and the tiny veranda was the perfect place to eat lunch. They wolfed the sandwiches down, accompanied by a can of lager each.

"We'll clear up when we get back," Harry said, leading the way down behind the house. "Isn't this fabulous? Peace and quiet, no traffic or pollution. A lot of people would give their eye teeth for this." He stalked along a small path, which led out onto a clifftop. Looking ahead, they could see for miles and miles across the sea. There wasn't sight or sound of anyone else in the world.

"It's wonderful," Gill agreed. "Imagine living here full-time. It's the perfect place for a writer. No interruptions. What a place to bring small kids for a few weeks. They'd have plenty of space to run around in and a lovely beach for sandcastles and paddling." She looked down at her feet. "What are those droppings?"

Harry stopped and glanced down at the ground. "Goats. There's still a small herd on here. I keep a check on their numbers and have to cull some from time to time. Otherwise they'd ruin all the vegetation."

"Not while I'm here, I hope?"

"No. Shall we go for a swim?"

Harry grabbed her hand and led her back down to the beach. The sun seemed hotter, once they were out of the light breeze from the cliff top, and they stripped off their clothes within seconds. As soon as Gillian entered the sea, she gave a shriek of delight.

"It's so warm! I've never swum anywhere as warm as this before."

"You haven't lived."

"We can't all be toffs."

Harry laughed out loud. "Is that what you think? You're wrong. True, I did go to public school in England, and my father did have money and land in these parts. But, that's as far as it goes."

"Well, it's beautiful here. Why don't you live here all the time?"

"I spend long periods here from time to time. But it really does need someone keeping an eye on the place, and I do have other things to attend to."

Harry chose that moment to swim away from her as if he was giving Gill the distinct feeling that she wasn't to bring up the subject again. She trod water for a minute and then dived down towards the bottom. When she surfaced, she shook the water from her ears.

"Harry! Was that a phone ringing?"

Harry swam back to her side. "What?"

"A phone. I swore I heard a phone ringing."

Harry blinked and shook his head. "No, it's impossible to get a signal here. You must have heard the wind blowing over the rocks. Sometimes you get the most unusual sounds."

"It sounded like one. Anyway, I know it couldn't have been mine, as the battery's completely flat. I'll recharge it some time."

Gill looked towards the direction of the house. It was a fair way from the beach. "I must have been imagining things." She glanced in the direction of where White Lady was anchored. The boat swam serenely on her anchor. She frowned.

Harry noticed her attention and swam closer to her. He encircled one arm around her waist. "Do be careful when you're swimming alone. Keep within your depth. I've rarely seen a shark in here, but there are plenty outside the lagoon, beyond the reef, and they can come in. Remember that, and don't venture outside or into deep water."

He stared into her eyes and was gratified to see them dilate with fear. Letting her know about the perils outside would ensure she stayed within the island's narrow confines.

Chapter Twenty - Gillian

Later that evening, Gillian's thoughts returned to the sound she'd heard from the beach. She didn't need to be reminded of the outside world, but the idea of being in danger, any sort of danger or emergency, kept returning. The last thing she wanted was to be found by the authorities. But knowing that help could be at hand if needed would have been reassuring. She was certain it had been a phone. If so, then why did Harry lie? Was she being stupid to think she could trust him even a little, especially knowing they had collaborated over Theo's disappearance? She felt as if cold fingers were walking down her spine, and she shivered. She didn't want to be controlled again.

She was sitting on the step of the veranda after their evening meal. Harry had cooked dinner, saying that since it was going to be two weeks before they saw each other again, he wanted the evening to be special. Afterwards, after pouring her a large gin and tonic (no ice), he insisted she sat still and relaxed while he cleared up. She could hear him whistling as he clattered away in the kitchen area. Was she being stupid? He seemed so agreeable most of the time. Much more chatty and amiable than when they'd first met. His smile seemed to be special and just for her that night. If he'd been younger, she could have easily fancied him, and that day, he couldn't do enough to make her feel happy and reassure her about being safe on Isla de Cabra.

Gill leant back against the step pillar with a sigh as she thought about home. Nathan and Rebecca. She took in a huge gasp of air, and somehow, it turned into a sob. She missed them so much. She put the empty glass down on the corner of the step and lowered her head to rest on her arms folded across her knees.

It didn't seem like any time had passed before she suddenly felt Harry's arms around her, drawing her against his chest and talking in a soft and gentle voice. "Don't cry. It's going to be all right," she heard him say. She knew she'd have to stay on the island for a short time; it was the only option.

"I've opened a bottle of wine. Look, it's still cold from White Lady's fridge." He picked up Gill's glass and filled it to the brim. "Shame to waste it."

They both took a mouthful. Gillian rolled it around on her tongue. "Nice. I know nothing about wine, but this is lovely."

"Sancerre. It was my...my late mother's favourite," Harry replied, pausing in the middle of his sentence. Gill flashed him a look, wondering if he'd been about to say 'my wife's', only to change his mind. She still knew little about him, and in all honesty, she'd have loved to have questioned him about the woman in his wallet.

Somehow, before she knew it, they'd downed the whole bottle, and she was actually feeling much happier. That night, when they shared the bed, Harry was a lot gentler than the last time they'd had sex, and he remembered to use a condom. Gill wondered if it had anything to do with being on his island and him leaving her for two weeks or if he genuinely felt remorse at the harsh way he'd treated her on the yacht.

She woke in the night to the sound of Harry snoring by her side. The beer and wine seemed to have knocked him out, and her bladder felt so full she knew she had to relieve it. Gill slid from beneath the thin cover and tiptoed out of the house and over to the toilet shack. The moon was well up, throwing a silver shadow over the tiny path she took, while all around, she could hear the rhythmic voices coming from the tiny colourful tree frogs.

Once back in the house, she remembered the ring tone. It would be easy to check through Harry's few belongings, but for what purpose? She was only going to be there for two weeks. What could happen during that time? The last thing she wanted was contact with the outside world. She wandered back through to the bedroom. She was going to stay, anyway; the solitude would do her good. She climbed back into bed, and Harry's arm snaked round her waist. "Where have you been?"

"The loo."

"You'll be fine here on your own," he replied as if knowing what she'd been thinking.

"I know. Two weeks is nothing."

***

Harry was up and about soon after eight o'clock. He made bacon sandwiches for them both and soon after, said he was leaving.

After they'd walked down to the beach, pushed the dinghy across the sand and said goodbye, Harry hesitated.

"What is it?" Gill asked.

"Nothing much. Few people ever come here, but if they do, I wouldn't approach them. I've never seen anyone come ashore, but just take care. See you in two weeks." And before she could argue, he was gone.

Gill watched the yacht with Harry on board disappear down the channel and then lost sight of them. All at once, she felt an overwhelming sense of isolation. She'd never been so alone in her life, so far away from another human being. She mulled over Harry's last warning and decided that if anyone did appear, she'd hide. It was probably all academic and Harry was being overly protective, but she'd be careful. She ran back to the house and stood on the veranda. Harry's yacht was nowhere to be seen. He must have gone around the island.

Puzzled, she frowned. She'd assumed he was sailing back to Antigua. For the first time, she realised she had no idea where he was heading.

Chapter Twenty One - Gillian

That day was just like any other on the island. Gill awoke after a cool and refreshing sleep to the sound of humming birds just outside the bedroom window. Their tiny wings beat so many times to the second, they were quite dazzling to watch, like tiny jewels fluttering around the plants in the overgrown garden. After a breakfast of a cereal bar, she wandered down to the bay. She realised from looking at the thin line of surf that the tide in the Caribbean was almost negligible and wondered whether this part ever suffered from the tropical storms that threatened the rest of the area. She sat down on the sand and looked up at the sky. There was a constant mewing from scores of birds, which Harry had informed her were terns, and she supposed they used the island as a nesting area. The trees at the back of the beach rustled with the breeze, and the tall sea grasses seemed to wave in response. Gill already felt at home on the island. She had a routine of sorts but generally pottered around for most of the days. After shoving her worries to the back of her mind, she realised that home back in England seemed so unreal. All she could remember was a place of cold and wet and years of deep disappointment.

Gill had walked around the island many times now. The whole place could be circumnavigated in just over the hour, and it was an easy walk for someone relatively fit. Whilst exploring, she discovered the island contained several animals as well as countless birds and frogs. At night, many bats flitted around the trees, and she guessed they were fruit bats out for their nightly forage. There were also glimpses of another type of animal which resembled a sloth, clinging to the upper branches of the trees, but being no zoologist, Gill couldn't be sure.

The goats came and went around the house. None of the animals seemed to fear her presence. She was a complete girl Friday without Robinson Crusoe. For the first time, she felt empathy for all those people who were slaves to a Monday-to-Friday job. She was happy there on a beautiful island, and best of all, she had it to herself.

After her walk and a half-hearted attempt to try her hand at fishing with the line Harry had left, she decided to take stock of the food left in the larder. Gill knew there was no butter or cheese left, and they'd scoffed the last of the bacon the morning Harry left. She found lots of tinned stuff: tomatoes, soups, pulses, a few stewed meat chunks in gravy. There were plenty of long life-milk cartons that were well into their use-by date, rice and pasta. The bread had all gone, and Gill had no flour to bake any…not that she knew how. All the foods were basic staples, but with the few fruits on the trees that she recognised, she knew she wouldn't starve. At least, not for a few weeks.

Gill had remembered to grab a few paperbacks off White Lady's shelves, and they helped while away the long evenings, which were dark from the time the sun set at exactly six each evening. Sunrise and sunset at six a.m. and six p.m. was something she could never get used to. She was more accustomed to England's longer days and nights during the summer months and shorter, darker, winter ones.

Once she felt sleep steal over her, she remembered to make sure the front door to the house was secured. Gill had always lived in a locked house, and despite Harry saying no one ever went to Cabra, she wasn't going to take any chances of someone creeping up on her at night. One of the chairs wedged beneath the door handle seemed to do the trick, and she slept with a hefty chunk of wood by her side. The window had a good lock, so that was safe. Nothing was going to happen, but it was better not to take any chances. Looking back over the preceding few weeks, Gill knew that living by and on the sea had done her good. She felt different, cleansed even. Maybe it was living without other people nearby: people and their toxic ideas and ways.

Late afternoon, the wind got up for the first time since she'd been on the island. It blew hard from the south-east, and the house was partly protected, being on the west side. The trees around her swayed, the grasses whipped around her legs. She wandered down to the beach for a swim and searched the sand for unusual shells before going into the water. The surface was disturbed by the wind entering the bay, and Gill swam further out than she had before. It was then that she saw the black fin rippling through the wavelets in the boat passage towards her. Panicking, she struck out for the shore and didn't stop until she'd reached about a foot of water. She hurled herself out, coughing and spluttering up onto the beach and finally collapsed after retching up a few mouthfuls of sea water. Looking back at the lagoon, she searched for the shark's fin, and saw it circling around and round. She was trembling with her lucky escape. Harry had cautioned her to be on the lookout and she had ignored his warnings.

For the first time, she felt lonely. Maybe not even that. Perhaps it was just a case of feeling sorry for herself. Gill suddenly realised she had been ticking off the days before Harry returned. But she had no idea whether it was company or him she craved.. It had been ages since she'd felt like that: confused and aimless.

She picked herself up from the sand and wandering along the water's edge, glanced down at the footprints she'd made earlier when searching for shells. As she walked farther and onto a new stretch of beach, she suddenly stopped and stared in horror. There, sketched out in the sand was her name. Not just Gillian, but her full name: Priscilla Gillian Hodges. She looked around her, staring into the dark shadows beneath the trees. But apart from the boughs stirring and waving in the strong breeze, she saw nothing else moving. Who knew her full name? Harry had never actually taken her passport from her, although he'd seen it. She'd never pointed out her first name was Priscilla. Gill studied the words, and her eyes darted across the sand, searching for another set of footprints, but it was smooth nearest the sea, and above, it looked as if it has been brushed.

She was frightened. It was obvious she wasn't alone.

Chapter Twenty-Two - Gillian

Gill hurried back up to the house. She was in three frames of mind, swinging from fear to panic and to anger. Fear that someone was out to scare her, panic that they knew who she really was and anger that someone, probably Harry, was playing silly buggers. She rushed into the bedroom and armed herself with her wooden club. She placed it behind the door of the main room. Lying around outside were a few large rocks, which she also collected. Finally, in the kitchen, she selected the largest and sharpest of the knives. She planned on tucking it into the back of her shorts and carrying it with her at all times. Once finished rushing around and arming herself, a new and sudden horrific idea entered her head.

What if...

What if Theo hadn't drowned at sea? What if, by some slim chance, his life jacket had saved him and he'd been picked up by another boat? Fucking hell! That meant not only did he know her true identity and secrets, but he'd know she and Harry hadn't bothered searching for him. Neither did they report his disappearance. At any rate, they'd be charged with attempted manslaughter or possibly murder. Together with Nathan's death and Lawrence's injury, in another life, she would have been hanged for her misdemeanours.

Evening was approaching, and as she hadn't eaten much that day because she'd been feeling queasy, she decided to make an early evening meal. It would help focus her mind on other things, if nothing else.

Gill rooted through the small collection of canned foods and plumped for stewed beef and onions. There were a few shrivelled potatoes and carrots left (nothing seemed to survive long in the heat), which would help make a nourishing stew. After peeling and washing the fresh vegetables, she cut them up into small pieces and placed them in a saucepan with a little water. The hob had worked well since she'd been there, and she hadn't needed to strike a match to light it. Nothing happened and after checking the burner, she assumed the gas had run out. It didn't matter—she recalled Harry saying he'd leave another gas cylinder, so armed with her club, she opened the door cautiously and slipped outside. It was nearly dark; there was no such thing as twilight in these latitudes, and she hurried around the back of the house to where she assumed Harry had left the spare.

She found the original gas cylinder sitting on the ground but of the spare, saw no sign. She rushed around, checking the house and immediate grounds, even the shack containing the loo, but couldn't find it anywhere. Frustrated and hot after her efforts, she returned into the house and barricaded the door behind her. Gill slumped to the floor in despair and thought about what she could do. The only alternative to heating the food was to build a fire outside, but she hadn't any immediate fuel and didn't relish the thought of scurrying around in the dark looking for firewood. Not with someone out there watching.

Could they have taken the cylinder? Her scalp tingled as pin pricks ran up and down her spine. If it wasn't Harry, then who was it and why? Gill's hands were shaking, as she scrambled to her feet. There was nothing else to do except be vigilant and take her mind off things by keeping busy.

After calming down, Gill gave herself a stiff talking to. She'd been living under Lawrence's thumb for too long, and now had to be stronger and firmer. Once Harry arrived, she'd give him a piece of her mind and insist he took her off the island at once.

First, she needed to eat. The only alternative was to find something else or just eat cold tinned beef. Feeling despondent and annoyed with Harry for forgetting to leave the extra gas cylinder, Gill switched on a light and sat down to a miserable supper of a cereal bar and a mug of room-temperature long-life milk. She resolved to get up early the next day, dig a small firepit and collect plenty of wood for burning.

Gill took a quick résumé of what she had: enough food until Harry returned; electricity and candles; warm water to bathe in and fresh water to drink. She felt relatively safe in the house and determined she could put up a fight if necessary. Even so, it took a while to drop off to sleep despite having many lit candles in the bedroom.

**

The next morning, the sun rose as normal, and as she looked out across the sea, the entire horizon was streaked with blood-red clouds. Gill had eventually fallen asleep in the early hours and as she gazed at the glorious scene, wondered what the new light and new day would bring.

Back inside the house, which was really nothing more than a cottage, she glanced around her surroundings. The place seemed so empty. She pulled her handbag out from under the bed and searched through her diary. She felt sure Harry was due back any day, and was surprised to discover she was delighted it was to be next day.

She had been stupid. She should have insisted on having some form of communication with him. What idiot lets herself be stranded on a semi-desert island with no means of calling for help? Anything could have happened. There was the shark for one thing and then no gas, and what about that unsubtle little message written in the sand? Sticking to her earlier decision, she resolved once again that as soon as he arrived, she was going to insist he took her somewhere more civilised. Maybe he had another house less cut off. Or maybe she could stay on the boat for a while.

Feeling suddenly dizzy and sick, Gill realised she hadn't eaten anything that day. She forced an over-ripe banana down and then set about collecting some wood. There would be a roaring fire, at least for that night.

Chapter Twenty-Three - Gillian

The next morning, after a handful of dried nuts for breakfast, Gill ran down to the bay to check Harry hadn't arrived early. The bay looked enticing, the water so clear and breath-taking, but completely empty. She dragged herself back up to the house and set about organising everything. She wasn't a particularly tidy person, but it gave her something to do, and she did want Harry to see she was capable of looking after his place, lent to her by way of kindness.

She stopped what she was doing and thought. Was it kindness? He'd said originally he had a house which needed tending. Looking around the place, it hardly needed the attention he'd led her to believe was necessary. What *was* his aim? Or was she just naturally suspicious after living with Lawrence? And how was she going to go about asking him whether it was he who'd drawn her name in the sand? He wouldn't think her insane, would he? Maybe she'd just forget it, as she was leaving the island anyway.

Gill packed her two bags and left them on the bed ready to be carried down to the bay. Harry might want a quick walk around the island after being at sea for a few days, as she presumed he'd come across from Antigua. There was no hurry to leave Cabra. She went outside again and scanned the horizon in the direction she believed White Lady would come from.

113

There was no sign of her yet, so she decided to wander down to the beach for a last dip. Rounding the hill, she couldn't believe her eyes. There she was—gently tugging at her anchor and Harry already rowing the dinghy in to the shore.

She ran down the hill. "Harry!"

He looked up from where he'd just expertly run the boat up onto the sand and was preparing to jump out. Gill didn't wait for him. Instead, grabbing hold of the painter she gave it a tug. The rubber dinghy slid a few feet up the sand, clear of the water. She then turned and gave Harry a hug. "I'm so pleased to see you."

Harry looked surprised but didn't push her away and returned her smile. "I said I was coming back, didn't I?"

"Yes, but…" she stopped. There was no need to let him think she'd missed him; they were hardly an item. It was a strange relationship. He bent down and picked up a couple of grocery bags. It was then she noticed he had more lying in the bottom of the dinghy. He handed her the two bags without a word and picked up another two.

Before she had a chance to ask about them, he got in first. "Have you any coffee left? I could do with a cup?" Without waiting for an answer, he started up the hill.

Chapter Twenty-Four - Gillian

Gill trailed after Harry up the hill. The bags were heavy and after peeking inside, she saw they contained fresh vegetables. Why on earth had he brought so many fresh groceries with him? Was he planning on staying on the island for a few days? After they reached the house, he dropped the bags in the kitchen area and then plopped himself down in a chair on the veranda.

She suddenly remembered the lack of gas. "I can't make coffee…there's no gas left. You said you'd leave a spare, but I couldn't find it anywhere."

He rolled his eyes. "I did, you silly woman. Did you look at the back of the house?"

"Yes." She let his derogatory expression of her go this time.

"I definitely left a spare." With a sigh of exasperation, he stood up and stomped round the corner to the rear wall. Seconds later, he reappeared holding a gas cylinder. "Try the hob now. This is the empty. I've connected the new one. Next time, you could try looking a little harder."

What the fuck? Gill was about to tell him there wouldn't be another time and that she had looked properly, when he forestalled her. "About that coffee…I'm parched, and I've brought some iced buns to go with it." He gave Gill that lopsided grin she'd become accustomed to, and despite herself, she couldn't help grinning back. She decided to let it go. What was the point of arguing? They needed to maintain a good relationship.

While they were sitting and downing their coffee and delicious buns, Gill asked him what he'd been up to. He shrugged. "This and that. I had some business to attend to and ended up sailing down to St Vincent. After I'd finished there, I called in to Margarita before coming here."

"You have a lovely life, sailing around all the islands. Do you…do you own property anywhere else?"

He hesitated a second before replying. "Just the one house on Antigua. I have some land there and a few acres elsewhere. If you've finished your coffee, shall we go and get the rest of the stuff down on the beach?" He stood up and gestured for her to follow.

The dinghy was as they'd left it, and he hopped on board and passed the bags over. She was again surprised at the amount of stuff and said so. He laughed. "It's not that much, and as I usually keep a good quantity of tinned stuff on here, I bought extra. Last time I was here on my own, I whittled the stores down. Plus, I did think about staying a few days here before moving on. Try a bit of fishing."

They carried the bags up the hill between them. Gill's first thoughts had been right. He needed a short break. She nodded and at the house, began unpacking the food. She was surprised to find a supply of women's sanitary products in with the new soap and deodorant. Gill looked across at Harry, who was staring at her.

He shrugged. "I thought you might need them."

In fact, thinking back, she hadn't menstruated since arriving in Lagos, and it was now getting on for seven weeks since then. She wasn't certain but assumed Nathan's death and stress had affected her cycle. One thing she was sure of—she didn't want Harry to know her personal problems. "Thank you. I've nearly run out, and these will do for next time. Oh good! You've brought some more bacon. I was dying for some a few days ago and steaks! Yum. This is like Christmas!"

"I thought I'd cook tonight. I see you've started a firepit. I can barbecue the meat over that. There's plenty of fresh stuff for salad."

"That sounds really good. I feel ravenous already."

He removed his cap and tossed it onto the table. Gill noticed his fringe was shorter than the last time they'd been together, and realised he'd had his hair trimmed. His face seemed fuller, rounder. Maybe it was the cut, or perhaps he'd been out wining and dining during the last two weeks on Antigua. She put their dirty coffee cups into the sink and suddenly felt him close behind her. She jumped and turning around, found herself imprisoned in his arms.

He kissed her, and she could feel the cupboard and sink pressing into her bottom as he forced her backwards. At first, she resisted, startled by his sudden pounce, then as

she felt his lips linger across her throat and down to the
hollow in her shoulder, she gave in with a shudder. She
was almost ashamed to admit it, but she was only human,
after all; it *had* been two long weeks since she last had sex.
She craved to be touched, and Harry made short work of
rediscovering all those secret places of hers. Within
minutes, they found themselves in the bedroom, and he
pushed her down onto the bed. Gill gave a cry of surprise
when he straddled her, pinning both wrists together in
one hand. She had forgotten how strong he was. Her lust
grew when he kissed her some more, and he thrust his
other hand up beneath her top.

Gill gasped as his fingers found her nipples, rough skin
against soft breasts. He released her wrists and used his
free arm to support himself while gazing down at her.
"It's been a while," he murmured as he slid his legs down
from her waist and alongside hers. He yanked her top off
and tossed it on the floor; her bikini pants following
quickly. She wanted him as much as he seemed to want
her and ground her hip into his groin.

***

It was late when they woke from their post-coital nap.
The pillows had slipped onto the floor; the top sheet lay
rumpled and damp beneath their sweat-dried bodies. A
cooling breeze filtered in through the window, and Gill
moved cautiously in bed to find out where she ached the
most. Harry obviously enjoyed rough sex, and she
wondered whether it was because he was older and not
getting it regularly or whether it was just the way he was.
She sat up and winced as she recalled the earlier pumping;

it seemed older men had great stamina. All the same, she didn't like it. It reminded her too much of Lawrence, and he'd forgotten the bloody condom again.

Harry stirred and blinked. He gave her a half-smile, yawned and then sat up after looking at his watch. "God. Is that the time?"

"Does it matter? You said yourself you needed a bit of a holiday."

"True." She was lying on her side, and he suddenly moved forward and slapped her bare bottom.

"Ow! What was that for?"

"Because I felt like it and you have a nice arse." He swung his legs to the floor and got up from the bed. He pulled on his tattered shorts and looked around to go out of the bedroom.

Annoyed at his arrogance, Gill suddenly decided it was time to air her fears that she believed someone had been on the island the day before. "So, you see, and I know this sounds daft, but what I'm saying is someone must have written my name in the sand. No one knows I'm here except you, and as my name is different to that on my passport…"

Harry looked surprised and did a double take. "Me? You think I somehow sailed in here without you noticing and wrote your name in the sand? Pull the other one, you silly woman." There! He used that derogatory term again.

"Harry, I'm *not* a silly woman and I'm bloody serious. If it *wasn't* you, it must have been someone else and I have no idea who that could have been. You haven't told anyone about me, have you? Sort of let it slip out in conversation?" She could hear the barbed sarcasm in her voice.

He walked over to the window. Leaning on the window frame, he gazed out over the garden. After a few seconds, he spun round. "No, definitely not. I tend to keep this island secret back in Antigua. Apart from a choice few, no one knows about Isla de Cabra, and I mean to keep it that way. You must have imagined it or written it in your sleep. Do you sleepwalk?" It was his turn to treat her words with derision.

She gave him what she considered was her best withering look. "No, I bloody don't. If it wasn't you, then the only other person I could think of was Theo."

"Theo?" Harry's expression was one of sheer horror, just how she imagined hers must have been when she first thought of it. "Theo? Now I know you've lost the plot."

"What if he didn't drown? Was found by a passing ship and somehow followed us here?"

"Not a chance in hell. Nobody can survive the Atlantic for long and being picked up by another boat is a one-in-a-million shot. As you saw yourself, there are plenty of hungry sharks following yachts across the ocean."

"I know, but who then?"

"Have you rubbed out the lettering?"

She shook her head.

"Then I suggest we go and take a look."

They dressed and hurried down to the beach, but in her heart, she already knew what they'd find.

Nothing.

"See. Just your imagination," he said scornfully and then seeing her look, gave her waist a squeeze. "It's easily done. The sea can make crazy patterns on the sand. Come on, let's get supper on the go. Sex always gives me an appetite."

Gill said nothing and let him guide her back up to the house. She knew she hadn't imagined it. But he was adamant it wasn't him and they'd agreed Theo had drowned.

He stopped beside the house and looked down at her pathetic attempt to dig a firepit and barbecue. "I think you need to gather some more wood in case you need a fire in an emergency. Get some small stuff as well as these big logs. Small twigs will catch light more quickly."

"Okay." She wandered around gathering wood. She felt tired and dirty after carrying all the food up, and then their afternoon of rough sex. She also ached inside. Harry seemed happy, stalking around, picking up a few fallen branches and stacking them in a pile, all the while whistling as he worked. As she watched him out of the corner of her eye, she suddenly realised what he'd just said. *Just in case you need a fire in an emergency.* Why? If she was going to leave with him after his few days' rest, then surely there was no need.

Was there?

Chapter Twenty-Five - Gillian

When she woke the next morning, she lay awake for a few moments remembering where she was and the events which had taken her there. She shifted around in the bed and saw from the empty space that Harry was already up and about. She relaxed, pleased to have a few moments to herself. She'd always enjoyed her own company. It gave her time to reflect and consider what her next action should be. She'd let Harry have his few days on Cabra, even put up with his rough sex if that's what it took, but she sensed the real need to move on. He already thought he knew what she'd done. Theo had seen to that. But the last thing she wanted was to let him have some hold over her, blackmail even. Most of all, she knew she had to keep him on side.

Gill rolled onto her side and left the bed. She deserved a bath after the previous night's sex. She picked up her towel and walked outside. She glanced around but saw no sign of Harry, and as the fishing line he'd brought with him was missing, decided he'd taken himself off as he'd promised yesterday. *A couple of freshly caught fish for supper would be lovely with salad and sauté potatoes*, she thought. It brought a smile to her face. They could use the barbecue again. There was something nice about outdoor living in a tropical place, and many people would have given their eye teeth to experience it.

She stepped into the natural bath and with a sigh, allowed the warm water to stream over her body. Harry had certainly found himself a little bit of paradise. She lay back, soaking her hair, and then standing up, soaped herself all over. It was easy to just dunk down and rinse afterwards. After a final soak, Gill left the bath and tucked the towel around her body. Her hair would dry naturally in the hot air.

Everything was so quiet as she walked back to the house; even the birds were silent in the lush vegetation all around. She reached the house and went inside, wondering if Harry was back, waiting for her to join him for breakfast. But the place was still empty. She pulled on a bikini and sandals and decided to find him.

She guessed where he'd be: on the other side of the island. He said the water was deeper and cooler that side and attracted better and bigger fish for eating. She wondered what he'd catch. Tuna or mahi-mahi? Or were they just deep-sea fish? She shrugged, knowing she was ignorant about fishing.

It was a beautiful day—hot and sunny. She felt the sun beat down on her shoulders and back. Within minutes, she knew she should have taken a wrap to cover up, but promised herself that she wouldn't stay out too long.

After a fifteen-minute-or-so walk, Gill reached the smooth granite rocks jutting out of the sea. The spot was stunning: a perfect photograph to grace the front of any geographical calendar. She paused and soaked up the view beyond the boulders. Apart from a pair of frigate birds and a white speck on the horizon, there was nothing but the varying shades of blue where the sea deepened to immense depths. She scanned the area, shading her eyes as the light was fierce even with sunglasses. Harry was nowhere to be seen in the vicinity. For good measure, she called his name, anyway. Her voice bounced back in a faint echo. The noise made her pause. Was that an echo or someone having a laugh? She cast a long look around but saw nothing but rocks and palm trees beyond. Imagination again?

Sighing, she climbed over the nearest rocks and headed for a small path between the largest two which stood as sentinel pillars before the real ocean began. The path wound round and upward as she climbed while far beneath, she could hear the gurgle and suck of the sea as it surged against the ancient granite. A white tern flapped away in fright when it heard her scrabbling over the rocks, and she paused to catch her breath. She had to be careful. Sandals were not the best footwear for climbing, but she'd left her trainers back in the house.

Gill was disappointed on reaching the end of the path because there was still no sign of Harry. She sat down and chewed on a fingernail. Damn the man! Where else would he go fishing? After a few minutes, she got up and began retracing her footsteps. A large wave forced itself up between the rocks, soaking the path, and she knew she had to tread carefully. One false slip and she'd have fallen between them. The rocks were smooth and without foot or handholds. If she plummeted down, she'd never be able to climb out. She shivered at the thought and picked her way across. It was only when she reached the end of the path that she could breathe more easily.

What should she do now? What if Harry had fallen? Had an accident somewhere? Knowing nothing about fishing, she hadn't a clue where else he'd be. She walked on, getting hotter, crosser and burnt in the process. Gill had been out for over forty minutes now, and there was still no sign of him. She had two choices: carry on around the island or go back to the house. She dithered while she thought. Would he have really bothered to go farther away from the house? She hadn't seen any signs in the kitchen that he'd had any breakfast before he left that morning and knowing his appetite, guessed he'd want something soon. She decided to go back. No doubt he knew a short cut and had already returned. She laughed at her foolishness. Harry knew this island like the back of his hand. No way would he risk an accident; he was far too crafty.

Back at the house, everything looked as it had when she'd left earlier. "Harry?" No answer. By now she was annoyed. Okay, so he was entitled to go off on his own. It wasn't as if they were an item. But he could have let her know out of courtesy. A simple note would have done.

Gill marched into the bedroom and peeled off her sweaty swimsuit. There was a blotchy mirror propped up against one wall, and she stood naked before it, studying the red parts on her shoulders and back. The sunburn felt hot as she gently rubbed some soothing after-sun cream into the worst bits. Blasted man! It was all his fault.

She dressed in a top and shorts, and then remembering she hadn't eaten either, sliced some of the bread Harry had brought and made a sandwich with some of the peanut butter. She swallowed it down with two glasses of water, followed by a cup of tea. Feeling better, and after washing up her plate and knife, she wondered what to do next.

Thinking he might have got back earlier and then gone out to the boat for something, Gill decided to go down to the bay. Perhaps she should have looked there first, but as he'd taken the fishing line, she assumed he'd gone to the rocks. She sauntered towards the sandy bay, and as she reached the brow of the hill, stopped. Her jaw dropped. White Lady was nowhere to be seen.

But when? Why? This was ridiculous. There had to be a good explanation. Gill stood completely still as if willing the yacht to suddenly appear between the rocks and motor towards the beach. But the channel was as clear and empty as the bay. Had Harry moved her for a reason? But to where? He'd said—and she remembered this quite clearly—that this was the only safe anchorage on the island. A breeze swept into the bay, causing the palms to sway and the fronds to rustle; little wavelets drifted into the shore. She ran back up to the house and scanned the horizon, but there was nothing to see but blue sky dotted with a few tiny clouds and an emptier-looking sea.

But wait…hadn't she seen a speck on the horizon earlier that morning? A white sail?

Gill slumped to the ground. The bastard had gone and left without her.

Everything rushed around in her mind. Had he mentioned going? Like popping back to…god only knew where. She realised the island was miles from anywhere. The nearest land, he'd explained, were tiny islands smaller even than Cabra. Colombia was the nearest mainland, and she shuddered to think of him going there, with its reputation. Eventually, she calmed down and took stock. No. Harry hadn't uttered a word.

Unless he'd taken off for a very good reason, like an emergency, she had to assume he was playing some sort of perverse mind game with her. That idea irritated her no end. Why on earth hadn't she seen it coming?

She had no communication with him—or anyone else, for that matter. He said phones didn't work there, although she still maintained she'd heard one ring that first day they'd arrived. But wait. She did have a mobile with her. She tried it a few times as soon as they reached the island but couldn't get a signal. Shouldn't she at least make one more attempt? Maybe even climb onto the roof to get a better signal? It was worth a try. There was plenty of electricity provided by the solar panels. She rushed into the bedroom and soon found her mobile. On switching it on, she found the battery was completely flat. No problem…it could be charged up. Gill stopped. Where had she put the charger? It wasn't in her handbag. She searched through the chest of drawers, swearing she'd put it there when she first arrived. She rummaged through every drawer and cupboard, looked under the bed, even checked the kitchen, but no charger was to be found. Okay, so no phone. Harry must have taken it for some reason. He should have asked first, though. Why would he? He had his own, didn't he? She felt like screaming. What cruel trick was he playing on her?

Gill willed herself to stay calm, be rational and think. Okay, so what should she do? She wanted off this bloody island. The whole scenario had become intolerable and…and spooky. She could build a whacking great big fire. Alert a passing boat. Would anyone stop if they saw a fire? Why would they? Wouldn't they just assume it was from some island native? Was it feasible to keep a fire going continuously? Anyway, she had no other choice or ideas at that moment. She really was a female Robinson Crusoe.

Chapter Twenty-Six - Gillian

The next morning, the first thing Gill did was to go down to the bay and see if Harry had returned. In her heart, she knew she was wasting her time, but it had to be done. Sure enough, an empty beach and lagoon confronted her as she rounded the hill.

She returned to the house and set about making tea and some breakfast. All the time, her thoughts were full of Harry: like, where the devil was he, and what the hell did he think he was doing, disappearing without a word? The more she pondered, the more she worried. What if he never returned? Was he some sort of maniac who enjoyed kidnapping people and then left them to die on Cabra? She hadn't found any graves, but who knew what secrets the sandy bay below held. If it was some malicious game he was playing, she had no way of knowing whether he planned on returning or not. Even if he did, something might happen to him, expert as he was at sailing a boat. Freak winds, seas or even falling ill back on land. The worst part was not *knowing*.

By now, Gill understood he'd schemed all along to leave her there, by the amount of food he'd bought. Thinking back, she should have been warier, on her guard and disbelieving, when he said he wanted a short break on Cabra. She was running true to form: a bloody fool. She was also positive it was Harry who'd written her name down on the beach. Despite what he said, there must have been another place off the island to anchor White Lady. What a liar. Once bitten twice shy. She should never have trusted him in the first place, and when they met again, she'd tell him.

After eating, Gill sat and thought. The first thing to do was check the food supplies. She needed to know exactly what there was, and if she eked it all out, how long it would last. She could add a few fruits from the island, and at a pinch, if she learnt to fish, add to her protein intake. There was another fishing line on the shelf. She walked over to the pantry and scanned the shelves. The quantities looked much the same when she arrived, so she supposed Harry had left two weeks' supply. Did she trust him to return, though? She trembled at the thought. No, she bloody didn't, but she couldn't dwell on that prospect. Also, as already surmised, if he took ill, he might take even longer to return.

She could survive for two weeks, but decided she wasn't going to take any chances. She needed to eat the perishable goods first, plus whatever else she could pick from the garden. The tinned foods would be her emergency rations only. Another thought crossed her mind: what if he returned and then left her alone on Cabra again? Or didn't return at all? She decided to hide some of the tins as an emergency cache. She sorted through the labels: meat, vegetables, beans, fruit and pulses. A selection was taken from each, and then she looked around for a suitable place to hide them. The cottage had nowhere to hide a cache, so she scouted around outside. Not far from the spa bath was a small outcrop of rocks. By moving a few stones aside, she discovered that beneath one, there was a small hollow—perfect for burying the tins. She scraped away some of the earth with her hands and deposited the hoard. Satisfied, she then rolled back the rock and smoothed the earth around it. The bruised vegetation would soon grow back to its normal luxurious state within a few days.

Feeling happier for resolving this problem and now hot after her work, she decided to treat herself to a swim. She walked down to the bay and lazed around in the shallows for half an hour. As she wallowed in the tepid water, she gazed along the beach. As far as she could tell from time spent on Cabra, this beach was the only part of the island clear of rocks or vegetation. It wasn't visible from land, but could she make some sort of SOS signal somewhere along the sand that could be seen from the air? But what could she use? There was nothing useful like a white sail she could cut up. She supposed she could find enough white rocks if she toiled all over the island. What about banana leaves or palm fronds? Could enough be cut and gathered? There seemed to be a plentiful supply, and they would be lighter to carry than rocks. Gill had been dealt a real dilemma. She didn't want to be found and identified by the authorities, but neither did she want to starve to death on the island.

She set to work, but first needed a good strong knife. Excited by the idea, she tore back up to the cottage. On opening the drawer containing the cutlery, she discovered to her dismay that almost all the cutlery was missing. She hadn't noticed the night before, as she'd had a simple meal of salad and cheese and used the plate and cutlery already out on the drainer. No sharp knife had been necessary then or at breakfast. Bastard! She felt tears of frustration well up, but she refused to let Harry get the better of her. She wouldn't fall prey to his pathetic mind games. He'd frightened her a few days earlier down on the beach...and then she remembered. After that episode, she'd removed the largest and sharpest knife. Unless Harry had found it, it would still be lying on the floor of the bedroom in the back pocket of her dirty shorts with the rest of the laundry. Bingo!

Gill worked hard all morning, dragging as many fallen palm fronds and banana leaves littering the ground from the immediate area into a pile on the beach. She scratched her arms and legs on some prickly bushes and discovered cuts and bruises running with blood. She washed these in the sea, thinking salt water was as good an antiseptic as anything found in a chemist and continued. After three hours, she sat on the sand, exhausted, and yet still the pile looked small. She needed to expand the territory and go further afield for more supplies. By this time, she was not only tired and sore, but hunger had set in. She limped back to the cottage and cut off a good slice of bread from one of the loaves Harry had brought, together with a piece of cheese. A quick calculation estimated the bread would last about a week if she kept it wrapped up and in the cool...the cheese a bit longer, but it did melt a bit with the heat. The first few weeks alone on the island, she'd suffered from an odd feeling on some days and put it down to dizziness and nausea. But the queasy symptoms had disappeared, and her normal healthy appetite returned. She knew the limit of the food stocks, though, and needed to manage it. It looked like she'd have to try her own hand at fishing sooner than she'd realised.

After lunch, she trudged back down to the beach and started arranging the branches and leaves into an SOS message. She had a pretty good idea SOS was universal, and as the beach was too small for any extra words, it would have to do.

Afterwards, she stood back and scrutinised her efforts. It was smaller than she'd have liked, but if she worked on it, adding more branches, it might work. She toiled all afternoon, knowing in her heart that being seen from the air was a long shot, but she had to do something, even if being found was something of a paradox.

After finishing, she stripped off and took a swim, all the time keeping a good lookout for telltale signs of a fin zipping beneath the surface of the lagoon. The encounter had made her wary, and she didn't dare venture out into the deeper, cooler water. The SOS was visible from the shore, but it still looked pathetic, and she wondered if she could replicate it on the cottage roof. On returning 'home', she stood and gazed at the building and decided it wasn't worth the bother. The cottage roof was far too small. Any message wouldn't have been noticed in a million years unless the plane was flying only a few feet up in the air.

Where was Harry? Why had he left her, the bastard?

Chapter Twenty-Seven - Gillian

A few days passed and before Gill knew it, she realised Harry had been gone for another two weeks. During this time, she hadn't suffered the same eerie feeling of being watched, so she'd learnt to relax a bit more. The days were spent keeping occupied as much as she could. She gathered plenty of driftwood and fallen branches, and piled everything up by the side of the house. She even ventured down to the rocks with the fishing line and a few lumps of mouldy bread on the hooks, but for all her hard work, she had yet to catch more than two fish.

She went through Harry's fishing tackle and found a couple of silvery hooks with coloured, feathery, rubber things attached. She thought he had called them lures when he and Theo were talking on board the yacht one day. Maybe it was time to try them instead of bread.

Gill took the line, complete with the lures over to the other side of the island. As it was a fair walk, and she meant to conquer her previous pathetic attempts at fishing, she packed a bit of lunch. Fresh water was a problem on the island away from the 'spa', and she realised how lucky it was to have such a reliable source. With a wine bottle, complete with cork and filled with fresh water, she shoved it into her backpack along with everything else. As she walked along the path between the granite rocks, she chanted a mantra in her head: tonight, she would eat fish.

The lures worked. Within an hour, Gill had two beautiful fish lying beside her on the rock where she was sitting. She couldn't believe how easy it was once she worked out where to throw the line and when to jag the wire to hook the fish. She had no idea what the fish were, but they were fish-shaped and looked perfectly healthy to eat. That night, there was going to be a feast. On the way back to the house, she planned her meal: fish, pasta and maybe half a tin of green beans. She was sure she could make some sort of sauce from the tubes of tomato and garlic paste. There was just enough left.

***

The fish was delicious, and Gill repeated the trip to the rocks the next day and the next. After the sixth successive trip, she caught just one much larger fish and called it a day. Watching it cooking on the barbecue, she realised just how huge it was; its teeth were gigantic and very sharp. That night, after she'd eaten it, she noticed a tingling around her mouth and in her fingers and toes. Puzzled, she wondered what could have caused it and decided it must have been the fish. Maybe it hadn't been cooked long enough; but what if it had been a poisonous species? Harry had muttered about not eating the larger predatory fish such as barracuda, but as she didn't know what a barracuda looked like, it was all academic.

Gill went to bed feeling tired and with a thumping headache, a few hours later, she awoke with a violent stomach ache. She stumbled along in the dark with just a

136

candle to accompany her towards the loo. She threw up immediately. Apart from aching all over, the subsequent diarrhoea and vomiting made her feel a bit better, and she crawled back into bed and pulled a cover over her shaking body. She eventually fell into a restless sleep, vowing not to eat fish for some time.

The next morning, Gill staggered out of bed and walked slowly down to the bay, just like every morning. She was feeling depressed and as weak as a kitten. She suddenly stopped and collapsed in a heap on the sand. Her heart leapt; her eyes transfixed on Harry's yacht lying peacefully at anchor.

Chapter Twenty-Eight - Harry

Harry strolled onto deck, stretched and turned toward the shore. The first thing he saw was Gillian, kneeling on the sand, and he lifted his hand to wave. There was no response, so he turned away, knowing the next hour wasn't going to be easy. The silly bitch was bound to give him grief for leaving without a word and staying away so long. He sighed and was about to turn away when he noticed a load of sticks and vegetation lying on the beach above the water line. He squinted to see better and almost laughed after making out the letters: SOS. As if! Stupid cow. Nobody was going to see that from there, and then he realised she must have been thinking about an aerial view. Even so, it was too small. She didn't realise no one would go to her aid. *Here, I rule.* He'd have words with her about that. She'd no doubt complain and shout a bit, getting all steamed up and angry, but it wouldn't affect him in any way. Quite honestly, he'd enjoy it even more. The last thing he wanted was a complete weak and compliant female. He wanted her vulnerable, but he also liked a spitfire who turned him on.

Harry took time dressing, drank a second cup of coffee and finished his breakfast. He saw she was still sitting on the sand waiting when he emerged back on deck, and he wandered aft to lower the dinghy into the water. He collected the bags of groceries and placed them carefully in the rubber boat. Spreading the weight was important, and dropping fresh meat into the sea would have soon attracted the odd nosy shark, which Harry knew inhabited the coral reef just outside the lagoon. He knew a shark's primary sense was smell, and it could detect one drop of blood in twenty-five gallons of water up to a quarter of a mile away. He knew that from experience. One day, a year or so back, he'd anchored in that very spot and decided to scrape the barnacles from the yacht's hull. He remembered cutting his arm on the sharp crustaceans, and less than three minutes later, three sharks had entered the bay. Luckily, at the time, he was near the boat's swim ladder and managed to haul himself out before they became too curious. Since then, he'd seen them inside the bay many times.

He checked that he'd locked the yacht up, the key safely in the pocket of his shorts and started rowing towards the shore. As he glanced over his shoulder, he saw that Gill had risen to her feet and was walking slowly down to the water's edge. Unlike last time, when she rushed down to greet him to help drag the dinghy up onto the sand, she stood well above the waterline. No doubt, she was feeling sorry for herself and about to let rip.

"Hi there. How have you been? No more problems with messages in the sand?" She didn't answer, and after clambering from the boat and catching hold of the painter to drag it from the sea, he took a good look at her. "What's the matter? You look like shit."

She scowled and muttered. "I've been sick. Food poisoning, I expect."

Harry tied the rope around a large boulder and approached her with a puzzled frown. "Food poisoning? I doubt it. You must be down to dried foods and tins by now."

"Yes, I am, no thanks to you. Why did you leave me without a word? I had to teach myself to fish, and the last one I caught didn't agree with me."

"Ah, that explains it. What fish was it? A large one with sharp teeth?" She nodded and he thought how sullen she looked, like a spoilt sulky child. "Barracuda, I expect. They're almost top of the food chain. It could have been a touch of ciguatera poisoning…it's a form of food poisoning caused by eating fish that have ciguatera toxin in them. The toxin is produced by a small organism, which attaches to algae in warm ocean-water reef areas. Small fish eat these algae, and the toxin accumulates and is concentrated in larger predatory fish, like your barracuda. It all boils down to where the fish are in the food chain. Think yourself lucky you're still standing. The poison is often deadly to humans."

"Well, thanks for bloody nothing. You were the one who suggested I fish."

"I suppose you ate fish one day after another?"

She flushed at his words and lifted her chin in defiance. She held her hands in tightly clenched fists as if she wanted to belt him one. "Yes."

"There you go, then. The toxin accumulated in you until it reached a dangerous level. Lay off the fish for a few weeks at least."

She raised her head and gasped. "A few weeks? I'm not bloody—"

"Can you give me a hand with the supplies? The weather looks like it might break. I don't like the look of those clouds. We might be in for a bit of a lashing." Harry gestured in the direction and she darted a look towards the south east.

"Why have you brought more supplies? You left me without any explanation. I want to leave here now."

"I had to leave suddenly. An emergency came in on the radio while I was on board that morning. You were asleep, and I didn't want to wake you. I didn't know I was going to be away so long. It couldn't be helped." He beamed at her in what he hoped was his best and most sincere smile before quickly looking away. She was being a right pain and he felt like slapping her.

"But more supplies?"

"You must have eaten your way through most of what I left before. Now, can you please take these bags while I bring the heavier ones." He stared back at her, keeping his expression as empty and docile as he could. He wanted her cooperation. He wasn't in the mood for games just yet. Harry pushed the bags into her arms and she staggered back. "Go on up and I'll follow," he said before reaching back into the boat and fishing out more bags. She didn't move, so he walked past her and began the climb up the hill. Perhaps ignoring her would teach her a lesson.

Once he reached the house, he turned around and saw she was just behind, so giving her his winning smile again, he took the bags from her hands. "Thanks. Why don't you make a nice cup of tea while I collect the rest? You look a bit peaky still, so don't overdo it. Then I'll do all the chores while you have a nice lie-down." That should take the wind out of her sails.

Her mouth dropped and she put her hands on her hips. "I don't bloody want to make a cup of tea. Not until you explain why you pissed off without letting me know. I don't go for your earlier excuse."

He stood composed before her and raised one eyebrow over her outburst. Then he shrugged and approached her with his hands held out in front of me. "Gill, Gill, calm down. You know you wanted to come here for peace and solitude. You needed to get away, somewhere to hide and get your thoughts together. You're full of emotion and staying here is the best thing for you. We agreed." He watched her carefully; her body looked as taut as a bowstring, her breathing ragged and shallow. He wondered if she'd react violently. She certainly looked like she might...or would she simply back down. Harry was enjoying this, observing her every move and reactions to his words. He could play her like a fiddle.

"No! I've had enough. I want to leave right now."

"I've just explained—we're in for some heavy weather, and besides, White Lady needs a bit of work on her engine."

"I don't believe you. You're lying."

He put on an injured expression and shook his head. "No, I'm not. Honestly, Gill. Look, I've brought you…us…some delicious food. More bacon. You love that, and steaks and a whole chicken. We can have that for dinner tonight."

"I still want to leave as soon as we can. Can't I come back to Antigua with you? I can look after your house there. I don't have to meet anyone, just stay in the background. Please."

Despite the waver in her voice, anger was building inside him. He didn't want her anywhere near Antigua and certainly not in his house. The place was still Marlene's…he could still feel her presence there. "Not just yet. You're not ready, sweetie," he said softly, moving towards her and holding out his arms. She stood completely still, unresponsive and compliant as he drew his arms around her. "I think the island's actually doing you good, you know. Apart from having a bit of food poisoning, you look far healthier than when I first met you. Blooming, in fact." He kissed her cheek and gently drew her head down onto her shoulder. He felt the tension leave her body as he rubbed her shoulders lovingly. After a few minutes, Harry drew back and smiled down at her, his look one of complete tenderness and desire. "Come on. I still have to get the supplies up, and then I can show you what I've brought. I've even bought you a few magazines. Put the kettle on, there's a good girl." He patted her bottom and moved off down the hill.

He walked to the dinghy, whistling like he hadn't a care in the world. Harry knew her mind must have been in overdrive, wondering whether she could trust him and whether anything he said was true. He chuckled while picking up the remaining sacks of supplies. It was all part of the elaborate plan, and he was loving every minute of it.

Chapter Twenty-Nine - Harry

Later that afternoon and after they'd had a tasty lunch of pâté and salad, he threw Gill a loving look as he withdrew a small box of chocolates from one of the bags he'd carried up from the beach and kept to one side.

"I didn't know if you preferred dark or milk chocolate, so I got a box containing both. I hope you like them. They've been in White Lady's fridge. You'd better eat them before they melt in the heat."

"I like all chocolate. Thank you." She took the box from his hands and put it down on the worktop.

"I've also bought some wine. I think I remembered which ones you liked best."

She looked at him with raised eyebrows, realising he was trying to wear her down little by little, one nasty deed followed by a nice one. A sort of nice-cop-bad-cop routine or a 'shit' sandwich.

"So how long are you staying this time?" Gill asked eventually. "Or are you going to disappear suddenly like last time?"

"No, I swear I won't. I've already explained, even though you don't believe me. Look…" he grabbed hold of her shoulders and spun her round to face the open doorway, "look at those black clouds. Do you seriously think I'd venture out in that?"

"No. I guess not." She shivered. "Will the storm be bad?"

"Probably. The roof's pretty good and well nailed down. We'll weather it out okay. Plenty of food and drink and electricity. Until we lose the sunshine. Then it'll get very dark."

He put his arm around her shoulders tentatively, and he felt her body tense and stiff beneath it. "You're very tense."

"I hate storms. How long will the electricity last, do you think?"

He shrugged. "A few hours. Why?" He couldn't help baiting her as he remembered back on the yacht's passage, Gill never wanted to sleep with the light off. At first, Harry had laughed at her and would switch off all the cabin's lamps, saying they were wasting electricity. Without fail, if he woke in the night or entered the cabin on his off-watch, he found she'd turned at least one light on again.

She didn't answer, and he guessed she was thinking about the darkness which was soon to hit the island. For some reason, she loathed the dark. He leant towards her and whispered spitefully into her ear. "Don't worry, we have plenty of candles. They'll be fine so long as the wind doesn't blow them out."

She broke away from him and wrapped her arms around herself. She walked further into the house, her steps jerky and agitated. He caught up with her and led her over to the sofa. "Sit down. You're as edgy as a cat on a hot tin roof. Let me give you a massage…it'll relax you."

He ran his hands over her shoulders, up around her neck and along her spine. Her body was rigid under his thumbs, and it took a lot of rubbing before he sensed her becoming more relaxed, her spine loose and less taut. "That's better," he murmured into her ear as he eased her into a better position until she was eventually lying on her stomach.

Harry moved below her waist, massaging her buttocks and along her thighs. He noticed she'd lost weight; he preferred skinny women. Her long slim limbs felt firm, and as he touched her, his groin ached as his penis hardened against his rough cotton shorts. He was also aware that like Marlene, she was younger than him by about fifteen years, and the age difference had always fired his blood.

He lifted her short skirt and tugged down her pants. Her smooth buttocks gleamed white in the semi-darkness. So far, she hadn't made any attempt to stop him, and Harry knew that once again, he'd won. Despite being pissed off with him, she still needed intimacy. As he turned her over and squeezed between her legs, he knew she couldn't resist any longer.

Chapter Thirty - Harry

The wind raged all around the house that night. The electricity fizzled out before it was time for bed, and as Gill made such a massive fuss about the dark, Harry lit enough candles to eat and read by if necessary.

"Why do you dislike the dark so much?" he asked eventually, after relighting them a fourth time.

"Just because."

"No, seriously. Loads of kids hate the dark, but you're a grown woman."

He felt the silence between them deepening and wondered if she'd dropped off. "It was my father. He insisted I didn't need a night light. It's just something I've never got over."

"But nothing can happen to you in the dark that can't in the light."

She looked at him and her eyes appeared enormous in her face. "You think so?"

"Try me."

Gill looked away and shook her head. Harry thought he caught a glint of tears in her eyes. Was this another of her feminine wiles? Thinking she could win him round by the threat of tears? He smiled a secret smile and plastered a look of concern on his face. It was easy to act as if he cared.

"You can trust me, you know." He rubbed her wrist gently, thinking of the sex they'd had that afternoon. It would be time for turning in soon. "I know I had to dash off last time, but haven't I brought you plenty of good food so you have a proper diet? I want you to be healthy and fit."

She stared at him for a minute before dropping her gaze and looking towards the nearest candles, their light flickering and guttering in the sharp draught of wind which entered under the main door.

"My father was very tough on me as a kid. He always wanted a son and just couldn't face the disappointment of my mother giving birth to a girl. I wasn't allowed to show fear or pain. It was a weakness, he said. Something I had to bear for being female. When my mother put me to bed, I used to beg for a night light, but he always laid down the law and removed the lamp from my bedroom. Later, when I could reach the switch on the wall, I used to turn the main light back on. He thrashed me and for good measure, made me spend my nights locked in the dark cupboard under the stairs. Every little thing I did wrong, he made me go in there." She shuddered.

Harry sat forward, fascinated. Was she finally going to tell him everything? Interesting. Perhaps this explained the scars on her wrists. Had she self-harmed because she had been punished? His instinct told him Gill hadn't been broken by him—yet. But if he was gentle and took it slowly, she might reveal more. "You poor girl. What a horrible thing to do to a child. What about your mother? Did she stand up for you?"

Gill fidgeted and shook her head. "No. Mum was completely under his thumb, always in awe of him. Downtrodden I suppose. But that didn't fully excuse her."

"Maybe, but I don't know the circumstances, so I can't comment. What about when you got older? Didn't you stand your ground?"

Gill's eyes widened and she took a deep breath. With one fluid movement, she stood up from the sofa and crossed over to the window. He could make out her outline in the semi-darkness and saw by the swift rise and fall of her chest, she was breathing rapidly. She suddenly whirled round. "Oh yes, I tried. I became a rebel, thinking I'd eventually break the old bastard down. I thought I had it under control until he...he stopped me." She paused and strode back to where Harry was sitting. She ran both hands through her hair, making it stand up on end, and looking at her, he wondered if she was about to have some sort of mental breakdown. He'd never seen her so agitated with those wild staring eyes. The thought excited him; he'd never witnessed anything like this before.

"Yes. Go on."

It was as if she had suddenly blinked and wondered where the devil she was and what she'd just said. Her shoulders drooped, she lowered her arms, and her mouth quivered. She reached forward and grabbed his hand. "No. No more. It's over and done with."

Harry smiled, wondering at her sudden change of mood. "Good for you."

Gill gave his arm a tug and looked over her shoulder in the direction of the window where flashes of lightning lit the black sky in sharp relief. An almighty crash of thunder followed, but she hardly flinched. Instead, with a strength he didn't know she possessed, she pulled him to his feet. "There's no point in sitting here. Let's go to bed."

This time—the first time—it was she who instigated the sex. She tore off her clothes, swiftly unbuttoned his shorts and tossed them onto the floor. Surprised, he sprawled on his back and watched in fascination as she lowered herself down onto him. Their coupling was rough and quick, but there was no doubt it was exactly what she needed. She climaxed first, and once they'd both finished, she snuggled against him, one leg thrown over his. She fell into a deep sleep minutes later.

Chapter Thirty-One - Gillian

The next morning, the storm had died down, but the sky still looked wild. Ragged torn clouds raced overhead as Gillian walked down the beach to check White Lady was still safe in the bay. The yacht was in the same place, so she knew she hadn't dragged her anchor. There must have been quite a surf beyond the inlet passage, as waves were creeping into the lagoon, washing the shore. Bits of flotsam littered the beach: palm fronds, coconuts and more than a handful of dead fish. It was hardly the typical Caribbean dream island she expected. Harry had stayed behind at the house to check on the solar panels on the roof after the strong winds.

Gill was happy to take a solitary walk and realised that as much as she tolerated his company, she was more than content on her own. Harry was a companion who was somewhat foisted upon her out of need. She felt nothing for him; and in fact, now considered him a complete and utter bastard for leaving her for those last two weeks. But he did present a lucid case when he wanted to…silver-tongued degenerate that she believed he was. He had a quick and devious mind, and she knew she had to be doubly careful not to be taken in by him again.

She did wonder whether he meant what he'd said about staying for a few days and then leaving her for a couple of weeks until he'd sorted his business. Part of her was okay with that, as she had another shocking problem she wanted to think about carefully when on her own again. And as for being alone on Cabra? Gill was almost one hundred per cent certain Harry had played that stupid trick on her with the sand. She knew the island well by this time and had covered every small path, entered each grove of trees and rock formation, and had found nothing to suggest anyone else had been there or still was. There were very few places in which to hide, as the island wasn't that large. Surely she'd have seen fresh, unfamiliar footprints?

She turned as a whistle sounded behind her. Harry was striding down the hill. "All looks okay to me. You've nothing to worry about."

She smiled, relieved to know that once the sun peeped out from behind the clouds, the solar panels would begin making and then storing electricity in the batteries. She loathed the idea of dark nights without power. Harry looked around him, his gaze settling in the direction of the east, towards the Caribbean island chain. Gill suddenly realised he had his rucksack with him and guessed he'd changed his mind and was about to leave immediately. She should have known. Or was this what he'd planned all along?

Should she try and delay him? Give him another night of unbridled sex? She glanced at him. The way he was standing…there was something about him that made her realise she'd be wasting her time. His mind was made up, and part of her felt relieved. She had other things to consider. Plans to be made.

"You're going?"

"Yes. Sorry my sweet, but there's a break in the storm, and if I'm lucky, I can use the weather window to make it back in time before the next tropical squall. I think the worst is over, and you'll be okay. There's nothing dangerous on the island, and it usually endures bad weather easily. I'll be back in a couple of weeks, maybe sooner if I get everything done at home, and we can talk about where to go next."

"I'll miss you," Okay, so it was a lie. She just wanted reassurance he'd be back.

Harry smiled and was about to carry on down the hill when he suddenly pointed to the pathetic SOS message. The branches and palm fronds lay scattered on the sand. There wasn't much trace of the message. "I meant to say something when I arrived. If that was meant to be an SOS, no one's likely to see it. The locals are miles away, and I doubt they understand SOS, anyway. I'd use the stuff as firewood. Make a pile in case you want to have a fire."

Gill followed his line of vision and nodded. "You're probably right. I can't remember the last time a plane flew overhead."

Harry looked satisfied and nodded in agreement. She assumed her words were what he expected to hear, and the feeling sent a wave of irritation through her. Control freak. She'd do it when she was good and ready.

"Clear it up soon as it looks a right mess. I like my island kept as pristine as possible. Do it … *today*," he said as he kissed her. The icy lingering look which accompanied his words sent a chill through her body. She had the distinct feeling that if she disobeyed, he'd find some way of hurting her.

She flinched as he moved, but he only hitched his rucksack up on his shoulder and marched down the beach to where he'd tethered the dinghy to a large rock. He pushed the rubber boat over the sand, and as it entered the water, he jumped in. The boat rose and fell over the waves coming in from the passageway, and pressing her trembling lips together, she turned away. Her last thought as she wandered back up the hill was that she hoped he was in for a bumpy ride back to wherever he was going.

An hour later, the skies darkened and rain began to fall. Huge drops fell, making holes in the sand outside the house, and bluish-purple clouds edged along the horizon. Gill, alone and dejected once more, watched from the doorway as the greenery of the garden took on a strange blue-green hue. The intensity of the rain increased, and as she looked farther out to sea, she saw nothing but a violent scene of frothy agitated violence.

She wondered if the storm had hit Harry.

Chapter Thirty-Two - Gillian Two Weeks Later

The last few days dragged. At first, Gill was mesmerised by the storm: the power and ferocity of something made entirely by nature. After a few days, the rains stopped, the winds died down, and the sea recovered to its normal state, waves no more than a metre high and rolling in from the south-east. The trees no longer dripped on her when she ventured along to the loo, and she could take a warm bath without being drowned by a tropical shower at the same time.

The rains brought forth a rhythmic cycle of chorus from the hundreds of tiny tree frogs all over the island. At first, she wondered what it was and then remembered Harry talking about these tiny creatures one day while they were still at sea. Together, their nightly song made a deafening cacophony. During the day, she noticed that overnight, new flowers had burst open on the surrounding bushes, and not for the first time recognised what a truly beautiful place a tropical island could be. The group of tiny jewelled humming birds still made their daily visits to the garden, and watching them hover over the flowers taking the nectar Gill found them fascinating.

She looked out to sea. Harry was due back the next day. He hadn't returned earlier as he'd indicated he might. The sun shone on the sea surface, and it looked calm and benign from where she was standing. There was no sign of a sail on the horizon, and she just knew he wouldn't arrive a day early, so she was wasting her time checking. A frequent and ghastly thought entered her head as she stood watching. What if he didn't come at all?

By now, she'd eaten all the fresh food. She was down to eating pasta, rice and crackers, with the usual tin of something not always very palatable. The stores had lasted, but she was craving something new. Fresh vegetables and meat. She hadn't risked fishing again, as she didn't want to be poisoned, although she'd found the odd crab and prawn, which she dunked in boiling water for a few minutes before shelling and eating. Those times, she'd been so desperate that she'd hardly waited for the cooked food to cool before picking at the shell.

The next day, she spent time on the beach, taking a dip and searching at either rocky end for a crab or two. She was absorbed and up to her knees in water before noticing White Lady had slid silently into the bay. Harry was on deck, getting ready to drop anchor. He straightened up, saw her and waved. She responded and was conscious of how much she wanted to leave the island. This time, she bloody well wouldn't take no for an answer.

The anchor looked like it dug in first time, and within minutes, Harry had lowered the dinghy and was rowing towards the ashore. Gill waded out to meet him and reached over to give him a hug. "I'm really pleased to see you," she said.

Harry pulled her towards him and kissed her gently on the mouth. "It's good to be back." She noticed supplies lying in the bottom of the dinghy. "Can I have a hand?" He gestured at the stuff.

"Let's leave them there. I want to go as soon as we can. It won't take me a minute to fetch my stuff."

"Are you sure you've sorted your head out? Only last time…"

"As sure as I'll ever be. I'm over Lawrence, well and truly, and Nathan's death was an awful tragedy I'll learn to live with. If anything, I'm going out of my head being here on my own." She laughed. He couldn't fail to take her off once he appreciated how serious she was and that she felt a lot better inside.

"That's good news, but I'd like to leave a few new supplies up in the house, anyway. I never know when I'm coming here next. It's good to be prepared."

She waited while he fetched a few bags from the boat. Her mind was whirling around. Was he for real? Why was she getting an uncomfortable feeling about this, a sort of déjà vu? "I suppose so. Can we go as soon as you've restocked the house?"

He laughed. "Give me a chance, will you? I'd like to have a coffee, stretch my legs and make sure everything's working. The solar and hob both okay?"

"Yes. Can we go after lunch then?"

Harry straightened up from the dinghy, and she wondered why he didn't look her straight in the eye. "It's a bit awkward right now. The house on Antigua…I have visitors coming in three days' time. You won't want to have them there at the same time. You might be recognised."

"I can stay somewhere else until they've gone. In fact, just drop me off on the nearest island, and I'll make my own way to wherever. I don't want to inconvenience you." She waved a hand dismissively. "Which island isn't important."

"But it is. Don't you realise the whole world is on the lookout for you? I read the papers. *Is* it true? You murdered your friend and tried to kill your boyfriend."

"No! Honest to god, I didn't kill Nathan. Lawrence had beaten me up, and Nathan came to my rescue, only Lawrence turned on him. It was Lawrence who killed Nathan, not me," she cried.

"Then what about Lawrence's injuries? The media says the authorities want to question you at the very least."

"I tried to protect Nathan and hit Lawrence over the head with a frying pan."

What if Harry didn't believe her? What would he do? He hadn't dobbed her in yet, and he'd known about Nathan ever since Theo went overboard.

"Look, you're safe here. Why push your luck?" He put the bags down at her feet and took hold of her upper arms. She felt his fingers pressing into her flesh. His grip was tight; in fact, it was pitiless and painful.

"Ow! Don't do that. It hurts." She pulled away and rubbed her arms. What a pig. He'd done that on purpose. "Look, I just want to leave here. I don't like the place. Sometimes I feel like I'm being watched, and quite frankly, I'm bored."

Harry walked away and then stopped, turned and confronted her. "Now you're seeing things. You have such a vivid imagination. I wonder whether you're quite right in the head! And you're bloody ungrateful, do you know that? I bring you to a safe place where you can hide out until the law has forgotten about you, spend *my* money on food for you, risk sailing across here and back, and all you can do is whine? Ungrateful bitch. I've a good mind to just go. You can spend the night on your own for all I care." He picked the last bag out of the dinghy and dumped it just above the water line. "Fend for your bloody self, I'm off."

Gill gulped. His words and actions frightened her. If he went, he might not bother returning. She had to placate him, make him believe she cared for him and was grateful for everything. "No! Please. Don't go, I really don't want you to. I need you here. I'm sorry. I just got a bit worked up, being alone and then seeing you…you know. I didn't kill Nathan." She fell to her knees and sobbed, this time not caring about keeping back the tears. They ran freely down her cheeks. He had to take her to Antigua. At the same time, she didn't like the look in his eyes, erratic and hostile, his tone unsympathetic and indifferent. Was he crazy? Gill lifted her face and whispered. "Please stay. I'll be good, I promise."

He stood with his head slightly tilted to one side. She knew he was weighing her up. She was rewarded by his nod. "Okay. I will *this* time. But you'd better behave."

They picked up the bags by mutual consent, and Gill trailed up the hill behind him. She vowed not to let him out of her sight in case he did another bunk.

Chapter Thirty-Three - Gillian

Although Harry had shown his nastier side, Gill had to say he was a far better cook than she first realised. On White Lady, she'd done most of the catering, leaving the navigation and running of the yacht to him. On Cabra, he seemed to relish doing cooking, whether it was indoors or on the barbecue. That night, before the sun set, he prepared a large joint of pork he'd bought with onions, herbs and potatoes, wrapped it up in a double layer of tinfoil and lowered it into the firepit. When she explained how hungry she was, he made a salad to go with it. The smell from the roasting meat filled the air, and Gill's mouth was soon salivating as she thought of the tender chunks of meat, which she hadn't tasted for days.

While he prepared the meal on the worktop, she put the remaining stores away. Thoughts of escaping from the island were uppermost in her mind, and she kept turning ideas around and around in her head. She reckoned she knew exactly how to get the anchor up, and she'd steered the boat numerous times. Surely it couldn't be that difficult to pilot a yacht through the channel if it was kept strictly to the deeper water in the middle?

She knew where Harry kept the boat key. He'd taken hers from her soon after they left Tenerife. He always wore shorts with pockets front and back. The right rear one contained a zipped pocket in which he kept the key for safety. All she had to do was get it off him. Gill assumed they'd sleep together in the double bed that night, and he always slept in the nude. She needed to ply him with plenty of alcohol and good sex to make him sleepy. Would that work? Would he see through her act?

Gill had another reason to get off the island now. She was convinced she was over three months *pregnant*. She hadn't had a period since before Portugal, and she'd stopped taking birth control when she was still with Lawrence. She wasn't shocked. Far from it—in truth, babies fascinated her. She thought back to Lawrence and what the brute had done. Her memories flitting before that to…that awful time when she was still a teenager. She shook her head. Enough of the daydreams. She was in the here and now. What about Harry?

Gill didn't want to tell him yet. She was still coming to terms with it, but when she did, she wondered how he'd take it. She assumed he hadn't any children of his own. What parent didn't mention their offspring, whether proud or ashamed of them?

She wandered through to the bedroom and stood in front of the old mottled mirror on the wall. She lifted her sarong and stared at her stomach. Still no sign. But within only three to four weeks at most, she'd develop a tiny bump. What if Harry did abandon her? Could she survive, deliver the infant on her own? She reckoned she could. She'd learnt a lot since she'd been dumped there: how to keep a smouldering firepit going, fish, recognise edible fruits.

"What are you doing?" Harry's voice suddenly broke into her thoughts and dropping the hem of her sarong, she whirled around in fear. Had he seen?

"Nothing. My skin felt dry and I was looking for the body cream."

"Dinner will be ready in a few minutes. Fancy a drink?"

She thought of pregnancy and alcohol but knew Harry would suspect something if she said no. Gill smiled. "A glass of wine would be lovely. In fact, let's drink the whole bottle to celebrate your return. I feel like getting smashed."

Harry gave her a look but said nothing. His brown eyes looked cold and unfathomable. She tried not to shudder, as she now recognised the dark side of his nature. She'd caught glimpses of it before, lurking beneath the surface, but latterly he'd shown his true colours, and she felt bloody nervous. Anxious for herself, and now, she had another being to consider. It was odd. She'd read about women who wished they'd miscarry under such circumstances. They didn't want a child conceived out of lust or rape.

But Gill felt different. She actually *wanted* this baby. It would be hers, something of her own she could love and cherish.

They eventually finished the meal, which was delicious and she said so. They had soon drunk the bottle of wine and Gill opened another bottle when Harry had slipped outside for a pee. She filled his glass to the brim, added no more than half an inch to her own and topped it up with water. The dark night lay all around, and she reckoned he wouldn't know the difference.

As the level in the bottle fell, she noticed Harry was slurring his words. He'd done most of the talking that evening while she nodded and agreed in all the right places, making out his conversation was stimulating enough for her to be interested. Without warning, he stood up, wobbled unsteadily on his feet and took hold of Gill's arm. "Bedtime," he leered and propelled her towards the door.

He pushed Gill backwards onto the bed and flopped down beside her. "Whassermatter? You've been moody and quiet all day." He reached for the knot in her sarong and fiddled with it, but it was evident he wasn't so drunk that he couldn't manage it. He soon pushed the folds of fabric aside. His eyes feasted on her breasts, which she believed were already a little swollen, and he grabbed one. She shrieked in pain and tried to pull away.

"Keep still, I've only just started. Why are you being so unfriendly?"

"I'm not. I'm just a bit tired…all the wine…"

He smirked. "You suggested it." Again, he pinched a nipple between his fingers, and she slapped his hand away. He grinned and slapped her back. "I thought you liked it rough? You always have before. Horny little bitch. I reckon you've always been loose." She flinched at the expression in his eyes; the malicious look sent a tremor down her spine.

"You hurt me."

He was all over her, the sarong tossed aside while he held her down with one hand, the other groped roughly between her legs.

"You're not a baby. Take it like a woman. If you complain, I'll lock you in the safe room. It's permanently dark down there."

Gill clamped her lips together to prevent her from crying out at the thought of it. As he mounted her, she shuddered, and immediately got the impression he thought she was enjoying it. He fucked her repeatedly until exhausted; he suddenly quivered and rolled off. Gill squirmed away from him. Disgusted with his actions and attitude, she planned that as soon as she knew he was completely out of it, she'd make her getaway. In the darkness, she lay as far away from him as she could; his snores and mutterings kept her awake in any case. At one point, he called out, and she thought he shouted a woman's name. It sounded like Marline or Marlene, and as Gill fought not to drift off, she wondered drowsily who she was.

Chapter Thirty-Four - Harry

He awoke later that night, his bladder felt full and achy. Harry noticed that the space next to him was empty and wondered if Gill's movements were what had wakened him. He sat up and saw by his watch that it was just after twelve. His mouth was as dry as a bone, and as well as relieving himself, he decided to have a drink of water. Walking through to the main room, he met Gill coming in the front door. She stopped in surprise.

"You startled me," she said.

"Not as much as you startled me. Why are you dressed in the middle of the night? Going somewhere?" She was wearing a pair of shorts and T-shirt, her feet encased in her leather boat shoes.

She looked down at her clothes. "I…I couldn't sleep. I went for a short walk after going to the loo. I'm going back to bed now."

Since she never wore anything except a sarong on her night-time trips to the loo, he became suspicious. Plus, she might have been unable to sleep, but go out in the dark without a light? He seriously doubted her excuse, as she never ventured anywhere in the dark without a torch.

"Get back to bed then. I won't be a minute."

She slipped past, and he stepped outside. The night air was still and fragrant from the flowers growing around the house. Harry wandered towards the path leading to the bay and could just glimpse White Lady nudging gently against her anchor chain. The sight of her gleaming in the moonlight held his attention, and he nodded to himself. Gillian had been about to try and flee the island. As he watched his urine stream down onto the sand, he smirked. It was just as well he'd removed the boat keys from his shorts before dinner and hidden them outside. He'd pre-empted any ideas of escape.

***

Gill's deviousness annoyed him, and although he felt jaded from their drinking session, he decided to punish her. Back in the bedroom, he rolled her onto her front and despite her cries of protest, entered her from behind. He knew she wasn't interested, and her body undoubtedly still hurt from the previous sex, but he didn't care. This was *his* island, and if he wanted to do what he liked with her, then he would. She owed him much more than she gave him credit for.

He was leaving the next day, and she definitely wasn't accompanying him.

Chapter Thirty-Five - Gillian

When Gill eventually woke, Harry was up and dressed. A cup of tea sat on the table by his side as he ate a piece of bread and butter. They grunted hello to each other as she walked past him on the way to the loo. She felt soiled and dirty after the night before and stopped at the spa bath. The warm water cleansed and soothed her body, and as she leant back in relief, she cursed Harry for making her body ache so much. The last episode had been awful, but at least he wasn't into sodomy, thank goodness. She felt tears sliding down over her cheeks. Was she ever going to get off the island?

She placed her hands on her stomach and willed the baby to be safe. Its survival was becoming much more important. When she finished bathing, Gill returned to the house and discovered that Harry had left. A feeling of relief swept over her, and she cried copious fresh tears. It was the first time she was glad of his leaving and the first time she hadn't wanted to go with him. When her tears had finished, she suddenly realised he hadn't mention how long he'd be gone, so she assumed it would be like all the other times and she'd see him about two weeks later.

By then, she reckoned she'd be about fourteen or fifteen weeks pregnant. She hadn't spotted blood since Harry's rough handling, and although she was aware the baby was still within the period for possible spontaneous abortion, she thought he or she stood a good chance of survival.

She tried not to feel emotional about the baby. She recognised that without it, life would be easier, and she had a far better chance of survival. But she'd been denied the opportunity twice before, and this time was determined it would happen. Gill wanted something of her own.

Chapter Thirty-Six - Gillian

True to form, Harry returned to Cabra fifteen days after he left. He leapt from the dinghy with a smile. "Hello, gorgeous," he said and pulled Gill into his arms.

She was astonished by his greeting, since they'd parted under very different circumstances. She was still furious with him; she considered unconsented sex a heinous crime. But as she still needed him to get off the island, she returned his smile and allowed him to kiss her. She even twined her arms around his neck to show how much she enjoyed his touch. Afterwards, she let her gaze linger on his face just long enough to see that his smile was nowhere near his eyes. Gill was no fool. He still held her in contempt.

"I've missed you. Let's leave the supplies and go straight up to the house." He made a grab at her, and she sidestepped out of the way. She wasn't ready for him to discover her pregnancy yet.

"What's wrong?" Harry asked in a demanding voice. His eyes narrowed as he stared down at her.

"Nothing...really. I'm just feeling a bit under the weather. It's been really hot at night since the storm, and I haven't been sleeping well."

"Leaving a light on won't help," he snorted. "Can't you just close your eyes and forget about everything? I never had you down as highly strung." His eyes had darkened even more, his mouth held taut in a thin line, and there was a flutter of nerves in Gill's stomach. She didn't like the expression on his face.

"I'll try, but the heat…" Her voice trailed off weakly, and she tried again, adding a brighter tone to her words. "Shall we have a coffee, or would you like something to eat?"

"Yeah, may as well." He grabbed two of the bags and then stomped past. Gill could feel his anger smouldering beneath the surface. For the first time, she felt more than just anxious. And it wasn't just for her, but for the baby as well now. Surliness she could put up with, she'd lived with it all her life. The odd beating now and again was just about bearable if she could shut her mind to it. But, with an infant growing inside her, she had to take extra care.

Up at the house, Harry upended the bags onto the table and selected a sealed packet of bacon. He stalked over to the kitchen area, and when she heard him slam the frying pan down onto the hob, realised he was making breakfast. Gill picked up some of the tins and sidled over to the pantry. The interior light of the cool house was dim, so she switched on the overhead light to see what she was doing. Harry glanced at the light for a second and then returned to the frying pan and bacon.

She made several journeys to put away the groceries in the larder and on the last, asked about his house guests. He looked at her with a slight frown and then dropped his gaze back to his cooking. "Oh, them. Yes, still with

172

me. They intend on staying another few weeks before moving on to the States. It means you'll have to stay here a bit longer."

He wasn't telling her anything she didn't expect to hear, but from his posture and the way his eyes slid away to the left, she knew he was lying. At first, he hadn't even known what she was talking about. *Liar!* Gill wanted to shout. She held her tongue, deciding she wasn't about to gain anything by arguing, so went along with it.

"That's a shame…for me, anyway. But it must be nice for you to have guests."

They sat and ate their fried bacon and egg sandwiches. Gill made coffee to go with it and tried to speak naturally. She mentioned the storm, talked about how many trees came down, and then afterwards, how everything was fresh and washed clean of dust. He nodded and added a few interjections of his own about the same storm on Antigua. She found she couldn't relax. Every word he uttered, she examined. She knew by now how the lies just tripped off his tongue. What else had he told her was sheer fabrication? She knew for certain there were no guests, and doubted he had a house on Antigua or land anywhere else. Gill glanced around the house as they finished the food. The building was plain and poorly finished, even if it did have a simple charm. Did Harry own it? Or the island, come to that?

She couldn't sit there listening to his rubbish, so she stood up and cleared away the crockery for washing. She put everything into a bucket to take along to the bath. As Gill walked along the path, she felt a slight movement in her tummy, a bit like a trapped butterfly beating against the palm of a hand. She stopped for a second and gasped. The baby! She had just felt its first movements. Now Gill knew for certain her child still lived within her. She *had* to get off the island.

After washing the dishes, she returned to the house and looked around for Harry. Sensing someone watching her, she glanced upwards and saw Harry was on the roof. She noticed for the first time there was a small makeshift ladder of sorts propped up against the side of the house. "What's wrong? What are you doing?"

"Nothing's wrong. I'm just checking the solar panels again. I do from time to time, especially after high winds and rain. Everything looks intact." He put what looked like a spanner into his shorts pocket and slithered across the roof to the ladder. Gill moved towards it and swiftly judged the roof height to be no higher than about ten feet. For a fleeting moment, she imagined pushing him off the ladder, but knew instantly that if she did, he almost certainly wouldn't be killed. It wasn't high enough to take that chance. The thought of killing Harry hadn't entered her mind before, and she put it down to the fact that now she had her baby's future to consider. But pretending to be anxious for Harry's safety wouldn't hurt.

"Be careful. That ladder doesn't look safe to me. If you fell and broke your leg, I don't know what we'd do."

He jumped down the last few feet. "It's fine, but thank you for being so concerned." He gave her a hug, and Gill, thinking of herself and the baby, asked him once again about letting her off the island. She didn't trust him as far as she could spit.

"Drop me off anywhere. I'm sure I can find somewhere discreet to stay. Or maybe hitch a ride on another yacht."

His arm was still across her shoulders, and he gave her what he obviously thought was his sympathetic and caring smile. "Gill, I honestly would love you to come back with me, but you know my position. Once the guests have gone, we'll see."

"What do you mean, *we'll see?*" She pulled away in anger. "You can't keep me here. You have to take me back sometime."

"It's...complicated. You're safe and protected here."

"Am I? I get the feeling I'm nothing more than a prisoner."

"No. No, you're wrong. Look, I've told you before...the authorities are hunting for you. You were seen and recognised in Portugal. Anyone would recognise you now. Your hair is longer and the red is clearly showing at the roots. The European police suspect you left for the Caribbean. Because of what they believe you've done, if you're found guilty, you'll be sentenced for murdering your friend. They want to question you, and your chances don't look good either way. You wouldn't last long in a normal prison. Someone would get at you...you wouldn't be safe. I expect Nathan has family left, eh? And then there's always Lawrence. I doubt he'd leave you alone. He'd come looking for you to get his revenge."

Gill felt her face grow taut as the blood left it. "I…I swear I…" She tried to speak to shout her innocence, but every breath had left her body. Locked up? She'd die…not again…she really couldn't bear it.

Chapter Thirty-Seven - Harry

Harry watched in fascination as her face turned white. He'd read about it happening in horror stories, but hers really did. She stood there, hand at her throat, gasping like a landed fish. Not a pretty sight. It was hard to stop himself laughing.

As soon as she'd recovered enough, she started shouting, which was something he couldn't abide. Marlene shouted just before she told him she was leaving. She shouldn't have done that.

"Why can't you be honest? I'm innocent, but this isn't about what you think I've done, is it? You have no right. I must get off this island, now! No one will learn about this place. Is this how you treat all your women friends? Bully and frighten them? No wonder you're on your own, never married. No woman in her right mind would put up with you for long."

He couldn't help it. History was repeating itself. He lifted his hand and hit her hard across the mouth. She staggered back, holding her hand to her cheek. A thin line of bloody spittle dropped from her lip. "Like I said, you're an ungrateful little cow. I've fed you for weeks. Given you this great place to hide…no one ever comes here. You're a murderer, and I'm preventing you from being locked up for good. Is this the way to repay me? You bloody mad bitch. You women are all the same. Grateful one minute and whining the next. I thought I'd put all that behind me, but no, you're all from the same fucking mould."

She wiped her mouth with the back of her hand. It shook, but he didn't know whether it was from anger or fear. Harry realised he'd said too much, and if he hit her again, he had no idea if he'd be able to control himself. So he stomped off down the hill. He'd taken nothing ashore apart from a couple of bags of food. The rest he'd eat himself. So what if she starved. She meant nothing to him and was fast becoming a real bind. He'd set out thinking keeping her there as a toy and sex slave would be an interesting and gratifying experiment. Now he wasn't so sure.

"Where are you going?" He felt her grab hold of the back of his shorts and the material ripped a little. He spun around and struck her hand away.

"Don't touch me, you mad bitch. I'm off."

"But you can't keep me here. You can't! You have no right."

"I have every right. It's my island. You know what? As far as I'm concerned I have no idea how you came here. Didn't know you existed, even." He carried on walking over the sand. She was right there, glued at his side like a rabid dog. Persistent and panting, almost frothing at the mouth in temper.

The dinghy was as he'd left it, and he pushed it a few feet into the sea and jumped in. Gill waited and watched in silent fury as Harry picked up the oars and started away from the shore. Then she lurched herself after the boat and landed face down in the bottom. "I'm coming. You can't stop me," she screamed.

He said nothing. Instead he pulled steadily for White Lady. As soon as they reached deep water and were about half way, he stopped and pulled the oars alongside the dinghy. Then he stood up and clambered the short distance to where she was sitting. Without a word, he grabbed her around the middle, gave her another clout for good measure when she objected and heaved her overboard.

She shrieked and hit the water with a splash. Harry climbed back onto the dinghy thwart and headed for the yacht. He laughed as she yelled and thrashed around and called out to her. "Don't make too much of a splash. Remember the sharks are attracted to it."

Chapter Thirty-Eight - Gillian

Gillian eked out the fresh food Harry had left as long as she could. But two bags didn't go very far, and she'd gone through everything within a week. Although the hot weather sapped her energy, she was thankful she wasn't a castaway on an island in the higher (or lower) latitudes where keeping warm was the priority. She would have spent a greater portion of her time scouting around for wood to burn if that had been the case.

Even so, she did carry home every piece of wood she came across. When she'd found Harry on the roof, she did wonder what he was doing. His story about checking the solar panels didn't ring true, especially since she'd already told him that everything was okay with the lighting after the storm. She was alarmed when he threw her into the sea and sailed off without leaving many new supplies.

But it was that first night she felt terrified. Once the sun had set on the horizon and she'd watched to catch that ever elusive 'green' flash, she went indoors. The recent rain had hatched many mosquitoes, and with the rising of the moon, they soon became active. Gill always lit a few candles; apart from a welcoming pool of light, she liked to think they kept some of the flying irritants away. Once the night shadows deepened, she resorted to her main form of lighting from the solar panels.

She flicked a switch and…nothing. Gill swore and wandered through to the bedroom, but the same thing happened in there. Every lamp in the house was useless. She tried changing a bulb, but in her heart, knew before she'd found the spare ones that Harry hadn't been checking the solar system at all. He'd been wrecking it. Bastard that he was.

Fear ripped through her. She didn't think she could get through a night in the dark, and so lit as many candles as she could. As the night grew blacker, Gill sat hugging herself, wondering what the hell she was going to do. She saw strange shapes in the flickering shadows, even imagining the face of her father at one time. A scream was building at the back of her throat. Terrified, she leapt to her feet. There were only so many candles in the drawer. She decided to light a fire outside. There was a good pile of wood by now, and if she positioned it near the bedroom window, the glow would comfort her through the long night.

Gill set to work, and later had a roaring fire for company as she ate her supper of pasta with a smear of tomato paste for flavour. It was plain and boring, but filled a hole. She had to keep fit and well for herself and the baby, and that included having enough to eat.

She checked through the stores. She still had the hidden cache she hadn't touched yet, and she'd managed to add a little to it every time Harry returned with new supplies. Gill remembered the fish she'd caught. She decided to try her hand at fishing again and only catch and eat one fish once a week to avoid ciguatera poisoning. There were other things to eat from the sea, which included crab, lobster and the odd conch if she was lucky. Gill was determined not to starve.

Sitting on the beach, she toyed with the idea of putting the SOS sign back, but Harry had been right. No one ever sailed past the island, and it didn't seem to be on any flight path, so it would have been a complete waste of time and energy. Besides, she got the feeling if he returned and found it resurrected, he'd have taken it out on her, and she had the baby to think about. He'd hit her already, and she hated to think what a proper beating might have done. There was also the threat of locking her in the safe room. When Harry had first shown her the dark hole in the floor, she shrank back in horror. The idea of venturing down there, let alone being kept a prisoner, would have turned her mind.

So far, she'd managed to keep the fire going. During the day, she let it die down. Old pieces of palm tree trunks were fibrous and although useless for making a blazing hot fire, they smouldered and kept the fire just alight during the day. At night, she added extra dry wood to make a more welcome and brighter light. Even so, Gill had gathered all the wood lying around the immediate area, and each day had to travel farther and farther away from the house for fuel. It didn't matter just yet, as she was now fit, and carrying the wood developed her muscles. She was far stronger than she'd been four months earlier. But the worry that she might eventually run out altogether kept her awake at night. Harry hadn't left anything which resembled a saw or axe, so she had no means of cutting down a tree. She kept her one good knife well-hidden as she didn't want him finding it and taking it from her. Instead of carrying the knife, she found an empty conch shell, which she smashed against the hard rock in the garden. The shell shattered into three pieces, and Gill selected the largest and sharpest shard to carry and use as a knife. The edge was razor sharp, and she asked herself if she had to use it, could she have sliced through an artery like a hot knife through butter?

***

It was still hot, the sun relentless, and to be truthful, Gill was bored with the monotony of it all. The storm was quite ferocious when it first hit, but its passing had added freshness to the air. For the first time since leaving England, she missed the rain. For all the colourful flowers and luxurious foliage, clear water and talcum powder beaches, it appeared that a paradise island was not all it seemed.

Gill's diary, which she'd kept out of Harry's sight, showed that he was overdue by four days. She stared at the date and couldn't believe she'd been there so long…kept prisoner all this time. Isla de Cabra had become her paradise prison.

The sun was well overhead by now, and she made lunch. She dipped into her tin cache and selected tomato soup (with one cracker) and a tin of peaches floating in thick, sweet syrup. She didn't bother heating the soup and ate both straight from the tin whilst sitting on the brow of the hill watching for a white sail to appear on the horizon.

She felt hot and sticky after she'd finished, and walked down to the beach for a refreshing swim. She walked out a short way until the water felt cooler than the tepid warm temperature in the shallows. Ever since seeing the shark, Gill kept a sharp lookout for a telltale fin, but there was no sign that day, so she lay back and relaxed…just a little.

Back at the house, she rinsed off the salt and hung her bikini up to dry. She could have swum naked, but since seeing her name written in the sand, she'd never quite been able to shake off the spooky feeling of being spied on. She stared down at her tummy, and with a jolt, saw that there was now a definite mound. Gill felt a flicker of fear and turned around, but there was no one watching— just dark shadows among the vegetation. She shivered. If she could see it, then Harry would, too. What would he say?

As night fell, she realised he wasn't coming. He wouldn't risk taking White Lady through the channel in the dark. He was too good a sailor to be reckless. But what about her? Surely he wouldn't abandon her altogether. Was he punishing her because she dared question his appalling behaviour of keeping her against her will? Or was it because she accused him of ill-treating all women, without any proof?

Chapter Thirty-Nine - Gillian

Four more days passed, and there was still no sign of Harry. By this time, Gill was more than anxious. She dragged everything out of the larder and totted up what was left of the food stores. They totalled a bag of rice, half a bag of pasta, half a packet of stale crackers, nine tins of soup, one of corned beef and two of fruit salad. The fresh food ran out days before, but thankfully, she had enough seasonings to add flavour to the soups and dried stuff. She hadn't had a cup of coffee in over a week, but there were enough teabags for about eight days. She'd got used to longlife milk in the tea, and knew she could drink it without when it eventually ran out. The recent fishing had been fruitful, but Gill hadn't been tempted to do it more than once a week. If she fell ill with vomiting and diarrhoea, then she'd have been laid up for ages. A lot could happen in a few days.

Gill's stomach cried out for more food, but she was more careful. At a pinch, she could make the rations last for about ten days. But what about the baby growing inside her? Would it be better to lose it? The idea gave her an added purpose to live. The raison d'être she and her baby were going to survive.

*****

Thankfully, she found a rock pool brimming with shrimps. Gill scooped them out with her hands and filled a couple of empty tins with the shellfish. Back at the house, she didn't bother to shell them before cooking but added an inch or two of water to a pan and boiled them for a few minutes. The shrimps tasted wonderful, although a bit fiddly to shell; she could have done with double the amount, but it filled a small hole.

She also found half a tree lying on the beach that morning. After snapping off what branches she could, she left them to dry in the sun. They made a welcome addition to her pile of firewood, which was always a worry. No wood, no fire.

Gill was about to go off foraging that afternoon, when she noticed Harry's yacht was approaching the island. Nervous with apprehension, she stood and stared, mixed emotions flooding through her. She was happy at the thought of food arriving but wasn't looking forward to seeing him. Her mind was in turmoil. She wanted to shout, hit him, but at the same time realised it would be nice to *talk* to someone. Gill decided to stay where she was. This time, she wasn't going to run down to meet him. He could go to her.

It seemed like hours, waiting up on the hill, and then finally, he appeared on the track. It wasn't long before sundown and would soon be dark. Gill had already rekindled the fire, and it was blazing nicely at the side of the house. She stayed where she was, sitting on one of the chairs beneath the window.

He stopped when he saw Gill and gave her a long lingering look. "Let's get one thing clear," he began. "This is my island. What I say is law. Unless you agree to everything I say, I'll go…without leaving you any more supplies. Understand?"

Gill remained silent at first. "If you did, it would be murder. I'd starve to death."

He sighed. "Haven't you understood anything yet? Anyway, it would take time to starve you. You hardly look like you're suffering. You've got the makings of a real belly."

She was wearing shorts with the zip undone, a T-shirt hanging loosely over them. As she was sitting down, she realised her bump must have been showing. *He thinks I'm putting on weight, the stupid man.* Gill sat up straight to disguise her pregnancy and heard herself answering him. "I understand."

He stared. "Everything?"

"Yes, everything."

He moved over to where she was sitting and stood in front of her. He was so close, she could smell his body odour. It smelt raw and tangy. "I want you to say sorry."

"Sorry."

"No, not that way. More than that." He unzipped his shorts and let them drop to the ground. Gill's gaze flickered down and then up at him. She bit back a retort and attempted to stand up. Not five minutes on the island and he was demanding sex. He pushed her back into the seat and stayed just inches away from her face. "No. Stay where you are. This position will do nicely."

Chapter Forty - Harry

Harry had never made her suck him off before because he'd always enjoyed her body. She was a good fuck, but feeling her gag once he ejaculated made it even more exciting. He recalled how a real feeling of power stole over him and knew at that moment he had her cowed. There was nothing more exciting than intimidating a woman into submission, but all enjoyment can grow thin and stale. He wondered how long he would carry on this little game.

They were up at the house that late morning, and so far, he hadn't made any effort to fetch the bags of food. They'd been in the boat overnight. He thought he'd let her sweat a bit more. "By the way, I see you've resorted to having a fire. That takes a lot of resources. I didn't see the smoke out at sea when I sailed past, so you're wasting your time if you expect anyone to come to your aid."

Gill stopped what she'd been doing and turned to give him a stunned look. Harry recognised she heard him right: that he'd passed the island many times and never called in. She eventually found her voice to reply, but didn't comment on his little taunt. That was a shame. He'd have enjoyed tormenting her. Instead, she answered him calmly. "It's not for that. I think you know the solar panels haven't been working since you left. I've kept the fire going for more light at night."

Harry raised his eyebrows. "The solar panels not working? Dear me. We can't have that. I'll have to inspect them while I'm here…if you're good." He gave her a wink and then yawned. "It might be time for a nap soon. Anyway, I don't advise keeping a fire going permanently, especially while you're asleep. Everything is so dry on the island now. A stray spark could send the island up in flames in minutes. Where would you be then? No shelter, no food. I suggest you put it out. *Now!*" Harry yelled the last word at her with the satisfaction of watching her jump. He waited while she stood her ground for a second and then smirked when she picked up the bucket from outside. He assumed she intended fetching water to douse the smouldering coals. He imagined she'd relight it once he left, but it didn't matter. All Harry wanted was to ensure she did everything he ordered her to. It was quite a powerful feeling to have complete control over someone.

While she fetched the water, Harry disappeared into the bedroom. He knew she kept a notebook in her bag as he'd read through it before. She hadn't written anything detrimental about him so far, probably realising he might read it, but Harry decided to nick it anyway. The loss would be a blow to her morale. He laughed. Everything was going just as planned. This time there would be no stealing away in the night. There would be no repeat of Marlene. Gill couldn't escape. She was his, to do with as he liked. She would stay there as long as he wanted, and after that, there were plenty of places to hide a body if it came to it.

With her notebook in his back pocket, he left the house and walked down to the beach, whistling to himself. It was a stunning view ahead. The bay lay undisturbed, hardly a ripple broke the surface of the clear turquoise water. The beach ran round the bay, pale fine sand rippling right down to the water's edge. The back was fringed by palm and casuarina trees and a smattering of lush shrubs covered with brightly coloured flowers. Gill was lucky to be in such an eye-catching paradise prison.

Harry pushed the dinghy a few feet across the sand towards the sea when he heard a shout. He paused and looked back up the hill. Gill was running across the beach.

"Wait! You're not going, are you? You haven't left me any food."

He carried on heaving the boat across the sand. As the 'rubber duck' entered the sea and floated, he held onto the side and stood in the shallows deliberately not looking at her. He heard Gill's panting from her short run. Her voice had quavered in alarm.

"No, I haven't."

"But you promised."

"I did no such thing."

"But, please, I need the food. I've almost run out."

Harry peered at her, knowing his look was unsympathetic and cunning. "No more tantrums. No more fires. No whingeing, or not only will I not leave any food, but I won't return. Ever."

Her body seemed to sag. "No I won't. I promise. Honest."

Harry waited. He enjoyed watching her squirm under his unemotional stare. Then he lifted the bags from the dinghy. He plonked them on the sand, thinking she could carry the lot up to the house. She had nothing better to do. She picked up a couple, one in each hand and stood as if waiting for him to help her. Harry ignored her and sat down on the thwart. The oars were stowed in the bottom of the boat. He fixed them to the rowlocks and without a word began the row to White Lady.

"Thank you," she called across the widening gap.

"Remember your promise." He said no more and didn't look back until he reached the yacht. Gill was still standing in the same spot. Harry ignored her. He hoisted the dinghy up on its davits and prepared to set sail.

Chapter Forty-One - Gillian

It took Gillian ages to carry every damn bag up to the house. She had to get them under cover, as she'd noticed that something had broken into some of the plastic bags during the night and disturbed the contents. She knew there were a few animals on the island and probably included rodents. The thought of rats clambering over her food was repulsive, but because she had to survive, she pushed the horrible notion aside. All food had to be eaten.

Even so, without Harry helping, she had to make numerous round trips, and once she'd dumped everything on the floor, realised there were more than the usual eight or nine bags. Was the bastard planning on leaving her longer this time?

Gill suddenly felt a flutter in her belly. The baby was beginning to be much more active, and she felt ridiculously pleased that, so far, there were no side effects with her pregnancy. Morning sickness was minimal, (she wasn't sure she'd even recognised it at the time), and apart from feeling miserable and alone, her overall health so far was good.

It was hot outside, so she walked over to the sofa and sat down for a rest. The stores could wait. As she sat, she pondered over the early years of her life.

Her parents were such stiff-necked people, especially her father, and over the years she'd grown to despise them. She believed the main reason was because her father was a vicar, a so-called man of the cloth. Gill was sent to Sunday school, and there, the lessons taught by the Sunday school teachers were the gentler stories from the bible about love and caring for one's friends and family. Gill's father's actions were nothing like that. He was strict, hard and unyielding. What made it worse was that her mother never contradicted him. Growing up was confusing. The stories said one thing, but her life simply wasn't like that. She still remembered that dark under-stairs cupboard and being locked in there for hours. Since then, she'd never ventured into caves or tunnels if she could help it. Harry's safe room and his threat had set her mind jangling with terror.

Once Gill entered senior school, she realised that other children led different, freer lives. She lived well on the fringe of pop music, drugs, soft porn and going out with friends at the weekend. When she was fourteen, she rebelled in a quiet roundabout way. Gill joined the library and later did some work for a charity. She spent hours at the library, poring over books which would have been banned at home. She had also made a couple of good friends by then, and they often met there before going into town for window-shopping and ogling boys. The charity work was a bit of a misnomer, as Gill did little more than occasionally help flog stickers on the appropriate charity day. Mostly, she spent Saturdays with a group of young people experimenting with smoking, alcohol and the first fumbles of underage sex.

Then all hell was let loose. At fifteen, she fell pregnant. There was no excuse; she wasn't under the influence of drink or drugs. Gill just wanted to *do it* and found out the hard way that babies can be made the first time.

Her parents hit the roof once they discovered that their 'chubby' daughter wasn't chubby, after all. She was over five months gone. Too late for a 'cessation'; they could never use the word termination or abortion. She was kept away from school (the head was told she was dreadfully ill) until the baby was almost due. Then things became very muddled and sketchy. Gill recalled going to a home of some sort and being delivered of a baby…but after that nothing. She knew she was ill afterwards and spent ages in some sort of hospital, but the time spent there was completely out of focus … she remembered almost nothing to this day. When she was eventually discharged, she was an adult.

The only thing she recalled with clarity was that it had all been her parents' fault, especially her father's. Gill's resentment ran deep, and she never went out of her way to see them again.

She shifted her position on the sofa and got up. Fully rested, she began restocking the pantry with the food Harry had left. Once again, she had a baby growing inside her. It gave her a new reason to live. She had to somehow convince Harry to let her off the island. She stopped what she was doing. It might take months. He was bound to find out about the pregnancy sometime and probably soon. How would he take it?

Gill selected some tins and set them aside on the table. They were to go into the hidden cache, which she'd already raided the week before. She had to make the food last. She noticed that Harry had left two half-kilo packets of rice this time. She added one of them to the growing pile on the table. If she wedged it inside an empty tin and pushed the lid back in place, it might stop the rats or mice getting at it. The thought of losing food to rodents made her feel giddy, and she realised she hadn't eaten since early morning. Gill tore open a packet of peanuts and allowed herself a handful. She had no idea when Harry would appear again.

Chapter Forty-Two - Gillian

The weeks passed, and Gill estimated it was almost a month since Harry had left. The weather had been mixed since then: hot, very humid with the occasional downpour of rain. It was fast becoming unbearable during the day and not much better at night. Some days she was plagued by mosquitoes and others flies, which she presumed were attracted by the goat dung all over the island. The island was getting her down and she couldn't wait to leave.

That day was like any other: get up, rush to the loo, make a skimpy breakfast and eye her fast-dwindling food with alarm. Gill had to resort to extra fishing again, as not only had she run out of protein, but she still needed to eke out her precious stores. She inspected her belly and guessed that as soon as Harry saw her without any clothes on, he'd know at once about the pregnancy.

The thought made her edgy, which increased as soon as she spied his yacht approaching the island. She rushed indoors and changed into her loosest dress. She could no longer wear shorts, as she couldn't get into them, and resorted to wearing the sarong all the time. The material was paper-thin and faded after all the washing and sun, but it was the most comfortable thing to wear. Gill smoothed down the cotton dress, and her bump seemed quite prominent to her eye. Oh, bugger!

She walked down to the beach just as Harry had lowered the dinghy into the water and watched as he piled plastic bags into the bottom. Her heart sank. He had no plans to let her leave this time then. She bit her bottom lip. She refused to let him see her cry again. Tears left him completely unmoved. It was at that moment when she finally understood he was never going to let her leave. She was his prisoner, and for some insane reason, he enjoyed her forced incarceration. She had to find a way to get off the island, or she and her baby would die there.

The dinghy hit the sand, and Gill grabbed the painter which Harry threw at her. She made a loop in the rope and started fixing it around the usual rock.

"Hi there," he said as he climbed out and gave the boat a nudge up onto the sand.

"Hello, Harry," Gill replied. She leant slightly forward so her dress fell away from her tummy. She didn't want him to guess just yet. She was terrified by what he might say or do. Gill didn't even want to look directly at him because she knew that if he caught her eye, he'd know at once that something wasn't right. Keeping her gaze down, she made a show of ensuring the rope was tied properly around the boulder.

"Here, come and give me a hand. I've bought some extra things for you. A few bars of chocolate and boiled sweets."

"Wonderful," She forced the words out. "Thank you."

He gave a short laugh. "You're welcome. Come here." Gill moved towards him and Harry pulled her into his arms. After the last time, she felt nothing but loathing at his touch and wondered how she was going to make it through the day. She had to keep up the play-acting because if she didn't, he'd end up hitting her again over some trivia and then pissing off with the food. She and baby would have been doomed. How could she have been such a fool to let things come to this?

Harry tilted her chin up and kissed her. He stretched his mouth into a smile, but it never reached his eyes. "Let's get the grub up and then we can relax," he said, releasing her and reaching down for a cluster of bags. He handed Gill a few, and she started the walk back up the hill.

She tried not to carry too much, but at the same time, she didn't want Harry to notice anything. They made a few trips, and then she timidly suggested Harry brought the last bags up while she made coffee and put the stores away.

The sight of all that food made her feel giddy: butter, bacon, loads of fresh fruit and vegetables, cooking oil and even a small tub of cream. Best of all, was a small box containing a selection of chocolates. If the situation had been different, she'd have felt like she was in heaven.

Gill gave Harry his coffee and fussed around him, offering him the choice of biscuits or cake. He seemed pretty much chilled, and she took the opportunity to ask whether he had time to look at the solar panels.

"I've cut down on the fires, as wood is getting really scarce," she explained. "It would be lovely to have a good light to read by at night. The evenings are really long otherwise."

He seemed to mull her question around in his head, as if weighing up the pros and cons. He nodded. "I'll see what I can do, but I'm not an engineer. It may need more than a simple adjustment."

"That would be great. Thanks. I would have looked myself, but I don't have any tools…not that I'd know what was wrong, anyway."

They sat and talked for a while. Gill made a huge attempt to be friendly and thought he believed she really was trying to be good. After a while, he stood up and said he'd go back to the boat and fetch some tools to look at the solar panel.

"I'll fetch the ladder for you." She walked around to the back of the house where the ladder was kept. She picked it up but decided it was too heavy for her to carry, so she dragged it round to the front, where the panels were fixed to the sloping roof. She eyed the roof gingerly. She hated heights.

Harry reappeared, and as she gawped at him, she saw that he was dripping wet. "What happened?" She couldn't resist laughing.

He shrugged, but she could see he was annoyed. "Bloody well tripped getting back into the dinghy. I fell overboard. Sorry, Gill, but there's nothing to laugh at. I've lost all my tools in the sea."

"Oh no!"

"Oh yes. The bay's too deep to retrieve them, so you're destined for more dark evenings, I'm afraid."

As he peeled off his T-shirt and shorts, she wondered if he'd made it all up. How convenient for him to make her suffer for longer. She also knew he kept a full set of diving gear on board, so he could have retrieved all his tools quite easily. He stood in his boxers and rummaged through the pockets of his shorts, tossing the boat keys and his wallet onto the table. The wallet fell off the table and opened to display the photo she'd seen before. Without thinking, Gill picked the wallet up and stared at the picture.

"She's pretty. Who is she?"

He snatched the wallet from her fingers and slapped her hand down. "Keep your bloody hands off my things."

Gill shrank away from the hostile glare in his eyes. "Ow! I was just saying. Don't get so uppity."

He continued to glare and then, as if something snapped inside his head, he shook it. "Sorry. I shouldn't have done that. It's an old friend. Marlene."

She attempted to get them back on a friendly footing. "She looks lovely. Not your wife then?" She smiled.

Gill didn't think he'd heard her at first, then after a minute he folded the wallet back in two and glanced up. "What? No. Not my wife, but a girlfriend from long ago."

"Did you meet her out here? In the Caribbean?"

"Yes. She was a white Caribbean woman. What's with all the questions?"

She gave him her best open and friendly smile. "I'm just interested. You're an interesting man...you must know that." She wondered if she'd overdone the sycophant bit, so left it there. She was rewarded by a self-satisfied grin.

"I suppose I am. There's not much to tell you about Marlene. We were a couple, but split up after a few years. She decided she wanted to go back to Trinidad despite coming from a penniless family and not having any money of her own. She gave up our beautiful home and everything else on Antigua. She just upped and went one day, out of the blue, and I haven't seen or heard from her since."

"Oh. Were you upset or was it mutual? When was this?"

Harry regarded her under hooded eyelids. "I was at the time, but it was for the best. We both wanted different things in life, and I couldn't persuade her my way was better. It happened some years ago. Now, enough, woman. Mind your own business."

"But I've told you about me, given you part of my life story. I thought as we were getting on so well today..." Her words dried up as she recognised the hollow look in his eyes.

"I know you for what you are—a cheat and lying murderer. I've never believed what you told me or your protests of innocence. Theo first mentioned it, and I saw that for myself, once I'd dropped you off here and sailed back to Antigua the first time. The internet holds so many riveting stories, doesn't it, Gill? Anyway, you can't compare my life with yours. I was blameless in Marlene's decision to leave."

Gill glared at him. Why did she get the impression he wasn't telling the truth? What poor white woman willingly gave up a 'beautiful home' to return to her destitute relatives? Was he playing her for a fool again? She believed so.

Chapter Forty-Three - Gillian

"I'm happy to cook for you," Harry said later that afternoon, and she smiled her thanks.

"Goody. You're a great cook. Better than me, and it's a treat to have someone else do it. What shall we have?"

"I've got lamb chops this time. We can have it with new potatoes and minted peas. Plenty of gravy and a squishy cream cake for pudding."

Gill's mouth watered at the sound of it all and watched as he prepared everything.

"If I get it all ready now, we can go for a walk, find you some wood maybe to replenish your pile."

She almost blinked. Why was he being so nice and amenable? She had to be on double guard. His good moods always seemed to lead to black or violent ones. Harry trimmed the fat off the chops and left them under cover in the pantry. He peeled the potatoes and put them in a pan of water to soak. Gill eyed the sharp knife which seemed to have appeared from nowhere. It must have come off the yacht, as she'd never seen it before. Could she use a knife on someone if her life depended on it? It wasn't like causing death from a distance, such as poison. Stabbing someone was so *physical*. Gill discarded the idea, as she knew she couldn't get to the knife without attracting his attention. Besides, she reckoned the knife she had already secreted away was bigger and sharper than this one. Just seeing it lying there seemed to have triggered her into thinking about killing him again, though.

As she thought about it, she trembled. Was this her, thinking about killing someone? She hardened her heart. She had to. She knew, given the chance, he wouldn't have hesitated to kill her.

***

Their walk took longer than Gill thought. Harry had decided to take a fishing line with him, and although she was adept at catching her own fish by this time, proceeded to give her a lesson on what to do. She let him prattle on, nodding at the right moments. He was full of himself. As he talked, she fantasised about slipping the knife in under his ribs. She'd seen a programme on television years ago, that if done correctly, the victim didn't feel a thing at first. Gill imagined using her knife on him…if the opportunity arose. Could she?

After the lesson and three medium-sized fish in hand, they gathered up a good armful of wood littered around the rocks and wandered back to the house. By now, it was late afternoon and Harry set about cooking the meal. While everything was cooking, he cleaned and gutted the fish, and Gill thought it odd that he never once asked how she usually managed this job, considering he'd removed all the sharp knives.

The meal was delicious, and afterwards, Gill felt completely full for the first time in weeks. She leant back in her seat until she remembered her bump and immediately sat upright. She refilled Harry's wine glass and added a smidgeon to her own. Harry was engrossed in some ramble about his house on Antigua and thankfully hadn't noticed either her blossoming body or that she was plying him with wine. The thought of him staying the night and running his hands over her body made her stomach lurch. For one thing, he repulsed her and more importantly, he'd discover her pregnancy. The day was drawing in, the sun setting when Harry suddenly sprang up and announced he was going.

"But it's getting dark," she protested without thinking.

"I can't stay tonight, and if I leave now I can just about make it through the reef," he replied, patting his pockets to check he had everything.

"Really? Are you sure you can't stay?" Gill was thinking of him snoring on his back in bed…her knife hidden outside, just waiting for her to slide it between his ribs.

Harry stopped in the doorway and turned. A smug expression appeared on his face. He walked back to the table and bending down, planted a kiss on her forehead. "Don't worry, gorgeous. I'll be back as soon as I can."

Chapter Forty-Four - Harry

Back on board White Lady, Harry had to laugh. The look on Gill's face had been priceless when he told her he'd lost everything in the lagoon. Silly cow! Hadn't he been sailing long enough to be extra careful when loading the dinghy with valuable items? He wasn't stupid. But she'd fallen for it and would have to suffer more of those long dark nights all on her own. The wood for burning was always pitifully hard to come by on Caribbean islands, so what she had in hand would soon run out long before he returned. He was gradually wearing her down; the game was going all his way, as he'd known it would. Soon, she'd be like putty in his hands, although the journey there was a thrill in its own right.

She annoyed him at first when she mentioned Marlene and handled her photograph. But Harry believed all women were the same: nosey, meddlesome pains in the arse. He'd been a little economical with the truth, though. Marlene and he had had one major row, which resulted in her leaving him. He hadn't known at the time how badly she'd taken it. Maybe he shouldn't have beaten her so hard. He took a little trip to Colombia, and when he got home, she'd cleared off. No warning, nothing.

Harry didn't worry so much about her leaving him, but he did care that she'd taken their daughter—Harry's first and only child. She shouldn't have done that. She didn't return to Trinidad, although he looked for her and made enquiries. It was as if she just vanished, their daughter along with her.

Harry weighed anchor and stowed it. He slipped the engine into gear and headed for the passage. The night was almost upon him as he navigated the yacht along the channel. The sentinel rocks of granite stood on either side, and the boat and Harry slipped from their embrace as they headed further out beyond the jagged reef lying on either side of them. The deep clear water was about two hundred metres out. Once clear, he turned the boat towards the wind and hoisted the sails. Happy to be at sea again, he looked at the electronic chart and turned the yacht onto its new heading. The destination was Colombia, where he had a bit of business to conduct. The deal meant nothing to him—he didn't need the money—but it gave him a thrill. He'd been doing it for years.

White Lady settled into her sailing groove. Harry set the automatic pilot and went below to make an entry into the ship's log. He made no mention of Isla de Cabra or Colombia but said he was heading for the Panama Canal. The authorities didn't have to know what he got up to.

Chapter Forty-Five - Gillian

Another month passed, and Gill's wood store was down to just a couple of miserable-looking sticks. She trawled all over the island and found next to nothing to burn. The nights were so long and dark, and she loathed them. The candle supply was also dwindling fast, and she was at her wits' end. Nothing could dispel her dread and hatred of the dark even if she could persuade herself there was nothing to fear. The shadows were still there. Her fear was becoming more than an obsession and she had to do something about it. But how?

Gill had no tools, and the roof looked bloody high to someone with an acute fear of heights. She thought of getting the ladder and scrambling over the roof to look at the solar panel, but the thought made her hands shake and sweat with fear. What if she fell? She'd harm the baby or miscarry. She had no medicines except for a jar of Vaseline, a few plasters and headache pills. If she lost the baby, she could bleed to death. Gill pushed the idea of traipsing across the roof to one side. She had to overcome her fear of the dark.

Her days were long and boring. Gill spent most hours searching for things to eat or fuel for the fire. She walked all over the island most days. Fishing trips had improved no end, and it was a rare day when she didn't manage to hook at least one fish. She was lucky not to have another bout of food poisoning and wondered if the fish she'd caught that time was just one in a million that was swimming in the waters of the island that day. Although her days were much the same with some sort of routine, she supposed it gave her a sense of comfort. But she wished she'd stop feeling so hungry all the time.

If only she had the internet, but that was impossible. Even if she could have charged her phone, she doubted there'd be any signal. Gill wondered about making candles from tallow, and she looked at the goats wandering freely over the island. Could she bring herself to catch one, slaughter it for fresh meat and then render down its fat to make candles? The idea was repulsive. She was an animal lover and wasn't quite that desperate yet. Maybe Harry would do it if she asked. That was if he returned. Gill pushed that idea away. Of course, he'd return. He loved making her miserable, the sick psycho. Why hadn't she seen it in the beginning?

The thought of candles from tallow gave her an idea. Because she caught fresh fish, the tinned ones were mostly left in the cache of hidden food. She knew there were plenty of sardines and tuna hidden. These were all canned in fish oil. It would be simple to drain off the oil, put it into something to store it and find something suitable to use as a wick. Corned beef also had a layer of fat for that matter.

Gill went over to the hidden food store and selected a couple of tins of sardines. She pierced the tin with the can opener. She'd torn a strip from an old skirt and used it as a wick by inserting it into the can. It was a bit floppy and needed something firm to make it stand up. Inside her handbag, she found a paperclip in one corner. She unbent half to create the bottom, poked it into the tin with the wick wound around it, bent the other half up and finally added a twist to hold the wick above the level of the oil in the tin. The wick stood proud and after a few minutes, the wick drew the oil up, and carefully, she applied a match to it. When the thing caught light, she felt immensely proud to have created light from something as simple as the oil from fish. While watching the candle burn with its small and smelly flame, she burst into tears. She couldn't help wondering why something as simple as a homemade candle should seem so important, but somehow it did.

The fish seemed okay after burning the oil from it, and she put it aside for lunch that day. She then realised that any oil, olive, cooking oil or coconut oil could be used to make a candle or more correctly, an oil lamp. Gill searched through all the food stocks and found a piece of mouldy cheese. The rind was waxy, ideal for making a candle. As for the Vaseline, wasn't that made from tar oils?

Gill knew the oil and candles wouldn't last forever, but this small discovery gave her hope and comfort that day.

Chapter Forty-Six - Gillian

Gill's stomach looked huge. She knew that when Harry returned, it would be the first thing he'd notice. She'd lost count of the days a week or two earlier, as she was too ill to bother. She remembered feeling very hot and shivery at the same time as she was sick, and her bowels turned to jelly. She spent most of the time lying outside before staggering to the loo in time. By her estimation, she was at least twenty-six weeks pregnant and felt like a beached whale. Harry had been gone so long, she'd almost given up thinking he'd return, but in her heart, knew he would. He enjoyed torturing her too much. Soon after he'd left the last time, she went to write in her diary and discovered it missing. This had to be his latest stupid trick. If she hadn't felt so afraid of him, she'd have laughed in his face when he returned. Instead, she bent over and collapsed in floods of tears. What had she ever done to anyone to make her life so miserable?

Gill felt renewed fear for herself and the baby. What if he decided she was no longer a good shag, especially now with this huge stomach? Perhaps he'd see her pregnancy as ugly. Some men would have. So far, she recognised that Harry had kept her alive because of some perverted idea of his to keep her a virtual prisoner purely to violate her body whenever he felt the urge. Would he even acknowledge the child was his? Not having seen a doctor, Gill had no definite way of saying when it was conceived.

She had to make plans. If he decided to just leave her there for good, then she had to stop him going somehow. How would she know beforehand? He hardly gave anything away. Gill made two decisions. She reckoned she could handle the yacht and reckoned she *had* to kill him first. The thought of killing anything filled her with loathing and trepidation, but in her heart, she understood there was no other choice.

She made sure her knife was as sharp as could be. Her hefty piece of wood was secreted under the bed along with the shard of conch shell. She could beat him around the head, bash his brains out. If they walked out to the fishing rocks, could she muster up enough force to push him down between them, where he'd never be able to climb out? She had a few alternatives to mull over.

The day had turned exceptionally hot and muggy, and Gill needed a refreshing swim. With her tatty sarong tucked around her bloated body, she trudged down over the hot sand to the beach. Gill was so lost in thought that the sight of Harry's boat approaching along the narrow inlet made her stagger with shock. Her nerves began to jangle; her heart beat painfully against her chest. She felt more afraid than she'd ever been, even when she'd been living with Lawrence.

It was the same performance as all the other times. Anchor down, dinghy launched, a pull to the shore, beach the boat. Then, as if in slow motion, it all changed. Harry walked towards her, bags in both hands, and she noticed immediately how his eyes were drawn to her stomach. His mouth opened, closed and then gaped open again.

"What? You're pregnant?"

Gill could only stand and nod, she was so terrified by what his reaction would be. Waiting for the outburst to follow, she lowered her head in submission. She couldn't put up with his anger, couldn't meet his eyes. *Please, god, someone help me.*

Harry dumped the bags on the sand and walked right up to her. He lifted a hand and touched her stomach gingerly. "Why? Why didn't you tell me?"

Gill was startled that he hadn't blown his top or raised a fist to her. Instead, he lifted a hand to her cheek and ran a finger lightly down it. She was astounded. Had she misread Harry? Was there a good side to him? Had taking her there been a genuine means of hiding her 'for your own good and then something happened and it all got out of hand'. *No!* She remembered how he'd hit her and deliberately wrote her name in the sand to terrify her, the stolen gas, and then there were the trashed solar panels. He'd even made a joke about the sharks. Everything was done out of spite once he knew how frightened she was of being alone and especially of the dark. He enjoyed torturing her.

"I didn't know what you'd say. I wasn't sure at first, as my periods are irregular, and the first couple of times we had sex, we didn't take any precautions. It must have happened then. Then this last time you were gone so long…I just grew and grew, and here I am."

He ran his hands through his hair and turned away, a stunned look on his face. He took a few paces away from her and turned. She noted his shocked look replaced by one of excitement. It was clearly plastered across his features. Gill stood perfectly still and silent. Was he pleased? She wasn't entirely sure. More like he was disturbed, hesitant about what to do or say next. A warning bell rang in her head. Harry was unstable, volatile, dangerous.

Without another word, he turned on his heel and walked back to the dinghy. He lifted the bags from the bottom and dropped them on the sand before pushing the boat back into the water.

Once again, she was alone on the island.

Chapter Forty-Seven - Theo

He couldn't believe he'd been thrown overboard. After telling Harry about Gill or more correctly, Priscilla Gillian Hodges, he'd acted completely out of character. Looking back, Theo believed Harry hadn't been himself since he'd met the woman. As the three of them sailed across the Atlantic, he couldn't take his eyes off her; obsessed, he thought.

At first, Harry completely refused to believe him, and then as it sank in, his expression turned more thoughtful. Harry could have even believed that the prospect of Gill killing someone turned him on. That realisation about Harry was an unpleasant surprise.

Of course, Harry hated that Theo knew what he got up to in the Caribbean. His father had dabbled in the business, and then Harry had taken over. There were more Coast Guard patrols around the coasts of Mexico and Colombia these days, but generally the big stuff took place in the Pacific. Harry was small fry; he enjoyed the thrill it gave him when 'sailing' the Caribbean waters and the Atlantic. Theo was only amazed he'd never been caught.

Truthfully, he wasn't interested in what Harry got up to. Theo knew he'd get caught one day, and it would be his own bloody fault. Theo had other matters to deal with. He didn't have time to worry about Harry. He had just risked life and limb getting out of Algeria and Morocco, and after passing on the info to his agent runner, needed to go to ground for a time. Harry provided him the means until he turned nasty.

So, there he was, barely afloat in the middle of the Atlantic, watching the light on the transom of White Lady slowly disappear in the direction of Antigua. He yelled himself hoarse, but Harry didn't turn the yacht around, and Theo guessed Gill didn't intervene on his behalf once Harry told her he'd disappeared overboard.

Why was that? At first, Theo assumed it must have suited her purposes, or Harry had some sort of control over her. He just didn't know. As he imagined what happened between them later, it didn't take Theo two minutes to understand neither of them did anything about searching for him. They both had a reason for his convenient disappearance and were therefore equally guilty, even if it had been Harry who'd pushed him. What a despicable pair.

Theo was wearing a life jacket, thankfully, complete with whistle. Big deal. Who the fuck would ever hear that in the middle of the Atlantic? There wasn't another ship in sight. He had no food, no water, and there was a hell of a lot of sea around and beneath him. He began to imagine sharks. He saw them in every wave heading his way. Within an hour, Theo was chilled to the bone, and he had difficulty staying awake until dawn. The one stroke of luck was that around six in the morning, he spied a large piece of wood floating near him. It was angled in the water, one edge about four feet higher than the other, and as he swam over to it, realised one end had two large metal barrels attached to it. The raft was unsteady, and it took him numerous attempts to drag his exhausted, cold body on board. As soon as he had, Theo sank into a troubled sleep.

He saw nothing the first day, and thirst and hunger set in. Theo knew he couldn't drink either his urine or sea water. Despite what some people thought, madness would have overcome him. On the third day, he caught a turtle. Raw turtle meat was…pretty unpalatable, the blood of a turtle even more so, but it kept him going. Days became weeks, and during that time Theo survived on fish, seabirds, turtles, turtle blood and rainwater.

After a while, he lost track of time. His hours were spent sleeping, having vivid hallucinations, and catching something to eat. Apparently, when Theo was eventually found, he'd been adrift for over two months, sunburnt beyond recognition and completely round the twist. He was taken to a hospital in Brazil, and spent the next five months recovering there.

Chapter Forty-Eight - Gillian

Gill lugged the bags up to the house and began unpacking them. This time, she was excited because as well as the usual stock items, Harry had included new candles, matches and more cartons of milk than he had before. He'd remembered that the oil was nearly finished, and as well as cheese and bacon, he'd added two tins of butter. A cardboard box contained six curried-meat pasties and two joints of meat. Cooked, the meat would last for days, with luck. Once the meat began to get a bit rancid, Gill could disguise the flavour with curry powder, of which there was plenty.

He hadn't taken the rubbish away this time, as he'd left so abruptly, even by his standards, and she knew that she'd placed the empty oil bottle in the plastic bag by mistake. Gill went and retrieved it. It was stupid she knew—the chances were minute—but every chance she got, she wrote a short SOS note and slipped it into an empty bottle. The bottles were taken to the rocky shore, well away from her bay and tossed into the water. Gill prayed that one day, someone would find one of these bottles and read her desperate message. If only Harry had brought more bottles, then she might have stood a chance. As it was, she knew that most glass bottles broke as soon as they were washed up onto a shore, but the small gesture gave her something to think about and a tiny measure of hope.

A few evenings later, it rained. Gill should have guessed, as the previous days had been muggy, sticky and unpleasant. The English would have called it typical thundery weather. She realised she was right in the hurricane season and hadn't yet experienced a real hurricane. Knowing the catastrophic destruction hurricanes caused, she hoped she never would. After the tropical storm Gill experienced soon after arriving on Cabra, Harry had assured her that the islands running along the north of Venezuela and off Colombia were rarely hit. Hurricanes were prone to drift up the Caribbean island chain and veer off towards Florida and sometimes more inland. She should be safe.

The rain turned heavy round about midnight, and the house shook and rattled with the wind and rain lashing against it. Gill made sure all the window shutters were locked tight and the front door securely shut even if there was no key. Within minutes, the place felt like hell. Sweat poured off her. It was like being locked in an oven. The storm lasted all day and the next night. The following morning, Gill woke to find sunshine streaming in through the cracks in the shutters and beneath the door.

Outside, it was a mess. The wind had torn branches from the trees, coconuts littered the beach, and everything dripped from the recent deluge. The firepit was a pool of sludge, and the spa bath was filled with hundreds of leaves. The roof looked as if part of it was about to slip to the ground, and she knew that sometime, she'd have to find the courage to climb up and see if she could do something to stop it from falling.

Her only consolation was that now, there was plenty of wood all over the island to keep her night fire going. Oh, joy!

Gill spent that day and the next collecting the wood. Some had piled up on the rocky shore on the windward side. She took care clambering over the slippery rocks to filch the wood before it got swept away by a large rogue wave sweeping in from the sea. There was little tide to worry about, but what she couldn't carry back home, Gill removed to well above the shoreline and left it in piles to be collected later. Taking it all back would have been a mammoth task, but she wouldn't have had any of it had it not been for the storm.

Nearly three weeks had passed since Harry left. Out of habit, Gill still went and sat on the hill just beyond the house for a few minutes each day. Sometimes she took a simple lunch with her. It felt peaceful, resting under the waving branches of the palm trees, and she often allowed her mind to wander. Gill's life had been one of deep lows and few highs. Nobody had ever put her first, treated her special. Had she been born so dreadful?

She cast her gaze across the sea, stopping at the horizon where the deep blue met the huge sky in a fuzzy line of what looked like prancing elephants. The storm might have left Isla de Cabra, but judging by this odd phenomenon in the distance, a new hurricane was still raging further east. Gill appreciated Harry wouldn't attempt putting to sea until everything had settled and returned to normal.

Chapter Forty-Nine - Gillian

Even though Gill had fish to eat, she found her body craved more protein. What she would have given to sink her teeth into a succulent steak or eggs and bacon. She wondered whether Harry would bring more protein now he knew she was pregnant. She'd been getting so hungry and raided the food cache more and more. Most of the canned fish had gone, and she was left with some bloody awful luncheon meat, corned beef or dubious casseroled chicken. Gill decided to stop being a coward and opened the chopped luncheon meat.

It tasted awful. It was so bad, she wondered who on earth would buy it in the first place. Gill decided it must have been because it was cheap. Harry wouldn't have wasted his money on a worthless captive, would he?

The weather brightened in the east, and she had the distinct feeling Harry would return that day. Sure enough, two hours later, she recognised the white sail with the red line along the leech and foot as White Lady made her way towards Cabra.

Again, Gill was in two minds about his return. She was desperate for good food but at the same time hated the idea of being nice to him. Was she ready, frantic enough to kill him? What if she failed and he went for her instead? Gill's head was spinning. It told her: Harry wouldn't harm me. The child was his, after all. Surely he believed that?

As she was so huge now, Gill wasn't sure she could handle the yacht on her own. She couldn't take that risk by killing him. She decided to take the reasonable tack. Make sure he had to see sense and take her to civilisation. She needed to see a gynaecologist and be examined. The baby had to have a scan. There were a hundred and one things to be done.

Gill went down the hill to meet him, all the time telling herself she was doing it for the baby.

She watched and waited. Could she tell from his posture what mood he was in? Gill noticed that as usual, the boat was full of stores and her heart fell like a stone. "Harry."

He jumped out and landed in the water. His bare feet looked long and boney in the shallow. Would their baby take after him? she wondered: all bones and angles. She couldn't read what he was thinking. She grabbed the painter and slipped it around the usual stone.

"I couldn't get here earlier because of the weather and I was busy making the house hurricane-proof. Sorry. Are you okay?"

"Yes, just about. I had bad weather, too. I'm nearly out of food."

"I've brought extra. You never know when the next hurricane will hit. We have two in succession sometimes."

Gill stared and wondered how he could be so calm and cold. Here was she, about thirty weeks pregnant and he was blithering on about making his house in Antigua weather-proof. As if she gave a shit!

She counted to ten. Keep calm. "Harry, I have to get off this island. Surely you can see that? It's not just me now—there's the baby too."

"I had nothing to do with that." He stalked past her with four bags of shopping in his hands.

"Yes, you did! It's your baby! You fucked me plenty." She lost it and yelled.

"Never heard you say no. What happened to your birth control?"

"No, I'm not saying I did. But you must take me away. I need to see a doctor because of the baby. For god's sake, can't you *see* that, you idiot?" Gill realised she was still yelling, and stopped when he whirled around to confront her. His face looked ugly.

"I don't *have* to do anything, and being rude will get you nowhere fast."

"You know you can't keep me here any longer. Be reasonable. It's not right. I've said before you can drop me off anywhere and I'll just disappear. I won't tell anyone about this or—"

He dropped the bags and twisted her arm. His fingers dug in so deeply she winced and yelped in pain. "Or what?"

He dropped her arm and laughed before picking up the bags again. He started for the hill. Gill darted after him and pulled at his shirt. "Really, I don't mind where you take me, or I can stay with you for a bit. We need to talk about the baby. Your baby."

Harry carried on walking and shrugged her hand off as she followed. "Not a chance. Besides, you're safer here. They're still after you."

Gill stared at his departing figure. Was it true? It had been months since Nathan died. They reached the house, and Harry dumped the bags on the kitchen floor. For the first time, he glanced down at Gill's thickened waist.

"I'll get the rest. Make some coffee, will you? And you can put this stuff away."

She felt her face blanch as he left the house. Would he just leave the rest of the bags on the beach and go again? Surely, he wasn't that inhuman. They had things to discuss. If he wouldn't acknowledge the baby was his, she'd simply go somewhere else. She didn't need him, and having him around wasn't what she'd planned anyway. A baby yes, him no.

Gill had no alternative but to do as he said at that moment. Maybe she'd get a chance to put a plan into action later. A walk along the rocky path out to the fishing headland or knife him when he was asleep. It all depended on what he truly intended doing about her…no…*them*.

She rushed into the bedroom and picked up her trusty wooden club. Gill was a bit unsure about knifing Harry. She was no anatomy student, so she could easily miss stabbing him in the heart. She considered it might be easier to bash his brains in instead and hid the club just inside the pantry. She then left the supplies still in their bags and hurried outside. The knife was hidden along with the food cache. She considered it wise to have that with her as well. She reached the rock and moved it to one side. The hollow was as it should be. At least Harry hadn't discovered her tiny secret hoard. He was sick enough to destroy it out of spite. Gill slipped the knife into the back of her bikini pants—they just about fitted, given her size, and pulled her not so baggy T-shirt down over them. It felt odd, but at least it was at hand and gave her a sense of security.

Gill walked back to the house and met Harry just rounding the hill path. "Where've you been?" he asked, his eyes narrowing.

"Loo. I have to go frequently—the baby pushes down on my bladder." She slipped into the house ahead of him and started putting everything away. Gill tried acting as normally as possible. She knew he was watching, and his whole manner seemed alert and suspicious. She looked up at him and smiled as if she was delighted with his purchases.

"Shampoo and conditioner. Folic acid and vitamin pills. You've even bought body cream! Thank you. I need all of these." Gill picked up some tins and moved them into the pantry. The club was hidden behind the makeshift door frame and at hand. Harry was still eyeing her suspiciously, so she left it where it was. She'd emptied nearly all the bags before Harry finally felt relaxed enough to ignore her and stroll outside. Gill walked the few steps back to the pantry and heard the faint pop as he opened a can of beer. Peering round, she could just make out where he was sitting at the table, legs sprawled out in front of him. The beer can clasped in his left hand.

She couldn't bear the tension any longer. Now was as good a time as ever. Gill lifted the club, positioned it in her hands to get the right balance and in bare feet, tiptoed towards the open door. She lifted the club and swung it at his head. As she did, he must have felt a change in the air movement, as he dropped the can and moved his arm up towards his head. The club connected with his bone, and she heard a distinct crack. Harry yelled and lunged to his feet, grabbing the club with his other arm. He yanked it out of her hands and stood there panting for a second as if gathering his thoughts about what had just happened. Gill went to take a step back when his injured arm darted forward, and he grabbed her wrist in a surprisingly bone-clenching grip. She screamed.

He was furious, his normally brown eyes as black as ink. "You bitch! You planned on murdering me, eh?" He lifted the club, and for one ghastly heart-stopping moment, Gill thought, *this is it. I've failed and he's going to club me to death.* She stared into his eyes, observed his insane smile and saw only her fate.

Chapter Fifty - Harry

Harry was livid.

After all he'd done for the ungrateful woman. He realised he was still holding the club and smiled as he raised it above his head. He meant to give the slut a taste of her own medicine. He was quite prepared to bring it smashing down on her head when she collapsed on the ground in front of him, her arm still in his grip. He let her go, the pain in his arm suddenly kicking in. He lowered the club.

Gill wrapped one arm around her head, the other round her bloated middle. "Please. Harry, please. Don't hurt the baby. I didn't mean to hurt you."

What? Didn't plan on hurting him? When she had a bloody huge chunk of wood in her hand? His top lip curled into a sneer.

Harry leant towards her. He could smell fear oozing from her body. Funny how fear has a smell all of its own. "You think I'm bothered? I care nothing for you or the brat. You can both die here as far as I'm concerned."

She gasped, tears gathered in her eyes. She was acting again, the little cow. "I didn't know what I was doing, I swear it. Please just let us go. I promise I'll never tell anyone about this. Never ever."

Harry laughed in her face. "Right. I don't think you will, as you'd soon be found out for what you are. Don't you realise, no one except me knows you even still exist? You just vanished off the face of the earth. They'll give up in a year or two. You'll be just one more missing person. A statistic. If I'm asked, I'll say you were hell-bent on going to South America...god only knows what happened to you there. Human-trafficking, body parts, drugs and whores. No one will care. You have no parents—you made sure of that long ago." Once he mentioned her parents, he noticed how she stiffened. "I see that connected with you. Parents died of natural causes, eh? I think not. You're one hell of a bitch, you know that?"

He watched the reaction in her eyes. He believed Gill was a triple murderer. She suddenly tried to stand up, twisting the arm he was still holding. Her resemblance to Marlene seemed to have disappeared as he glared into her face.

"That's utter rubbish. You've just made that up. I'm no murderer! Why do you keep me here if you hate me so much?" she screamed.

Harry laughed in her face. "Because I enjoy it, and I can," he replied. He remembered he was still holding the stick. He drew back his arm and hit her hard over the head. She pitched forward; blood pooling beneath her. He tossed the club far into the thick vegetation at the side of the house. When he returned, she was still lying in the same position, but he knew she was alive because he saw the faint rise and fall of her abdomen.

Harry stared down at her in disgust. She could die for all he cared. Without another thought, he turned on his heel and ran down to White Lady.

Chapter Fifty-One - Gillian

When Gill opened her eyes and came round, she couldn't remember what had happened. She groaned and using her elbows, pushed her body up into a sitting position. She was shocked to see a thick congealed slick of blood on the veranda floor and more covering her right arm and chest. Her head throbbed, and she raised a hand to touch the throbbing spot gingerly. Her hand touched something sticky, and when she looked at it, saw that it too was covered in blood. Shit! What the hell had happened to her? More importantly, where was she and…oh my god…who was she?

At that moment, she felt a strong movement, and put her other hand to her belly. What? She was *pregnant*? Still sitting on the floor, she looked around. Was she alone? A feeling of horror stole over her. She couldn't gather any thoughts. Had she lost her mind? She'd forgotten everything.

She stood up and everything swayed. After steadying herself against the door frame to get her balance, she peeked inside the cottage. She thought she recognised it, but a violent pain shot through her head, and she staggered into the nearest chair. Think! She had to think and remember what had happened.

She listened. There was birdsong and wind soughing through the tall palms overhead. Palms? It was somewhere tropical then. Her dizziness came and went. She needed a pee, but where on earth was the bathroom? She staggered indoors and noted the kitchen, groceries on the table, an open door leading to a small walk-in cupboard, which on closer inspection proved to be a larder. There was another doorway, and she walked slowly towards it. It was a bedroom with a small double bed and a few pieces of wooden furniture. No bathroom but there was an old speckled mirror. She studied the reflection and despair flooded through her. The thin and haggard face staring back was a stranger. Dark shadows ringed her eyes. She sort of recognised the facial features but didn't. Dried and congealing blood trailed down from a wound above her temple. What had she been doing to get this? She felt panicky. She couldn't remember anything and seemed to be alone. The baby kicked again, and she remembered her immediate mission: find a loo.

It had to be outside. A track led behind the house, and she followed this to a small cabin. Success. As she sat on the seat, she tried to recall anything about herself, her past, what she was doing there.

She walked back down the path and explored the simple cottage. It was tiny, and it didn't take her long. The clothes in the chest of drawers were all women's: a handbag contained a purse, mobile phone—dead and no charger in sight—and a passport. She recognised the photograph in the back as being the woman in the mirror and discovered her name: Priscilla Gillian Hodges. She screwed her face up at this. She didn't feel like a Priscilla at all. She spoke the name aloud. Priscilla Hodges. No. It didn't feel right. Then she said Gillian…it felt better, more right.

Her head still ached, and she searched through the drawers for some painkillers. There was a packet of paracetamol, and she took two with a glass of water from a jug in the kitchen. She decided she was obviously living there for some reason, but the more she tried to remember the more her head hurt. By now, it was nearly dark outside. She flicked a switch for the lamp in the bedroom and nothing happened. Candles…She'd noticed some in the other room. She lit as many as there were lying around, and once she'd got used to the gloom, she knew she'd done this before…many times.

Feeling sick with her headache and overwrought with worry, she closed the main door to the outside and wandered through to the bedroom. She eyed the bed and lay down. She sniffed at the pillows, but they held no answers. All she could smell was a slight mustiness and a faint whiff of sweat and shampoo.

She closed her eyes and in panic, let the tears flow. She rolled over onto her side and drew up her knees, wrapping her arms around them for comfort. What was she going to do? She was obviously heavily pregnant and apparently alone. She had no idea where she was or whether there was anyone within calling distance if she needed help. And she did now. Eventually, sleep must have stolen over her, as she slept restlessly with visions of different faceless persons and a shark with a wide-open mouth showing rows and rows of vicious sharp teeth.

Chapter Fifty-Two - Gillian

Since finding herself prone on the floor of the veranda, she kept a record of the days by scratching marks on the wooden veranda floor. Two weeks passed, the initial terror had subsided, and she began to remember certain episodes in her life. She knew she had no family. She wore no ring, so she obviously wasn't married, but she was sure she must have had some sort of partner. She was pregnant, after all, and the strange thing was, she knew it wasn't her first pregnancy. Then everything went muzzy. She remembered being on a yacht, looking up at the tall mast in the moonlight, and there was a man. Or were there two men? What happened to him or them? Not her partner, she believed…probably not her type. But then, what was her type? She didn't feel as if she was in love with anyone. And the baby? The worst and most sickening thing was because she couldn't remember much beyond a feeling of intense panic, she couldn't feel much about that, either. Who was she? *What* was she?

She'd gone right through the cottage. The food in the walk-in cupboard wouldn't last much longer, and she was scared to death at the thought of dying there. She must have been living in poverty, as all the clothes in the drawers looked threadbare and soiled. Because of her pregnancy she had very little to wear. She discovered she didn't possess one item of maternity clothing.

Once her headaches and the feeling of nausea and dizziness had disappeared, she explored the land. She discovered the sandy bay leading down from the cottage and the gorgeous lagoon of crystal-clear water. It looked so inviting that first time, she immediately took a swim. She didn't go too far out as she didn't know her abilities as a swimmer, and with her pregnancy, she felt heavy although buoyant, which was a strange quixotic experience. She swam every day thereafter. She felt a connection with the bay. It was as if she was bound to it in some way. Was that the first place she set foot on, on this land?

Later, she traipsed farther away from the cottage and discovered she was living on an island: a small one, at that. Where? She screwed up her eyes as she thought. By now she was certain she'd been taken there by yacht after crossing an ocean. It had to be the Atlantic. So there was a good chance she'd come from England or the UK, at least. Her passport was British.

She explored the island as best she could with her pregnancy curtailing any clambering over slippery rocks and uneven ground. Her body felt and looked huge, and although she guessed she wasn't a nurse, as she had no inherent knowledge of medical things, she estimated by her size that she was either expecting twins or her due date was less than two months off. The thought of giving birth filled her with trepidation, especially when she had found she was all alone on this speck of an island, which she guessed from its tropical plants and climate to be somewhere in the Caribbean, off the coast of Africa or even South America.

She was filled with a sense of despair and loneliness. No one to help, little food and hardly any painkillers once her baby started to arrive. She might die giving birth, or she might kill the baby in her ignorance. God help them.

She'd found a fishing line with hooks and brightly coloured plastic things on it, like prawns and small fish. She decided the bay would be useless for fishing, as the water was so clear, and although she saw fish darting along the sandy bottom, they usually swam away far too fast to catch. Rocks appeared to be the best place. She walked to one place where the rocks were the tallest and largest in the island. An odd feeling came over her. She just *knew* she'd fished from there before—when she closed her eyes, she could visualise pulling in a line with a largish fish struggling on the end. She was proved right when she hauled in her first catch and something triggered a memory in a flash. *Don't overdo it…one fish and no more than two a week.* She recalled with clarity being told this by a man, but somehow, knowing it didn't fill her with joy. Instead, she was filled with a sense of foreboding and dread. Was he why she was there? Did he leave her?

The next day she was shaken beyond belief. She went down for her usual morning swim and found about eight plastic grocery bags lying on the beach above the water line. When she opened the first one, she found it contained food. Was this for her? If so, then why hadn't the person who'd put them there made their presence known? What mystery was surrounding her and this island? And now she had an anonymous benefactor. Did she? Or was there some other sinister reason for her being there? It wasn't as if it was a tourist place.

She scanned the bay. It looked just the same as it did when she first woke up with a head wound. The palm fronds swayed in the gentle breeze, tiny crabs scurried over the sand down to the water. Colourful birds called from the tree tops. She peered into a thicket of wavering grasses. Was someone spying on her? Then she heard hooves over the stones farther up the hill, and realised it was a small herd of goats passing through. All the same, she shivered, and the odd sensation of being watched didn't leave her all day.

She lugged the bags up to the cottage, making a few trips as they were weighty. She knew pregnant women shouldn't carry substantial loads. She unpacked them all and without thinking, put everything away in the larder. The food would keep her going for a few weeks. As she worked, it dawned on her that she'd done this many times…this, and again the feeling of being watched made her feel edgy. She felt her heart flutter in her chest. Who or what was out there? Food had arrived, and she'd taken it because she knew intuitively it was meant for her. It gradually dawned on her, with terror, that she was a prisoner. What had she done to deserve this?

She made dinner late that afternoon. She couldn't wait for nightfall. She found two succulent-looking steaks, and the sight and smell made her stomach rumble and mouth water. As she sat chewing the meat, an image suddenly entered her mind with a blinding flash. Harry. His name was Harry, and he was dangerous. More than that. Harry was deadly.

Her head ached, her heart thumped so hard it hurt. She felt sick and faint at the same time. Everything came flooding back with clarity. She'd tried to kill him, and somehow failed because his body certainly wasn't on the island. She realised he'd turned the tables on her and bashed her over the head with her own weapon. Had he left her for dead? No. He must have known she'd survived. Why else would he have come back and left food here? The baby! It was his!

So, if he left food, did that mean he'd forgiven her? Was he still coming to terms with the baby? Surely he'd come back and take her off the island soon?

Chapter Fifty-Three - Gillian

Two more weeks passed and Gill hadn't seen Harry in over a month. She stared at her reflection in the mirror every day; her bump was enormous, but the rest of her body looked pitifully thin. Gill's hair was a proper mess and needed a cut. The dark-brown dye was just visible on the last three or four inches of hair. She looked like some sort of wild woman, with dull shadowed eyes staring from an emaciated face. Worse, some of her teeth had become wobbly, and she knew she was going to lose at least two of them.

Three days later, Harry had been and left more supplies without a word. This time, there were twelve bags, including a few items for the baby. Gill found disposable nappies for newborns, nappy-rash cream and about a dozen tiny little garments. For some reason, the sight of the baby clothing filled her with sadness, tinged with guilt and very little joy. A new birth should have been a time for rejoicing, but instead, she was filled with sinister thoughts. Last time…last time… Lawrence had beaten her so hard, she lost the baby she was carrying. Gill sensed there was something else in her past life but guessed she'd blocked it out because it was too painful.

The one thing Harry had forgotten was to include a good supply of candles. Since regaining her memory, Gill had gone back to needing light throughout the night. She felt thoroughly pissed off with his forgetfulness. Or was it on purpose? She noticed he'd brought the last two lots of supplies during the night or very early morning when the dawn was just lighting up the sky. Did he venture ashore and spy on her at the house? The hot muggy weather continued, and she had to sleep with the window shutters open to let the cooler night air in, or she'd have died in the intense heat. Did he stand just outside the bedroom, watching her while she slept? She reckoned he did because she always felt more edgy on the mornings after his visits, even before she knew for certain he'd been to Isla de Cabra again. The idea was unnerving, spooky, but then, she soon learnt that everything about Harry was creepy. How she wished she'd never set foot on his yacht. Of all the mistakes in her life, this was the worst.

After long hours spent agonising, Gill decided she couldn't risk having a baby in the dead of night without proper light. Before Harry stopped going to see her, she'd asked him to look at the solar panels. He made a stupid excuse about having no tools, as he'd dropped them overboard. She knew he lied that day and ever since. Gill studied the roof. Part of it had slipped to the ground due to the savage wind that accompanied a squall every time it passed through the island, but in the main, it looked sound and solid enough. She made up her mind to take a look herself. It was better to do it then and not leave it to the last minute. She estimated she had only two weeks left before the baby was due.

Gill fetched the ladder and leant it against the house. She rolled some large boulders at the base of the ladder to keep it in place. There were no tools on the island except her knife and a tiny screwdriver she kept in her purse for repairing sunglasses whenever the screws fell out. After testing the ladder, she felt confident it was secure and sturdy, and she climbed to the top. Gill recalled that the photovoltaic system Harry had installed was simple...often used on caravans or boats. He explained it to her once, and she wished she'd paid more attention at the time. Looking at it, she recalled him saying it wasn't what could be called a solar panel at all. It consisted of some solar cells stuck on a wooden board and wired together. She could see where Harry had linked each one: negative to positive, before joining them to a solar battery and inverter. She traced the wires and then thought she'd found the problem. Surely, there was no link to the solar battery. The battery was farther over, so she shifted her position to get a better look. As she crawled forwards a few feet, she felt the roof move and creak at that moment. Two of the beams had been exposed to the elements. One end looked odd, and it flashed through her mind that it was rotten. As she looked more closely, she noted with horror that the whole thing was one big tree-termite nest and riddled with ants. In panic, she began edging back towards the ladder, but too late—the whole thing gave way, and Gill fell, crashing to the ground, taking the termites down with her.

The air was forced out of her lungs, and at first, she could do nothing but try to gulp in more air. She was covered in hundreds of wriggling termites; they were everywhere. She flapped her hands, trying to brush them off, and finally, they disappeared. Tears streamed down her face with the effort of trying to draw breath, and she wondered if she'd injured herself. Eventually, she breathed properly, and dragged in air like she'd been drowning. She could move her arms and legs. Her back and right hip ached where she'd taken the brunt of the fall, but she was amazed to discover that apart from a few cuts and bruises, she'd escaped unscathed.

Gill rolled over onto to her side and stood up on shaking legs. Damn the solar electricity. Damn Harry! She'd been stupid to even try getting on the roof. She stepped towards the house, and as she did so, felt a pain shoot through her abdomen. Crap! What now?

Chapter Fifty-Four - Gillian

The pains lasted for the rest of the day, and Gill knew they'd continue into the night. She didn't feel much like eating, but was very thirsty. She filled the one and only jug with water and took it with a glass outside. Harry had included some fruit with the new delivery, so she picked at some grapes. Gill didn't feel like sitting, so she wandered around. That evening, down in the bay, the water looked alive; she watched a display of silver and gold flashes winking back at her. She realised she was watching an exhibition of bioluminescent plankton, no doubt drifted in on the gentle tide.

The candles were lit, the groceries put away, and the fire was ready to light as soon as real darkness fell. The oppressive muggy day gave way to a cooler evening, and she sat watching a group of fireflies as they flitted from bush to bush in the garden. If she felt miserable before, then that evening Gill felt utterly desolate. She knew she was in for a horrendous experience and was completely alone.

She realised she had nothing much to prepare. Harry had bought only a few baby clothes and nappies. No painkillers, no fresh sheets, no baby crib…nothing. Restless, Gill roamed around the house and garden, willing the pain to go away. It wasn't time; it was far too early. She believed she had another two weeks to a month before reaching full-term. It was pitch black. She lit the fire. It flared up, and as everything was so dry, it caught almost immediately. She stared at the pile of wood she'd collected. Would there be enough for the night and the next few days? She doubted she would be strong enough to go out scavenging if something went wrong. She was so bloody afraid.

So far, the pains hadn't been bad. Gill timed them on her wristwatch and from the onset, saw they were at least twelve minutes apart. As the day progressed into evening and then into night, things speeded up and the contractions were closer together—eight minutes between them. She was sweating. This wasn't a false alarm, a trial run, this was the real thing.

Gill stepped back from the fire and glanced around. Just a few feet from the blaze, everything was in dark relief. The night was as opaque as she'd ever seen it; no moon had risen to soften the edges. The garden looked gloomy, shadows cast by the fire made her imagine phantoms waiting in the murk beyond. She needed to pee urgently, and grabbing a flaring piece of firewood, she shuffled down the path to the outside loo. The sound of the water running into the spa bath caught her ears, but she ignored it and sat on the seat, grunting as a new pain shot through her abdomen.

Finished, she walked back to the house, the firelight guiding her over the path. What should she have been doing? What was a woman supposed to get ready for a birth? Hot water—she could boil the kettle, she had gas. She filled the bucket with water, too, just for good measure. She hurried indoors, and the gas popped as she turned it on. Clean cloths, towels. There was another in the bedroom. Jesus, that one hurt. Hospitals gave you gas and air, didn't they? And pethidine, if she remembered…all she had was about sixteen paracetamols to chew on. They wouldn't do much good. Gill found the tablets and took two. They were better than nothing. She didn't expect the pain to disappear completely but hoped they'd dull it. She tucked the pills inside a drawer in the kitchen for safekeeping and walked back outside. There had to be light; she couldn't have the baby in the bedroom. It was too dark, even if there was a glow from the fire flitting around the room. She trembled; she was so terrified.

Gill realised she was sweating, and poured a little water from the jug over a flannel. It felt nice and cool, and for a minute she forgot about her predicament until the next contraction took her by surprise. By her watch, she saw it was nearly midnight, and the pains were getting stronger and closer. She groaned and stood up, gripping the back of the chair as she leant over it. Gill knew she was swearing as she imagined red hot coals in her belly. She suddenly felt a warm dribble run down her legs.

She looked down and saw yellow-tinged water pooling at her feet. Her waters had broken; the next stage of labour was imminent. Another contraction hit, and she heard herself whimpering as she grabbed hold of her stomach. She tried to remember a television programme she'd watched about labour…she knew that when the head presented, she had to pant before the next contraction struck. Was she that far gone already? She had no idea.

She just wanted the whole frightening and agonising thing to end.

Gill wished someone would come…even Harry would have been some sort of comfort. Another human being to just *be there*. A contraction was building. She screamed…felt faint, but it passed.

More cramping, they kept coming and coming. Gill barely had time to draw breath in between. She knelt over the chair, in a sort of squatting position, knowing that if she lay down, she'd never get up.

Gill felt the next contraction travel up her back and felt an urgent need to push. Was she ready? She didn't want to tear herself. She reached down, and put one hand between her legs as the pain ebbed and felt what seemed like a bulge. It must have been the baby. Within what seemed like seconds, another almighty contraction started, and this time she gripped the chair seat and pushed with all her might. The contraction was longer than the others, and she stayed in the same position, pushing down as hard as she could. As the pain passed, she sobbed and tried to relax. She felt between her legs again and found what she guessed to be the head. Her fingers slipped around the tiny neck; it seemed free of the umbilical cord. Five seconds and another contraction began. Gill pushed again, and another guttural scream escaped her lips. Then there was a sort of relief. She felt a slithering sensation as the baby began its escape from the birth canal. Reaching down as soon as she could, Gill guided the baby onto the wooden floor.

She found she was still squatting over her baby. She panted, knowing it wasn't quite all over. The baby girl seemed tiny. Far smaller than she thought her enormous stomach had indicated. She didn't move or make any sort of noise. As Gill peered more closely, she thought she was tinged with blue. She picked the wet, slimy, little body up and inserted a finger gently into her mouth. Up close, her nose looked gummed up with mucus, so Gill placed her mouth over her nose and mouth and sucked. She spat out the goo and repeated the action. This time there was a definite movement in her chest. Gill stared and was about to repeat the suction a third time when she opened her mouth, inhaled and let out a tiny cry. She lived!

Gill gave her chest a gentle rub to encourage her breathing. Within seconds, she let out more of a yell. Fascinated, Gill watched as her daughter's skin became pinker with each cry. Gill couldn't believe that not only had she given birth but that this infant, who'd come early, was alive and kicking.

She settled into a more comfortable position, waiting for the afterbirth to expel and nestled the baby against her chest. The baby's head turned instinctively towards Gill's breast, and she remembered reading that letting the infant suckle helped deliver the afterbirth.

She latched on at once, and as Gill watched, she felt a tear trickle down her face. She named her Ella.

Chapter Fifty-Five - Gillian

That night, Ella and Gill shared the double bed for the first time. Gill finally delivered the placenta about twenty minutes after Ella was born and cut the cord with her sharp knife. Somehow, she remembered to tie the cord attached to Ella into a knot as near to her body as she could. By this time, Gill was exhausted. She gave the placenta a cursory glance and struggled over to the fire with it. She didn't want it lying around as the blood would attract rats. After tossing it onto the fire, she added a few more logs and then staggered back to the veranda. Ella was cradled in her arms and fast asleep. She knew she had to clean up a bit, or by morning, the place would be infested with flies drawn to the blood and mucus. Gill threw the remains of the bucket over the mess she'd made and then walked through to the bedroom. She emptied one of the drawers and lined it with the clean towel she'd got out earlier. The drawer made a good crib for Ella.

Once she'd thrown more water over the wooden veranda, Gill closed the door and got ready for bed. She felt dog-tired but elated as well. She picked Ella up from her makeshift cradle and rewrapped her in the towel. She spent a few minutes gazing down at her beautiful little daughter before exhaustion overcame her. She knew she'd have to sort out some clothes for her to wear the following day. Gill laid her in the crook of her arm and within minutes, they'd both fallen asleep.

***

Next morning, Gill was awake just as dawn was breaking at its usual time at around six. As she glanced down at Ella, she stirred, and within seconds, she was awake and bawling. She put her to her breast and miraculously, the noise stopped as she began to suck. Gill studied her child. She was tiny and perfect. She had all ten toes and fingers, a head of fuzzy, white, downy hair and her grey-blue eyes. As she fed, Gill planned to put her in a nappy and dress her in one of the little cotton vests Harry had left her. She suddenly stopped sucking, and from her facial expression, Gill realised she was having her first poo. She parted the towel and eyed the black sticky stuff with disdain. Was it meant to be that colour? She had no idea and was too tired to think about it. Maybe Harry would know when he next visited. She drifted off back to sleep.

When she woke a bit later, Ella had fallen asleep. Gill stared down at the tiny child and considered what she truly felt for her. She was beautiful, and Gill pondered how something so wonderful could be created by two people who disliked each other so intensely. Harry clearly hadn't given a thought to what their sexual activity might produce. The idea of having a baby hadn't been on her mind, either, but this way? Was it right?

As she stared at her, a sudden horrible notion crept into her head. Harry might want her or he might not. If he did, would he try and take her away from her? Gill hardened her mouth. He could go and screw himself. She realised she'd been kidding herself. As soon as she set eyes on her, it had been love at first sight. Ella was hers and he wasn't getting a look-in.

Chapter Fifty-Six - Harry

He had no idea how far gone Gillian was with her pregnancy, but she looked huge the last time he saw her. He'd returned to the island a few times, sometimes with supplies, but occasionally just called in overnight after passing through from Central America. Standing in the shadows, he'd watched her as she wandered around the house and garden. She'd taken to sleeping with the shutters open; it would have been easy to smother her as she slept.

After she tried to kill him, he wanted nothing more than to strangle her, but something made him stop. His senses told him she hadn't lied. The baby she was carrying was his; the dates added up, just about. At first, he didn't know what to do. After Marlene cleared off with their daughter, he felt so incomplete. He hunted for them, all over the Caribbean and beyond, but Marlene had obviously found herself a good hiding place. It was his fault. He should never have treated her that way, but she knew what he was like from the beginning. Anyway, it wasn't her leaving that hurt the most. It was more to do with stealing his daughter. Now, it seemed like he was going to be a father all over again. He had a second chance.

But what to do about Gillian? Despite her protests of innocence, he still believed her to be a murderess. Plus, she was an ex-inmate from a psychiatric hospital. Highly volatile and as Theo said, possibly dangerous in more ways than one. Harry decided to bide his time until she delivered his child.

His visit to Isla de Cabra was overdue. Harry set about purchasing supplies plus extra things for when the baby was born and then set off in White Lady to see how Gillian was faring. He hadn't forgiven her but was curious to see how she was coping.

As he approached the island, he sensed a difference. It looked the same, but he just knew something was afoot. Maybe she was ill? What if she'd had an accident and lost the child? Maybe she'd died, even. He anchored and lowered the dinghy complete with the supplies.

The morning was still young, the sun just rising. He opened the door to the house and paused. Everything was quiet, and he realised Gillian must have still been asleep. He put the bags of groceries on the veranda floor and was about to walk through the house to the bedroom when he stopped. The room ahead was untidy and needed sweeping, crockery littered the worktop, but it wasn't that which caught his eye. It was line of tiny little clothes hanging out to dry along the side of the house. He gawked. So, it had been born, then?

Harry walked through the house and stopped at the doorway into the bedroom. She was in bed asleep, and the baby was lying next to her. Gill must have sensed he was there, as she opened her eyes and looked straight at Harry. He witnessed a series of expressions cross her face before she half sat up and pulled the baby closer to her side.

"You've had it, then." He indicated with his head in the direction of the sleeping tot. "When?" Harry watched as she swallowed before answering. She feared him. Good. Perhaps it was because he walloped her last time. As if he'd let her get away with nearly killing him.

"Three days ago."

"How was it? I'm sorry I wasn't here. I'd have liked to have been." He peered down at the baby. It looked so small lying in Gill's arms. He felt his heart begin to melt. It was like remembering when Marlene had their daughter. "What is it?"

"A girl."

Harry moved closer and gently stroked the baby girl's clenched fist. It felt so soft and vulnerable to his touch.

"Her name's Ella." He jumped back as if he'd been scalded. How could this be? Gill stared at him with surprise. "What?"

He backed away, shaking his head. "Nothing." Was the bitch playing a nasty little trick on him? "I was surprised at your choice of name, that's all. Why Ella?"

"No reason. The name just popped into my head almost as soon as she was born. It seemed to suit her. I went through names before I had her, but funnily enough that one didn't cross my mind. We ought to get her checked out by a doctor soon. She seems okay, but there are special tests they do to make sure a baby hasn't got anything nasty like a heredity disease or anything."

"All in good time. The main thing is for you to rest and for her to gain a bit of weight. She's awfully small. Is she feeding okay?"

She nodded. "She came early. I had a fall and it brought her on. She really does need checking, as she's premature."

He studied the pair of them. They looked healthy enough, although Gill had a bit of a flushed face. Harry moved a bit closer and then perched on the side of the bed. "I'd like to hold her." He watched her closely as her arm tightened around the baby.

"She's only just dropped off. Maybe a bit later when she wakes for a feed."

Harry smiled and nodded. "Of course, there's plenty of time. You and your daughter are still joined together as one. It'll take time for you to feel comfortable with anyone else touching your baby. Don't look so surprised. I know quite a lot about kids." He looked around the untidy room. "Can I get you anything? It's early, so I doubt you've had breakfast. Bacon and eggs do? I've got all your favourites with me."

He sensed she was still wary of him. He didn't suppose he could blame her, really. He thought it was time to get her to let her guard down. He wanted to hold his daughter.

"Look, you stay cosied up here while I put the kettle on and rustle up some breakfast. Then when you feel able, I'll help you down to the spa for a bath. You'd like that. Afterwards, you can sit in the fresh air on the veranda until you feel like a nap. I can bring all the supplies up and give the place a bit of a sprucing up as I go."

She looked doubtful, and he decided to leave her alone. He bent down and kissed baby Ella's cheek and then Gill firmly on the mouth. Harry smiled and murmured into her ear. "I'm delighted to have a daughter. Well done, she's beautiful, just like you. You rest easy, and I'll bring you that cup of tea, my love."

Chapter Fifty-Seven - Gillian

Gillian was confused by Harry's behaviour at first and then as she thought about it, more than a bit suspicious. He'd waltzed in and asked about her labour without waiting for a reply and then as if nothing had happened between them the last time there, said how pleased he was with Ella and how he was prepared to look after her mother. Had he conveniently forgotten he was keeping her there against her will?

She didn't trust him one bit. Not until she was on that boat with Ella and they were safely on their way back to civilisation.

Gillian could hear him, rattling around in the kitchen. As the frying pan hit the stove, she caught a faint pop and whiff of gas as he lit it. What was his game? Was he making some attempt at throwing her off balance and catching her unawares? Would he snatch her baby away? He couldn't. She was her mother, and Ella needed her. All the same, Gill decided Harry needed close watching. She gazed down at her baby—*her baby*, not his. He just happened to be the father by default. If only she could raise this child this time. See her grow to childhood and on to womanhood. She stopped her apprehensive thoughts. Why was she thinking of that? Of course she could do it. Millions of women did. Why not her?

Gill laid Ella down and slid from the bed. Up until then, she hadn't ventured far from the house, only to the loo and back. Her legs felt a bit wobbly, but she reminded herself she was a young woman and would heal better and more quickly if she got her circulation going and had some decent food. She'd given birth to a baby, she hadn't been ill. All the same, she did feel as if the room was particularly hot that day. Perhaps Harry was right. A refreshing bath would do her good. She'd see. She slipped into her dressing gown and pulled the belt around her waist tightly. It was amazing how slim she was now she'd had Ella. A lot of it had been fluid, of course.

Gill turned and gazed at her. She was fast asleep, and it seemed silly to disturb her, but she couldn't leave her on her own; she was far too young and precious. She had to have her within an arm's length at most. She walked over and gently picked her up. Gill was pleased that she didn't even notice. She knew this perfect state of babyhood didn't last, though. Babies developed their own patterns of sleep.

"I thought I'd join you, Harry, as I'm not sleepy now. I'll sit on the veranda."

"Good idea. Breakfast is nearly ready. I'll bring it out in a tick. There are some more baby things for you out there. You can look while you're waiting if you like."

Gill took a seat at the table, laying Ella across her knees while she went through the bags. There were loads of baby things. He'd even thought about her, as he'd included two nursing bras two sizes up from her usual measurement. How had he known that? She found more nappies, nursing pads, nipple cream, wipes, a baby bath towel, more unisex clothes, feeding bottles and three containers of milk formula. Why had he brought milk powder? Surely, he knew Ella would have her milk? Unless…the other thought was unbearable. He couldn't steal her away!

Harry must have had someone help him choose everything in the shop. Gill pulled the wrapping from the last and largest item and discovered it contained a Moses basket complete with soft cotton sheets. Her head swam. The things must have cost him a lot, as they looked good quality. Had he accepted Ella as his daughter and was prepared to do the right thing by her? Why spend good money if not? As Gill fingered the baby clothes, she wondered what his ultimate decision concerning her was. She was very aware he'd bought these items before even seeing Ella or knowing he was the father of a girl.

A sound made Gill turn her head, and Harry approached with a cup and plate in his hands. "You've had a good look at everything? Have I chosen well? I had to make some educated guesses, not knowing what the baby would be." He smiled, and in that split second, Gill felt like screaming. What was he playing at? He'd left her for dead the last time they spoke. Okay, so she struck the first blow but only because he'd made her a virtual prisoner on Cabra. She said nothing about that, instead nodded and thanked him in a quiet voice.

"Tea and eggs and bacon. Get stuck into that. This is just what you need to build yourself up to feed Ella. Why don't I take her and put her in the basket? You'll find it easier to eat without having her on your lap."

"She's fine. I'll try her after her next feed. This looks great."

Gill made sure Ella was safe on her lap and picked up the knife and fork. The food tasted delicious and she *was* ravenous. It had been ages since she'd tasted anything so good. Since Ella's birth, Gill had only managed to boil up a bit of pasta or rice and add a squirt of tomato paste for flavour. She was ready for her taste buds to explode as she wolfed down tender back bacon, bright-yellow egg yolk and a slice of crusty bread spread with a liberal dollop of rich creamy butter. It was heaven.

Harry joined Gill and sat opposite her. He slurped his tea while watching Gill eat. Ella moved, and he shifted his attention to her, staring as she stretched and made little farting noises on Gill's lap. Eventually, Gill finished her breakfast and wiped the plate clean with the last of the bread. Ella was making that mewling noise that only newborn babies can.

"I think she's hungry," Gill said. She pushed her plate away and picked Ella up. "I'll go and feed her."

"You can do it here if you want."

"No, I think she likes peace and quiet when she takes a feed," she replied in panic. She didn't want him watching her. It was Gill's time alone with her, and she didn't relish the thought of him staring as she latched onto her breast.

Almost in panic, she stood up and hurried back to the bedroom, closing the door behind her.

Ella was wide awake and rooting eagerly around Gill's dressing gown for her milk. Once she offered her breast to her she immediately settled down. Gill felt thankful her milk had come in quickly. She guessed Ella was getting enough as she sucked hard with her tiny mouth for about ten minutes and then promptly fell asleep. Even though she was premature, Gill thought she had a good suck for her size. She lifted her to her shoulder and gently patted her back. She didn't know for sure but supposed it was instinct that guided her...like knowing she had to offer the other breast as well even if she was sleepy.

Gill shifted Ella from her shoulder and jiggled her a bit to wake her up. A few minutes later, the door opened and Harry stood there with another cup of tea.

"Thought you'd appreciate another cuppa. You need to drink lots to keep your milk supply going. As soon as you feel thirsty, you must down a glass of water." He placed the cup down by the side of the bed and watched mother and baby for a moment. "She's got a healthy appetite. Must be my side of the family," he said with a laugh. When Gill didn't answer, he moved to leave the room. "I'll be outside if you need anything."

"Thank you for the tea. You know, I've been thinking. Ella should see a doctor...and me too. She seems okay, but I keep getting stomach ache, and I'm still bleeding. I also keep having hot flushes."

"You will for a short while. The stomach ache comes from feeding Ella. When she sucks, it triggers a response and your uterus contracts. It'll wear off, as will the bleeding."

"But I do feel very hot. If you won't take us off the island, then maybe you can bring me a book about rearing a baby as I know next to nothing," Gill persisted. She wished he'd bugger off and let her finish feeding Ella in private.

Harry shrugged. "It's the time of year. Hot and muggy. Why do you think hardly any tourists visit the Caribbean during the summer months? Anyway, it's far too early for either of you to travel anywhere on a boat. What if we ran into a storm? How would you cope, hanging onto a baby in a rough sea? You know the rule—one hand for you and one for the boat. Wait a while."

"I could strap her into her Moses basket. If it was tucked behind a lee cloth, she'd be safe."

Harry sighed. "When she's bigger. Anyway, both of you look as healthy as anything."

"Yes, but babies have to have tests as soon as they're born ... there's one called phenoketo something."

"I know. Phenylketonuria. Relax. That's a one in a million chance of that happening. Look at her. Truly beautiful and she'll be a bonny bouncing baby in a few weeks. You don't need a doctor. I can take care of both of my beautiful girls." He gazed down at Ella and then turned his attention to Gill. His mouth smiled, but his eyes were as empty as they ever were. He bent towards her and kissed her cheek. "Have I thanked you yet for giving me a new daughter?"

Gill felt a fresh disgust rise in her as his hand wandered across her uncovered breast, giving the nipple a vicious tweak. She couldn't help wincing. Her body was not his to do what he liked with and besides, it bloody hurt! Harry's moods flitted from one extreme to the other. Gill knew she had to tread cautiously—being around him was like living with an unstable volcano. Harry wasn't about to let her off the island yet, and she had to be a good girl and bide her time. But, by God if he prevaricated again…she just hoped she had it in her to kill him if necessary.

Once Harry had left the room, Gill's eyes flooded with tears as she began to worry about whether he was staying. She desperately wanted to leave, and knew she'd have to go at it from a different angle. But if he wasn't about to take them with him, then she didn't want him on the island either. She loathed the way he looked at her and Ella. The word predator crossed her mind, and she wondered if he was insane or just plain cruel.

Of course, if he did stay, it would be another opportunity to kill him. Was she strong enough to strike him? Gill wasn't sure. Ella gave her another vital reason for getting away, but she wasn't fully recovered from the birth.

Gill finished feeding Ella and burped her over her shoulder. She brought up a posset of milk, and Gill reached for one of the wipes Harry had bought. She knew she couldn't stay in the bedroom all day, so she wandered out into the main room. She also wanted to keep tabs on Harry while he was around. The house was empty, and she found him outside, looking at the damage to the roof.

"I'll take a look at the solar panel while I'm here. I've brought a few new tools with me this time. The last storm certainly did a good job on this." Gill followed his gaze to the roof. No way was she going to admit she'd already been on the roof. The sicko might have taken it out on her and blame her for endangering his daughter's life.

Gill watched from her chair as Harry positioned the ladder and edged gingerly along the better side of the roof. Fifteen minutes later he joined her on the ground with a self-satisfied grin. "All done! Tonight, you should have plenty of light. I'll just go and check."

"What was the problem?" She knew full well he'd pulled one of the wires out the last time he was up on the roof.

"Quite a tricky one and a bit technical to explain. Nothing to worry your pretty little head over. I'll replace the wood next time when I bring some fresh timbers with me."

"Thank you. I appreciate that. You know how Ella and I rely on you for everything."

Harry smiled some more. "I'll do anything for my girls. Tell you what…make a list of anything you and the baby need, and I'll make sure I'll bring it all back with me next time."

"That's kind. I'll have a think and write it out later. Do you have any paper? I seem to have lost my diary. I could have torn a page out of that. You didn't see it when you were tidying up, I suppose?"

"No, sorry. Now, what about that bath I promised you? I do a fine massage too."

Gill shook her head. "I'm fine, except I might go and have a lie-down with Ella now she's asleep. Maybe later."

She slipped away while Harry was fiddling around with the ladder and went back into the house. What a liar. He didn't blink an eye when she mentioned her diary. She hesitated between the bedroom and the main room. If she stayed at the back of the house, she knew she couldn't see what Harry was up to. What if he wrecked the hob this time? She wouldn't have way of heating food. If she rested in the main room, he'd be nearer. She opted for the lumpy sofa, wedged Ella in between her and the back and prepared for a fitful doze.

Gill needn't have worried about Harry getting up to anything malicious. He wouldn't have had time, as when she awoke later that afternoon, the creep had gone. So much for waiting for her shopping list.

Gill lay there listening to the calls of the tropical birds. She'd seen a pair of parrots a week before, and wondered if they were still on the island. They were beautiful: mostly green-feathered over the main parts of their bodies with a red forehead, deep-blue outer-wing feathers and a red rump. She hoped they'd come again and wondered if she could lure them down from the trees with a piece of fruit or nuts. Not that she could afford to give food away. Gill turned her thoughts to Harry sailing back to civilisation and whether she was angrier he'd left them or relieved she wouldn't have to be on her guard with Ella. Gill couldn't rely on him not to snatch her baby away. She also remembered what he'd said earlier that day. "Have I thanked you for giving me a new daughter?" *New* daughter?

It sounded like Harry already had a daughter. Was Marlene the mother? Gill wondered what had really become of her…and her daughter.

Chapter Fifty-Eight - Harry

Harry didn't trust the woman and was in a quandary. When he first saw Gill, he'd been struck by how much she resembled Marlene. Both in looks, colouring and build. That was as far as it went, because strangely enough, although the resemblance was great, her temperament was different, and he didn't desire her half as much. That came later, and it was more because she seemed indifferent and unavailable that he made it happen. Then he indulged himself with one of his greater fantasies: the initial chase, culminating in keeping a woman on an island and bending her to his will. Harry should have taken Marlene there when they first met, but that was another story. For now, he had Priscilla Gillian Hodges in his hands.

Knowing her history, that which he'd gleaned from media reports over the previous few months, he should have stayed well away. Once he discovered she was pregnant, things had to change.

But it was when she told him the name of the baby— their baby—that Harry felt as if he'd been gutted. How on earth had she found out that Marlene and he had given their daughter the same name? He kept nothing in his possession or on the yacht relating to her. Had it been coincidence? He doubted Theo knew about Ella, as he hadn't seen him during the short time Ella lived with Marlene and himself on Antigua. Did Theo find out somehow? He always enjoyed winding him up about his 'darker side of life', as Theo put it. He knew about his Colombian ventures and held him to ransom whenever he needed a favour. Had Theo found time to tell Gillian something when they were halfway across the Atlantic?

Anyhow, it was all academic. Theo was somewhere at the bottom of the ocean, thankfully, and couldn't blackmail him anymore. Harry wanted to get his daughter out of the arms of that murdering bitch before disaster struck again. He needed to plan this carefully.

Chapter Fifty-Nine - Gillian

The next week passed in a blur. As well as the temperatures soaring and bringing with them a few days of tropical downpour, Gill began to feel off colour. Nothing drastic, but a general malaise. She slept as much as she could. Every time Ella had a sleep, Gill got her head down for a nap. The routine was a round of feeding Ella, cleaning Ella and putting her down for an hour or more. Gill had a raging thirst, little appetite, although she knew she had to eat to keep her strength up, and very little energy. She was still bleeding and it was becoming annoying. Gill had no idea when it was supposed to stop but thought it should have lessened by now. She hoped that when Harry returned, he'd bring her the book she asked for. Hopefully, it would have all the answers she needed.

At first, Ella slept most of the time, but after a week she became grizzly and restless. Gill suspected she might not have enough milk for her and thought she'd have to resort to the milk formula. If only she slept for longer periods, Gill would have more energy to cope. She could hardly handle washing her tiny clothes and hanging them outside to dry. Gill resorted to rinsing them through and leaving them in the sun on the veranda floor.

When Gill was awake, she flip-flopped between hoping Harry would show up that day or wished he wouldn't and someone somehow would discover them. A rescue was top of the list. She guessed he'd come when he was ready, and she'd have to surrender eventually and let him hold Ella. Harry was her father, but Gill hated the idea of him, or anyone, cuddling her.

Was she a bad mother? Was she coping? Who knew. Gill slept as much as she could get away with. If only she didn't feel so yucky and if Ella didn't cry so much.

Ella woke again. Her pitiful little cry told Gill she was hungry. Gill's breasts no longer responded automatically to her wails, and she wondered if her milk supply was drying up. She struggled to her feet and wandered over to the kitchen area. The kettle was full of boiled water, still hot. She unwrapped the baby bottles and gazed at the writing on the box. She knew they needed sterilising before she used them. But Ella was screaming, and Gill had no time to immerse the bottle in a solution of Milton. She scalded the bottle with the boiled water and then read the instructions on the tin containing the milk formula. Once she understood what to do she made up a feed according to her age. Gill had no idea about her baby's weight and had to estimate the amount. It looked small, but then she was a tiny baby.

Gill picked Ella up from her basket and cuddled her close. Ella stopped crying long enough for the formula to cool down, and Gill sat down on the sofa. She hoped desperately she'd take to the bottle, as she knew she'd never be able to satisfy her herself, feeling as ill as she did.

Ella gazed up at her mother with what seemed like perfect trust. Gill felt a pang of regret. She wanted to feed her baby herself, and she'd let her down. She was a lousy mother. She let Ella nuzzle against the teat of the bottle. She baulked at first and turned her head aside towards her mother's chest. Gill almost cried in frustration, and then as she squirmed in her lap, she suddenly opened her tiny mouth and Gill eased the teat in. She sucked and sucked. In less than five minutes, she finished it all, and after Gill had changed her, she fell into a far longer and deeper sleep than she had the previous two days.

While Ella slept, Gill thought about what to do. If she couldn't supply her with enough of her own milk, then surely she could give her both. She was certain some mothers supplemented their own milk. That had to be the best solution. Besides, Gill didn't want Ella to become completely dependent on something other than her. It would have made it too easy for Harry to steal her if he knew he could give her formula. Gill closed her eyes, fighting the ache of disappointment in her throat. She had to persist with breastfeeding and make sure Harry knew nothing about the supplementary milk when he returned. With her mind made up, she grabbed the bottle, washed it thoroughly, and put the milk formula at the back of the pantry. If she was going to conduct this little subterfuge, she couldn't let Harry find out. Later that morning, after tidying everything away, Gill felt happier and fell into a deep sleep.

She awoke much later to the sound of something heavy being placed on the floor in the main room. Filled with alarm, Gill sat up, and grabbed hold of the club she kept under the bed. She swung her legs round just as Harry gave a cursory knock on the door. He stood framed in the doorway with a big smile across his face.

"Good morning and how are my favourite girls today? You can put that down, Gill. I haven't come to hurt the mother of my child." He strode across the room and after giving her a long kiss, looked down at Ella with a fond look.

Gill tried not to squirm under his embrace, but knew it was something she had to put up with, especially if she was to stay in his good books. She smiled back. "Sorry, I didn't know it was you. We're fine, thanks. You've returned early. Not that I'm complaining."

"Yes, I decided two weeks apart was too long, and I wanted to see you both."

Gill didn't argue that he had actually left her for a month at one stage. Disagreeing wouldn't have helped their case. "That's nice. I'm really pleased."

"Good. I've brought you lots of goodies and a big fat steak. I know how much you enjoy them. Afterwards, there's apple pie and cream."

"Fab! Are you going to cook as well? You're much better than I am."

He put his arm around Gill's shoulder and gave her a squeeze. "Of course. Did you think I'd let you slave over that stove? You know I love cooking for you."

That day was much like many others. Gill dealt with Ella while Harry messed about outside. He brought all the supplies up: ten bags, so maybe two weeks before visiting next, checked the solar stuff and that the lights worked and generally cooed over Ella and herself. His manner and mood swings were amazing. If Gill didn't remind herself he was *keeping her there by force*, they could have passed as any ordinary happily married couple.

So far, she hadn't let him cuddle Ella. Fortunately, she'd been grumbly and needed more nursing. Something Harry couldn't do. He watched as Gill fed her. There was something about his intense stare that made her feel uncomfortable, and she asked as pleasantly as she could for a cup of tea.

"Of course, my sweet. Then I'll start dinner."

Gill almost sighed with relief. If his hands were busy, he wouldn't have time to fret about holding Ella. When it was time to eat, Gill placed Ella in her basket and kept her within arm's reach at her feet. Harry didn't seem to notice, as he was full of himself that afternoon. He mentioned work to be done on White Lady, plus his Antigua house and how he was having it decorated. Gill hoped it meant he was doing it up for them…slim chance. She was almost one hundred per cent certain he meant to keep her—at least—there.

As the sun began to melt slowly towards the horizon, Gill decided to have one more try. "Harry, I really would like Ella to have a check-up. Don't you think it would be wise to be on the safe side?"

He glanced down at the sleeping Ella. Nothing could have looked more perfect and normal. He laughed. "She's doing fine. You're doing a great job, you know. She looks perfect. Why risk her among other kids and their germs in a clinic?"

"But…"

He put his dessert spoon down on the plate, drained his wine glass and stood up, pushing back his chair. "Time to be making tracks. I'll see you soon."

Gill sat open-mouthed at his decision. Had he made his mind up to go *before* she'd broached the subject of Ella's health, or was she the one who triggered it? She knew he had nothing personal ashore with him and guessed he'd never intended staying. Of course, she was still out of action sex-wise, maybe that had something to do with it as well.

Harry paused at the doorway just long enough to give her a disdainful look and then he was gone. Effing creep.

Chapter Sixty - Gillian

Just over a week later, she took Ella for a short walk as she'd been fretful since the early hours of the morning. Gill still felt kind of off-colour—she wasn't totally well. She was still getting stomach aches, but thanks to the good food Harry had bought, she was eating better. On their return to the house, she was surprised to see Harry had returned. She wandered up the steps of the veranda and met him coming out.

"Hi!"

"Hello yourself," Harry replied. "So how are you both? How's my little Ella?" He reached out and stroked the top of her head. "Let me hold her." He held out his arms and carried on speaking. "I've brought you lots of things, including a couple of Motherhood magazines. I had a flick through, but you might find them useful." He indicated over his shoulder towards the main room.

"Oh, thanks. I'm not sure about Ella—she's been very miserable today. Keeps crying and she didn't sleep most of the night. That's why I took her for a walk."

"Even more reason for me to hold her then. She probably wants her dad."

Ella chose that moment to open her tiny mouth and let out a not-so-tiny yell. "See, she probably wants feeding."

"A few minutes won't kill her. I'll be very careful."

"Well …" Ella's cries increased, and Gill wondered if she could sense her agitation around him.

"Give the child to me. She's my daughter. I have rights."

Gill blinked at his words. Rights? What about mine? Then as she paused, he placed his hands beneath hers and said very softly and forcibly between his teeth. "Give her to me."

"Be careful. Support her back and head."

"Shh. There." As he held Ella firmly against his chest, Gill saw at once that he knew what he was doing. So, she was right. He knew how to hold an infant. She couldn't relax. Harry had her daughter in his arms and his boat— the only means of escape off the island—was only yards away down the hill. What if he made a dash for it, taking Ella with him? Her stomach gave an almighty lurch and she felt physically sick.

"Why don't you sit down with her? She likes it if you lay her on her tummy across your legs." Gill realised she was possibly talking to someone who knew far more about holding a baby than she did. The idea made her feel as mad as anything.

"Have you had lunch?" she continued, hoping he'd suggest he make it like he often did on the island, although he'd never offered on board the yacht. Odd that.

"I had a big breakfast, but I'd love a sandwich. You'll see I've brought fresh bread and more butter. Plus, you'll find a large slice of pâté. A pâté and tomato sandwich would go down very nicely, thank you."

Gill hovered around, anxious, not knowing what to do. "Come inside while I make it. You can talk to me while you're holding Ella. It's nice to have someone to talk to."

Harry was making cooing noises to Ella, and she lay quietly in his arms, gazing raptly into his face. Gill swore she thought she saw her first smile. She was filled with jealous rage. She wanted to tear her from him.

He looked up with a soft look in his eyes. "What? Oh right." He stood up and Gill followed him into the house. "Go on, make those sandwiches then."

Gill was furious. Not only had Harry enjoyed the first of their child's smiles, but she was lying perfectly content in the arms of this monster. She sorted through the bags until she found the stuff for their sandwiches. The pâté looked delicious, and she cut doorstep bread slices and slathered them with butter and filling. Fresh salad— wonderful food. Gill handed Harry the plate and remained standing in front of him. Her eyes flicked over the bags. She could only see four. Did that mean he was taking them back with him that day or the next?

"Right, here you are. Hand her over to me now, she's due for a feed, and I don't want her to get out of routine."

"Babies this age don't have a routine. Don't be ridiculous, woman. She's perfectly happy and safe with me. Sit down and eat your own lunch. I can manage with one hand."

Harry gave Gill a glare as if he knew what she was thinking.

They sat and ate in silence. Harry gazed at Ella with keen attentiveness, and for the first time, Gill felt the odd one out. She must have recognised Harry was calm and unruffled. Minutes later, she kicked her little legs and then turned her head towards his chest.

Harry chuckled. "Uh-oh. I think it's your turn now. That's one thing I can't give her. I enjoyed holding her, though."

The moment Ella was back in Gill's arms, she felt relief sweep through her. It was stupid really; she knew Harry was far stronger and could easily have wrestled Ella from her arms at any time, but just holding the baby soothed Gill. She pushed up her T-shirt, and soon she was nursing normally. She still experienced odd stomach pains from time to time and felt bruised and sore from the birth, but unless Harry had brought her more painkillers, there was nothing to be done about it. Common sense told her she'd return to normal when her body said so.

"Right. While you're doing that, I'll go and get the rest of the stuff." He turned and left the house. Gill followed his progress with narrowed eyes. So, he wasn't taking them off the island that day after all. Bastard. She wished she'd killed him that one time she had the chance. She'd been so stupid not to plan it more carefully. Now he'd be on his guard as much as she was on hers. They were treading on eggshells. Who was going to make the first mistake?

While Ella fed, Gill's mind wandered. Were there any poisonous plants on the island? Could she make up a brew of something that would make him sick enough to knock the stuffing out of him. If he was ill and weak, she knew she could overpower him enough to kill him. Gill thought of her knife hidden along with the hoarded tins. With a sleepy Ella over her shoulder, she walked across to the doorway. No sign of Harry. She just had time to make a dash and grab the knife. She could hide it in the bedroom. Gill hurried along the path, moved the boulder and seized the knife. She tucked it under her T-shirt and scurried back to the house. There was no sign of Harry, so she carried on through into the bedroom and slipped the knife out of sight under the mattress. It would have to do for now. Gill didn't have time to think of anywhere else to hide it.

She wandered back into the main room and looked out of the front door. Where was he? A wind suddenly blew up from the south-east, picking up sand and whipping it against her legs so hard that it stung. She glanced at the heavens. The blue sky was being taken over by grey-purple clouds. Gill heard a shout and saw Harry climbing the hill.

He walked past them and dumped the bags on the floor. "Changed my mind. Looks like there's going to be a bit of a blow. I have to go to Colombia this time, so the wind will get me there nice and quick. See you when I come through on my way back."

His manner had changed again. He didn't even attempt to kiss Ella goodbye, let alone her. Gill stood with the baby in her arms. Her breath came in great gasps. How could she kill him if he didn't stay long enough for her to carry out a decent plan?

"Bastard! Bastard! Bastard!" she screamed after him but knew he'd never hear her yell over the sound of the wind and the rustling trees overhead.

Ella chose that moment to wake up and cry. Her cries turned to high-pitched yells. Gill felt like running out to the granite rocks with Ella in her arms and jumping into the storm-tossed sea. What kind of life was this?

Chapter Sixty-One - Harry

The woman was driving him insane. *She* was insane. Harry knew his rights; the child was his, and he was entitled to hold and be involved in her upbringing. But that was as far as it went. He didn't want an unstable woman, mother or not, anywhere near his daughter, and he had to do something about it quickly. Mind made up, he turned White Lady's wheel, reset the sails and headed not for Colombia but for home.

Once Harry reached Antigua, he set about organising his household. He had a couple of local women who kept the house neat and clean, and they cooked for him when he couldn't be bothered. The mother, Hannah, had been with Harry for fifteen years and Amelie about five. Both women were loyal and trustworthy, and he knew they'd keep their mouths shut. Amelie was the mother of two small boys, aged three and about eighteen months, as he recalled. She still breastfed the younger of the two. With the right disbursement, Harry knew she'd take charge of one more tiny baby.

It took no time, and arrangements were swiftly put in place. Harry gave Amelie a wad of dollars to buy everything she needed for Ella, plus a generous gift for her mother and herself. They were instructed to reorganise the bedroom next to his and turn it into a proper nursery. All he had to do was return with Ella. Harry knew various people in local government on the island. A generous greasing of palms was all it would take to get Ella swiftly registered as his legal daughter. Money worked wonders in those parts as it did over most of the rest of the world.

Hannah was quick on the uptake, asking a few leading questions, and he knew he'd have been a fool not to be at least partially straight with her. Harry said the baby was his own daughter and currently in Colombia. The mother, a local girl from one of the many offshore islands, had died of malaria, and Ella was in grave danger of being sent to an impoverished orphanage. As she was his blood, he wanted to do the best for her. Hannah frowned and fixed Harry with a curious stare, but nodded agreement that bringing her home was the Christian thing to do and the only solution.

"An innocent child is never to blame. Bring her home, and we'll make sure she's loved and cared for, Mister Harry. By the way, someone was asking for you yesterday."

"Oh? Who was that?"

"He didn't leave a name, but said he'd surprise you with a visit sometime. He said he knew your father too."

"Curious. Maybe it's an old friend or business acquaintance of Dad's. They're often popping up when they visit the Caribbean. Dad certainly knew some characters in his lifetime. Anyway, if he calls again, tell him I'll be back in two days' time unless I run into really bad weather." Harry hoped it wasn't one of his father's more dubious contacts. He'd had one or two, but he gave the matter no more thought, as he had plenty to keep him occupied. Time was pressing down heavily on him.

Harry had the yacht restocked with food and water, cleaned and filled with diesel on his return. He added some vital baby items, including a bassinet, and in less than thirty-six hours, he was back behind the wheel, under full sail.

Chapter Sixty-Two - Gillian

With Harry gone, Gill had time to make a sort of plan. She didn't have many choices. Harry was evidently intent on keeping her there. The only way to get off was to either kill him and steal the boat—could she manage it with a baby in tow?—or somehow convince him he had to take them off the island. The second was impossible, as he obviously didn't want Gill as well as his daughter. Tough, they came as a package or not at all.

Harry turned up early one morning only a few days after he'd left. Gill had spent a ghastly night. She was hot and almost feverish. Ella sensed her discomfort and refused to nurse. Gill resorted to using a bottle of formula and despite her inept mother, she seemed to be thriving. Luckily, Gill had got up and tidied away the feeding bottle and tin of baby milk before Harry arrived. Ella had slept for a couple of hours and awoke just before Harry turned up.

Gill still felt odd as well as hot and shivery and put it down to lack of sleep. When Ella started crying, she explained to Harry what a bad night they'd had.

"What a greeting for your father. Hello, Gill." Harry was all eyes for his daughter and after dumping a few carrier bags in the middle of the room, he walked over to where Gill was sitting, trying her best to pacify Ella. "How is she?"

"Not so good, I'm afraid. We had a lousy night."

His face showed concern. "Why? Is everything all right here? The solar lighting still okay?"

Gill waved a hand dismissively. Time to get on with her scheming and make up a few symptoms. "Yeah, that's fine. No, baby Ella couldn't settle. I think she's coming down with a tummy bug or something. She's had a bit of a runny tummy, smelly nappies, and I've been wondering if she's got a cold too. She was a bit snuffly this morning." Gill lowered her head towards her and took a sniff. "I thought she'd done it again—another runny poo—but it must have just been wind. Poor little mite."

"Has she been feeding?" Harry sat down next to Gill and gently stroked Ella's downy cheek.

"So-so. Not too bad but nothing like her best. I might be exaggerating a bit, new mums often do, I believe. I don't suppose you have any baby medicines in those bags you've just brought us."

"No. I didn't anticipate needing to…what do you need?"

Gill paused as if thinking. "Um, something for colds? The baby equivalent of paracetamol, I suppose. A loose tummy will probably have to run its course."

"Poor little mite. I've got stuff on White Lady, but it's all for adults. There's no way she can have any of that. Even a tiny amount would be too toxic for a baby. She doesn't have anything serious, does she? Just a common cold?"

"Maybe. As I said, I'm probably panicking, Ella being my first baby, but where would she pick a cold up from? It's not as if we're overrun with visitors."

Harry looked like he was about to say something, and she wondered what he'd thought of. Was he at last making up his mind to take them off the island?

"What?"

"I didn't say anything."

"No, but you looked like you were about to."

"No."

Gill withheld a sigh. Pathetic man. How she detested him. "I'm sure it's just a mild cold. As you've said before, she's a picture of health normally. Just get me something and bring it here next time. A doctor will only say I'm worrying over nothing."

"If you're sure. Just supposing she got worse…it's a full day-and-night sail from Antigua to here. Babies are so vulnerable. She wouldn't stand a chance if it was something serious."

Gill almost laughed out loud. It made a nice change for him to be on the receiving end of oppression. "Harry, it's okay. I'd never put our baby at risk. Just come back with a few baby medicines. Maybe something to stop diarrhoea. I read somewhere that babies die of diarrhoea more than anything else. Did you know that?"

Harry's face turned white as he looked from Gill to Ella and back again. "No. I didn't."

She nodded. "So get the best medicines and oh, what about a thermometer as well? That would be really handy."

"She hasn't been sick too, has she?"

"Not yet, although I did think she might have been about to after her last feed."

He peered more closely at Ella and then shot Gill a look of pure venom. "Maybe it's you. You're the carrier of something—a cold or a bug. You said you felt shivery the other day. And what have you been eating? Whatever you eat will pass on to her. Have you been careful and washing your hands before feeding her?" He sat back and regarded her with an expression she didn't like. She almost felt the anger rising in him. He was blaming her for not taking proper care of his daughter. What an effing cheek!

"Of course I bloody well do. What do you think I am? An idiot? I'm very careful with hygiene and I wash every piece of fruit or vegetable before I eat it. I don't eat anything on this island I don't recognise. I don't want to end up poisoned. But let's get this clear…I practically starve sometimes between your visits, as you're so unpredictable with your timing, so I have to supplement with local fruits and fish."

"Calm down. You could have asked me for more."

"What? Would you have even listened? Did you hear every time I asked you to take me off this island? I said I'd be perfectly happy at home with you in Antigua. You could see and hold Ella every day then." If he was angry, then she was feeling furious with him now. Harry drew back from her onslaught and stood up. He walked over to the doorway and leant against the wooden frame. When he spoke, he didn't face Gill. "This wasn't entirely my choice."

"What?"

"All this. I hadn't planned…I knew you were hiding from the police. I knew you'd done some awful things. But this just happened."

"You're not making sense." Gill felt her body stiffen. *Things*, he'd said. What did he think he knew about her? "What things? I—"

He interrupted before she could finish. "When I first saw you in Portugal, you reminded me of my ex-partner, Marlene. Your looks, something in the way you walked. I dunno, you just did. And then you orchestrated that little meeting between us in the marina bar. Later, at dinner, I learnt you wanted a berth to take you away from Europe. I thought, why not? I sometimes take passengers, and you said you could cook and sail a bit. You were cool, uninterested in me as a person, and I like a challenge. Plus, I recognised something in you that spelt mystery. It was written all over your face."

She shrugged. "So I wanted a lift. You know why. We were both getting a deal."

"Yes, but then Theo showed up. You know we talked about you, that night on watch. I told you what he said.

At that time, I wasn't wholly sure I believed him. Anyway, it seemed a good idea to let you hide out on here for a while. I made up my mind later that Theo was right. Your excuse about getting away because you'd lost a friend was only half of the full truth."

"That was true, but I was afraid I'd be blamed for Nathan's death, and I was grateful at the time to hide away on Cabra. But you left me here for far too long." Her voice became shrill, raised, startling Ella as she slept in her arms.

Harry lifted his shoulders, hands palm upwards towards Gill as he turned around. "Things just happened. I didn't mean to keep you here that long. I suppose it became a sort of game. I enjoyed it. It was something I'd imagined doing. Call it a fantasy."

"Game? Fantasy? You fucking nutcase. I wanted to leave, and I told you countless times I wouldn't tell a soul. I'd have done what I said—disappeared into South America. How could I have harmed you? You made up an excuse that there were drug smugglers in these parts and it wasn't safe to attract their attention. Why would I have gone to the police if they were after me?"

"Like I said, I wanted you here. You reminded me of Marlene. Things happened, just took over." She stared into his eyes and saw cunning, a cold blackness. He was making it up. He was an insane psycho who preyed on women. She trembled. What had happened to Marlene?

She got herself together. "Not good enough reason, Harry. You could have taken me off, called me by a different name." Ella stirred and she glanced down at her. She was beginning to wake up. Maybe their agitated voices were getting through to her? As much as she loved her daughter, Gill recognised that she was her liability, her responsibility. Was she really cut out for motherhood? She hadn't made a good job of it so far.

Harry laughed. Not in a friendly way. "The locals are naturally curious. Don't you think they'd look at you and notice the resemblance to Marlene? She disappeared…I never found her. At one stage, I was suspected of doing something terrible. Besides, everyone knows me on Antigua. They'd have wondered who you were, where you'd come from. Someone would have soon found out the truth."

"Maybe. But that was my choice. You have no obligation to me. I'm not even your new girlfriend. So, I'm to take it you didn't kill Marlene? She realised what a sick fuck you are and left instead."

Harry threw her a look which was full of spite. It was as if he hated Gill knowing anything about his background. "How dare you! Don't you dare speak her name. As if you can compare yourself to her. She was worth ten of you."

"But she obviously didn't feel the same."

Harry balled his hands into fists, and Gill shrank back against the sofa. Ella was still in her arms, and she felt threatened by the ugly glint in his eyes. He drew in a deep breath and relaxed his hands. "Apparently not. But this isn't about her. This is about you. When I discovered you were pregnant and worked out the dates, I realised I was going to become a father again. I was being given another chance. Ella would become my heir, and I liked the idea."

She almost gasped. "You said 'again'. Did Marlene have a baby?" Gill watched closely and saw his eyes clouding with pain.

"Yes," he muttered hoarsely. "She had a daughter. Her name was Ella, too. I thought you'd somehow found out and were playing a cruel trick on me."

She blinked and slowly shook her head. "No. I never knew that. I swear I didn't. The name just felt right."

Harry didn't answer. His eyes locked onto hers, and she almost dropped Ella with fright. Dark pools of resentment and loathing glared back at her. She stood up and put Ella over her shoulder. "Honestly, the name…I just liked it." Gill had to break his stare. She felt as if she was in the presence of a deadly stranger. "But Harry, you have a new baby daughter, but what about me? I've told you I'll never say a word, I swear. But I must know. I'm Ella's mother—she depends on me."

"Fuck that. I know it all, Gill. Or I should say Priscilla Gillian Hodges. It's amazing what you can find out on the internet these days. I traced back to when you were fifteen. You fell pregnant, and your upright parents, pillars of the local church, hated the shame of their one-and-only daughter producing a bastard. For fuck's sake, it was the nineties. They sent you to a special place to have the child, and you agreed to have it adopted."

"Only under pressure. I wanted to keep him." Gill felt herself go hot and cold all over; her skin prickled. It was hard to breathe. Her legs were shaking as she took a couple of footsteps away from him. She had to get to the bedroom.

"Oh yes, so you said at the time. But that's not entirely true, is it?"

"Don't. Don't say it." She squeaked, gasping for air. Everything began to close in on her. She backed away…the knife in the bedroom was just a few feet away…

"Oh yes. I'm going to shout it at you. You killed your first baby, didn't you?"

Chapter Sixty-Three - Gillian

"Well, you're not going to kill mine. You're not fit to be a mother. No child should be left alone with you. I have no choice. She's coming with me."

"No! No I didn't. That's not true. I swear I didn't kill him. It was my…my father," Gill replied with a sob. "He said he was the spawn of Satan and smothered him when I was asleep."

"Lying bitch!"

Harry flew at her, and Gill sidestepped to miss his oncoming fist. Somehow, she made it into the bedroom just as he grabbed her T-shirt. She felt it rip, and the tear gave her a chance to make it to the bed. Harry made another lunge and grabbed her hair. She shrieked in pain and slipped, falling onto her knees. Ella was miraculously still against her shoulder. Gill's eyes drew level with the mattress. Harry roared in her ear as his fist finally made contact with her head. On impact, she thought it would explode. Unconsciously, her hand scrabbled beneath the mattress, and she felt her fingers nudge around the handle of the knife. Once again, she felt Harry's fist thump against the side of her head. Tears and stars filled her vision as well as pain. He stumbled against her, and she felt his hands take hold of Ella's shoulders.

"Murdering bitch," he gasped. "Your baby, your friend. Did you kill him because he found out the truth about you?"

"No!" Gill heard herself scream, her fingers frantically clamping tight round the knife handle. "No! I didn't kill either of them. You can't take my baby. You can't have her."

Suddenly there was a void as Ella was snatched from her shoulder. Harry rolled onto his side and away from Gill. She watched in desperation as he got up on one knee and then stumbled from the room. Ella was firmly held between his hands. Gill pulled the knife free and staggered to her feet. The room swayed as she ran after him. Harry had made it as far as the sofa; there were shopping bags in his way, and he paused to find a path through them. Gill made a flying leap onto his back and felt the knife score deeply across his skin. Blood gushed from the wound, as she took another stab, this time feeling the blade slide deeper into his flesh. Harry roared and fell, hitting the stone floor heavily. There was blood everywhere, and Gill shrieked as she tried to rescue Ella from beneath her father.

Ella screamed back, her little arms waving. Gill pulled her free, and tucked her under one arm. In the other hand, she still held the knife. Harry made an almighty bellow and attempted to get into a sitting position. Gill was panting from fear and exertion. He struggled to stand, and she swept the knife in front of her, stabbing at his face, arms, and hands, anywhere she could make contact. It was as if a red mist had come down in front of her—all she wanted to do was thrust and stab. Erase the sight of him. Save her baby from this monster. All she could see and smell was blood. Harry raised one arm above his head to protect his face, but her panic lent strength to her arm. She had to save Ella. Gill slashed and slashed. Then, when the fight seemed to have gone out of Harry, she turned away and ran from the house.

Chapter Sixty-Four - Harry

He didn't know how long he'd been lying there. It couldn't have been that long, as the sun was still high in the sky. He remembered groaning as he attempted to stand. The floor was slick with blood, the arm and one side of the sofa drenched. Harry lurched to his feet, swaying as he looked around the room. There was no sight or sound of Gillian or his baby daughter. He glanced down at his wounds. Blood still ran freely, while his back and lungs felt like they were on fire. He'd never felt such agony. He found it hard to catch his breath and realised she must have perforated one of his lungs.

Harry knew he'd die on the island if he remained there. He had no doubt that if Gill returned and found him alive, she'd waste no time in finishing him off. There were no medical supplies in the house. White Lady was lying in the bay, a full medical kit on board and a fully working ship's radio. He could easily bind his wounds temporarily and make an SOS Medical call.

He managed to drag himself out of the house, across the veranda. No sign of Gillian anywhere. He hoped to god she wasn't down on the beach and thinking the same: the yacht was the only way out of there. His breath came in gasps; it was torture. Slowly, he teetered his way down and across the sands, a bloody trail following his laboured progress.

The rubber dinghy was where he'd left it, the bows out of the water, the stern resting in the shallows. He needed to drag it farther into the sea for it to float. Harry prayed his energy wouldn't give out before then. He pushed against the bows, and the boat moved a few inches. He gave another shove, and it moved some more. Eventually, it was free and floating. All he had to do was climb in and somehow propel himself to the yacht. Harry wasn't sure if he could row twelve foot of rubber to the mother boat.

He stumbled against the side and clung on, each breath becoming harder than the last. Harry knew he couldn't find the strength to clamber over the side into the dinghy. If only he could cling on, grasp a hold on the rope along the sides and paddle the boat out. He gave a kick and the dinghy moved. It was hard going, but he was making headway. The cool water lapped over his wounds causing fresh pain as the salt ate into his flesh. He left the shallows and headed for deeper water. Harry felt a new surge of energy. It was going to be all right. He'd get on the yacht and make that call. Medical help would arrive and they'd find his daughter. That sad bitch would get her just desserts and be carted off to whichever psychiatric hospital prison would take her. Guilty or not, he didn't care one jot about the cow.

Harry didn't see the shadow following him until he'd just about reached White Lady. As he looked down, he noticed the sleek grey body slowly turning round and round as it pushed its nose into the long trailing tendrils of blood Harry had left behind him. The gigantic mass of fishy cartilage suddenly rose to the surface, its wide mouth agape, showing row upon row of savage teeth. As it bit down upon his torso, Harry wondered why he suddenly couldn't feel his legs, then found he was being dragged down beneath the turbulent surface. Blood and flesh swept past his face, and the last thing he thought of was Ella and how he'd failed her, like he had his other daughter.

Chapter Sixty-Five - Gillian

Gill had no idea if she'd killed Harry, but the image of him suddenly finding the strength to run after them lent energy to her flagging body. With Ella once more held tightly in her arms, screaming her head off, Gill fled from the house and headed for the opposite side of the island. She stopped every hundred yards or so to catch her breath and looked fearfully over her shoulder in case he was following. The farther east they went, the more her mind was put at ease. Not that they were out of danger yet. She paused at the granite rocks, and after finding a place to rest and hide, set about feeding Ella. Her face was still red from her screaming, and the poor little mite had fallen asleep, no doubt due to exhaustion.

Gill eased her into a more comfortable nursing position and tried to wake her. Ella screwed up her face, but before she had time to yell, Gill offered her breast. Peace reigned for a few minutes, but all too soon, the baby pulled back her head and gave a thin cry. Gill changed her position, but like before, she soon gave up sucking. Gill's heart plummeted. Her milk was almost gone. She had to return to the house and supplement her feed. Gill had no way of knowing how long it was since they'd fled along the path, but her watch said it was nearing three thirty. She estimated they'd been gone well over an hour. Her mouth felt dry and her throat parched. She moved her cramped legs and inched round into a kneeling position before standing up. Gill glanced down at the ground and saw she'd left some blood on the rock. Her pad must have leaked and she needed another. The running must have made her bleed more profusely. It smelt odd, too.

Gill had no choice but to return; everything she needed was back there. She hoped Harry was dead. Surely he couldn't have survived the stabbing she'd inflicted on him? With him lifeless, they were both safe. Tears of fear and desperation ran down her face. Truth be known, she'd never wanted to kill him. If only he'd done what he said he'd do when they first met. She glanced down at her baby, and as she did so, his words fluttered back to her. *You killed your first baby!*

She knew she hadn't. What she said about her father was all true. Gill felt fresh tears running down her face as she sobbed, and she held Ella close to her. Her head had been hollow, a dark empty void, for so long, but Harry's words had freed her mind so that she remembered everything now. Before, she'd remembered so very little…the clinic…feeling so utterly useless and numb with shock when her father told the doctors she'd smothered her baby boy. Another memory suddenly came back to her in a flash…*in a maelstrom of fatigue and mental disorder…for the remainder of your life, you will have to live with the fact that you killed your newborn baby son…that burden will never be lifted.* She was filled with horror. The court. And then she was then sent to that awful psychiatric hospital. All for something she hadn't done.

Ella let out a wail, and Gill put her finger into her mouth to suck. As she quietened down, Gill started back along the trail. She wiped the tears from her face.

Ella moved her left arm and edged her own fingers into her mouth. She sucked hard. Gill would love and care for her. If only she could get to the yacht and off the island. She started the journey back, resting every few minutes as exhaustion seemed to have caught up with her.

The house loomed up ahead. Everything looked still, so silent. The veranda was covered in dried blood. Gill could see where Harry had dragged himself from the house, across the wooden decking and onto the sand. There was blood there too…flies were already feasting. The trail seemed to lead down towards the lagoon. She decided to leave Ella at the house. Her Moses basket was in the bedroom, and Gill laid her in it gently. The walk seemed to have quietened her temporarily—her eyes were closed.

Gill looked around for some kind of weapon. She had no idea where she'd dropped the knife. If Harry was still alive, who knew what state he was in. He could have even found and picked up the knife. She selected a thick piece of wood; it would have to do. A minute later, she was down at the water's edge after following his trail of blood.

The beach was empty. White Lady lay silently at anchor. The surface of the bay was unruffled, as calm as a mill pond. Something looked different…the dinghy wasn't in its usual place. Scuff marks across the sand showed where it had been pushed into the water. But it wasn't tied to the stern of White Lady. Gill cast a long search around the bay, and at the far end, in deep water by the channel entrance, she saw the dinghy lying off the rocks. She narrowed her eyes and noticed it was untethered, floating freely. The stern also looked different, and she realised it had been deflated. But why? Where was Harry?

She shifted her feet in the shallows. Something hard and gristly seemed to be trapped under her right foot. She looked down and as she moved her foot, the water swirled over the object. Blood rose to the surface, and Gill realised with horror she was gazing down at Harry's mutilated head.

Chapter Sixty-Six - Gillian

Her milk had completely dried up. For now, Ella was thriving on milk formula. The last two days had passed in a haze. Gill was hot and feverish, craving nothing but water. Anything she ate, she brought up. She knew she had to eat to survive. She had to stay alive for Ella. Having a baby gave her a reason for living.

Once she'd got over the shock of finding the grisly remains of Harry's head, Gill looked for other parts of his body. A few scraps of flesh were washed up on the shore, and she put everything she found into a shallow scrape she'd scooped out farther up the beach. She shoved the piece of wood she'd been carrying as a weapon into the sand marking a sort of grave. At one end of the beach, the water was tinged pink, and once she saw the shark's fin circling farther out, she guessed what had happened. Harry, the psychotic control freak, the one who practically kidnapped and kept her prisoner on Cabra had come to a violent end. The shark had been attracted by his wounds once he'd entered the water.

Gill couldn't find it in herself to cry for Harry's ghastly death. His appalling cruel behaviour towards her decreed otherwise. But she did regret that Ella would never know a father. But Gill's greatest distress was on seeing the dinghy up on the rocks and severely punctured—no doubt by the shark's jaws. They were marooned on the beach. She had no way of getting out to White Lady and no way of leaving the island. Ella and she were doomed.

As the hours passed, Gill's abdomen felt as if it was on fire. The pains came and went, each one more violent than the last. Gill recognised she could die, especially when the bright red trickle of blood she'd been passing since having Ella became a sudden gush.

Ella. She had to do *something*. She couldn't leave her to suffer and die of starvation. Gill felt so weak and wondered what she could do to save her daughter. Her muddled brain eventually worked out that her placenta hadn't completely come away and she'd retained a chunk of it. For the last two—or was it three?—weeks, the remains had continued bleeding. She gave Ella one last big feed, and she instantly fell into a deep sleep afterwards. Gill kissed her on the forehead and laid her in her Moses basket before placing it on the bed.

As Gill was pondering what to do, she heard a noise outside; it sounded like an anchor chain being run out. She couldn't detect for certain what it was from the house, and in her fevered state decided that anything on the island spelt danger. Harry had mentioned drug runners in these parts. Could it have been them? Where could she hide Ella? Gill staggered a few steps into the living room, and her eyes fell on the rug covering the 'safe' room. She'd certainly be safe down there until she could investigate the noise.

Gill rolled back the carpet and lifted the trapdoor. The cool, dark, earthy smell hit her. The top step was deep and wide enough to place Ella's basket on it, and Gill crawled back to the bedroom to fetch it. Then afterwards, summoning up what remaining strength she had, went outside. She picked up one of the conch shell shards for protection and headed across the sand. The path down to the beach seemed to go on for ever, but before she reached the crest of the hill, her legs gave out. Gill slumped down and lay looking up at the brilliant blue sky. A coldness took hold of her fingers and toes, spreading along her arms and legs. She imagined she could see Nathan beckoning her, her unnamed baby boy cooed in her arms, and Ella lay sucking her fingers contentedly before the blackness overtook her mother ...

Chapter Sixty-Seven - Theo

Following his discharge from the Brazilian hospital and with help from the British Consulate, Theo eventually made his way back to England. During his last few weeks of recovery, Theo spent most of the days glued to the internet, researching Gillian.

Gillian's name was plastered over every tabloid during the preceding months, and there was plenty more on the internet. It didn't take him long to discover where she lived and who her friends and family were. She came from Petersfield, Hampshire, and as far as Theo could tell, she had no living relatives and just one close friend, Rebecca Holmes.

Theo had recently read the piece about the death of Nathan and Lawrence's involvement. Gillian's blood was discovered under Lawrence's fingernails, and the consensus was that he'd assaulted her before she disappeared. The police still wanted to question her, but only to rule her out. They discovered that Lawrence had previous form, and Nathan's death was almost certainly at his hands.

It was easy for Theo to find Rebecca Holmes' address on the electoral roll. The next part would no doubt be harder. There was he, a middle-aged journalist, turning up and asking a young woman, who apparently lived alone, if she knew where her friend might be. She'd been interviewed by the police, but denied seeing her after their mutual friend had been found dead at Gillian's house. Theo wasn't expecting the moon. At worst, she'd bar him; at best, she'd repeat her story.

Theo had been doing his job for years, and he still stuck to the adage: intuition or a feeling rather than pure fact. Rebecca was Gillian's only true friend. She had to know more than she was letting on. He hoped Gill had managed to contact Rebecca sometime in the last year; the idea wasn't a long shot by any means. They'd been friends a long time.

Theo's only concern was Rebecca. If she thought he was looking for Gill for revenge, he'd never get a foot through the door.

He found the house—a neat, semi-detached, Victorian house—at the end of a cul-de-sac. Theo dressed casually smart for the occasion and apart from a phone and small notebook in his pocket, arrived empty-handed. There was a blue Ford parked on the tiny drive.

The door was opened after a short knock, and Theo found himself staring in surprise at the leggy pretty brunette standing in front of him. She smiled and for a moment, he felt at a loss. Her expression seemed so open and friendly, and here he was, about to shatter her composure.

"Hello, can I help you?"

Theo may have been a hard-headed journalist, who'd seen countless horrors and atrocities around the world, but he also liked to think he still possessed a heart. Completely off balance, he said simply, "Gillian."

Her face turned pale, and then as she recovered, her brow creased into a frown. "Sorry, you've got the wrong house." And went to close the door.

Theo put up a hand inside the wooden frame, thinking she could hardly trap his fingers. "I think I might know where she is."

Her mouth opened and shut, and then she cast a swift glance over his shoulder towards the open road. "Who are you? Reporter or police? I've told you, I've no idea where she is."

He felt bad when he replied. "I have to admit I *am* a reporter, but that's truly incidental. I last saw Gill on a yacht crossing the Atlantic. We were on the same boat. Look, my name is Theo Jerome. Here's my press card. I swear I don't want to hound you, just talk. Maybe we can help each other?"

***

At first, she was hesitant and suspicious, and he insisted on telling his story first to allow her time to get used to him and relax. After he finished, she sat very still and silent. Her remarkable violet-blue eyes were flooded with unshed tears. When she spoke, her voice was low and husky.

"That's quite a story. You're a journalist, used to writing a good yarn. How do I know you're telling me the truth?"

Theo sat forward in the armchair, elbows on his knees. "I know it's unbelievable in many ways, but Harry was acting out of character, I think. He seemed besotted by Gill. Followed her every move on the yacht. It only came to me last night, but I wondered if she reminded him of someone else. They were sleeping together, by the way."

"That's what I find so odd. Gill had an awful life with Lawrence. He often beat her, and he would never let her see me or Nathan alone. He was always there. He was so very jealous and controlled her completely. I begged her to leave him, but she said she couldn't. He locked all the doors and windows, and kept her a prisoner. The only time she went out of the house was when he took her. He made her suffer, so I'm surprised she formed any sort of relationship with this Harry. I'd have thought she'd be off men for good."

"Harry treated her well on White Lady, if a little controlling. I think she saw him as some sort of saviour, and he was older. Maybe even a father figure? It was definitely Harry who pushed me overboard. I was standing on the outer deck, having a quick pee. Stupid of me, as I wasn't clipped on. Harry obviously saw an opportunity and turfed me into the sea."

"But why? You mentioned drug-running. Why didn't Gillian react?"

"She was below, fast asleep. She might have done…that's something we don't know. But you must realise this, even if Harry treated her well, she was ultimately under his control."

Rebecca sat still for a moment, and then got out of her seat. "Gill suffered a lifetime of control freaks—her father, then Lawrence and now it seems this Harry too. Gillian was gentle and a lovely girl. I wished she'd found the strength to stand up to people, but I think her father was to blame for that. I know it's early, but I need a drink. Fancy one?"

Theo smiled. "A small whisky if you have some, please."

Rebecca returned with their drinks and sat back down. "Cheers, although I'm not sure what there is to be cheerful about."

"I don't know. The latest report found traces of blood under Lawrence's nails, so he obviously hit her, probably first. The consensus is Lawrence is the guilty one, especially as the police have found evidence of previous form. Do you feel able to tell me a little about your side of things?"

She opened her eyes wide and gave him a wary look. "Who said I knew anything?" Theo waited and eventually, she sighed. "Okay. But, please, this won't go any further?"

He assured her it wouldn't, and she sat back and told him all about Gillian and her life.

***

As Rebecca talked, Theo began to get more of a feel for Gillian. Rebecca said there were a few gaps, but she pieced things together from snippets she'd read in the press. When she told Theo about Gill's strict and religious father and the death of her baby boy, he felt uneasy. Rebecca noted his tenseness and nodded. "I know what you're thinking. Gill never said anything much about that time, but I had my suspicions. She rarely spoke about her parents either. She blocked most of that dreadful period out."

She continued, saying how Gill came to her that fateful night and how distraught she was. "She wouldn't hurt a fly, let alone her best friend. And what Lawrence said was pure fabrication. Nathan had a boyfriend. He wasn't interested in girls that way."

Theo nodded and finished his whisky. Lawrence sounded like a real piece of shit. What man beat his girlfriend so badly that she miscarried? He felt his face grow taut and asked Rebecca if he could trouble her for another whisky. She returned with the bottle and told him to help himself.

"So, if all this is true, and I believe you, then Gill's somewhere in Antigua?"

"Yes. You said she phoned you?"

"Yes, just the once. She was in Portugal but wouldn't say where. Neither did she mention a yacht. I think she was just being cautious and didn't want to land me in it as well as giving away her whereabouts. I almost wish I'd gone with her. We could have looked after each other. What kind of friend am I to let her go off alone?" She looked completely miserable, and if Theo had known her better, he would have comforted her. As it was, he simply gave her a reassuring smile.

He remained silent as an idea was forming in his head. He took a sip of whisky and then carefully placed the glass back on the coffee table.

"You can still help her. I'm going out to Antigua. Why not come with me and help solve this mystery? Hopefully we can find her and bring her home."

Chapter Sixty-Eight - Theo

Theo booked them both on a British Airways flight to V C Bird International, Antigua, two days later. Rebecca, or Bex as she liked to be known, had plenty of leave owing, so getting time off wasn't a problem. Theo even managed to wangle a couple of upgrades to business class, and as she was pretty and warm-hearted, he looked forward to sharing her company for eight hours.

She was proper but friendly, and he respected that. Even so, her company made the journey pass remarkably quickly.

In Antigua, they had a forty-minute wait while they went through customs—some Caribbean procedures never changed—and then picked up the hire car Theo had booked. They checked into the hotel and after relaxing for the rest of the evening, went to bed. The following day promised to be an interesting one.

***

Theo had only been to Harry's Antiguan house once, but he remembered it well and recalled where it was situated on the island. Harry's father had been a wealthy man, much of his money probably gained from smuggling. He was never caught handling the goods himself, but he'd been on the radar of various coast guards. He handed everything over to Harry when he died.

Theo told Bex that Harry was idle, basically. He didn't need to work and apart from the odd trip with choice cargo hidden in a spare and empty diesel tank, whiled his time away.

Theo learnt from the grapevine some time back that Harry had met a woman he loved, and at the time, he wondered if he might settle down. But after a year or so, she disappeared back to her home island of Trinidad, apparently. The thought crossed his mind that Gill might have reminded Harry of this woman but decided it was too far-fetched and he let the idea go. It wouldn't have helped, anyway.

Now, as Bex and Theo waited on the doorstep of the large gracious house, he wondered how Harry would react once he clapped eyes on him.

The door was opened by a young woman. From her dark eyes, skin and hair, Theo assumed she was from Antigua. When she spoke, he knew he was right from her attractive lilting accent.

"Mister Harry, he isn't here right now."

Another older woman peered around the corner of the door. "Was it you who called about a week ago, sir?"

"Yes, I did, and this is my friend, Miss Holmes. We're here for a short holiday. Do you know when Harry is due back home?

The two women exchanged looks. "He should been back two days ago. He gone sailing. He said he no late unless the weather she be bad," the older woman stated.

"And has it?" He thought it hadn't, as the hurricane season had officially ended but needed to check.

"No, sir." They both shook their heads.

"Did Harry say where he was going?" Rebecca asked.

The women glanced at each other again and paused. Then the younger woman seemed to take charge. "Mister Harry went to fetch his baby girl. She is on an island off Colombia."

Theo raised his eyebrows in response and heard Bex stifling a slight gasp. "Really?" he replied. "What about the mother? Was she coming home too?"

His brain was thinking rapidly...seven months...was this woman Gillian? Had they found her? Harry needed locking up, but since meeting Bex and what she'd told him, he seriously doubted Gillian was guilty of anything truly bad.

"No, sir. She passed away...malaria. Mister Harry order room be fixed for the child and everything. We gone and fixed it good. Do you want see?"

"Dead?" Bex whispered.

Theo sensed Bex's dismay as she stood by his side and slipped her hand into his for reassurance. "It might not be her and it might not be true. Don't worry, we'll find her," he murmured into her ear. Theo turned back to the women servants. "Yes please."

They were shown into the room, and saw immediately it was equipped for an infant. Theo's mind raced, but he said nothing more to Bex. So, if Gill had died, then was Harry rescuing their baby? He turned abruptly from gazing at the collection of nursery items. "Do you know where this island is? Mr Harry is an old friend of mine and might be in trouble, ill perhaps, as he's now overdue back on the island. We need to find him."

The older woman nodded. "It was his father's island. There's a map downstairs."

***

The channel looked as if it was too small and shallow to take a forty-five-foot yacht. Thanks to a forward-looking echo sounder and depth sounding, they passed safely over the rocks below and squeezed into the lagoon beyond. Harry's yacht, White Lady, lay immediately to their right.

Theo and Rebecca had teamed up with an Antiguan skipper, Trevor, who was happy to take them to Isla de Cabra for an attractive sum of cash. He'd heard of the place and the rumours surrounding Harry and the island but never had any cause to venture that way. Trevor lowered his yacht's dinghy, and they all motored across to the other yacht. There was no sign of anyone on board. Everything looked orderly. Harry must have been expecting to return as it was left unlocked and open to the elements. As they stood on deck, Theo suddenly pointed to the rocks off to their right side. "Look! That must be White Lady's tender."

They motored over and found the rubber dinghy in a sorry state. One side was completely deflated.

"By the looks of it, it seems that this was attacked by something big. Jeez. Look at the size of those holes." Trevor whistled and indicated with his hand. "Bloody big shark, I reckon."

They looked at one another. Theo knew they were all thinking the same thing, and Bex looked completely shocked. "Shit. I think it's time to go ashore."

The ride over the bay took them straight to the sandy beach. It appeared empty except for the usual flotsam which drifted onto any shore around the world. Theo noticed some of the rubbish seemed to have a pink tinge, but he said nothing and hoped Bex hadn't noticed. Trevor had, and the two exchanged glances. This was one bay they certainly wouldn't be taking a dip in. They beached the tender and trudged across the sand towards a path that appeared to wind around and up the small hill overlooking the bay.

Theo paused as they came to a small mound in the sand. A piece of wood was dug in at one end, making it resemble some sort of crude grave. He felt a prickle run along his spine and shot a look over to Trevor.

"Are you thinking what I'm thinking?" Theo asked and Trevor nodded. Bex groped for Theo's hand, and he gave it a reassuring squeeze. He looked around. Nothing stirred under the bright harsh sun, and then he felt a slight breeze over the back of his neck.

"Jesus, what's that smell?" Trevor gasped, taking an involuntary step back and clapping a hand over his nose.

Theo looked towards the hill. "Coming from up there, I think. We had better go and see. We can take a closer look at this afterwards. Bex, I think you should stay here. I recognise that smell…I'm warning you, what we find won't be pleasant."

Bex looked around and gripped his hand more tightly. "This place gives me the creeps. I don't want to stay here alone. Can I come? I'll close my eyes if it's bad." She stopped and looked distraught. "It's Gillian, isn't it? She's dead." Her breath caught in a sob.

Theo pulled her to him and murmured into her hair. "I believe so. Stay behind me."

She nodded. "Okay. I'm okay."

They climbed the hill and at the top stopped. An emaciated-looking woman was lying on her back, arms outstretched. A brown stain covered the sand around her lower abdomen. Bex gave a short cry and sank to her knees. "Gill?"

"It looks like we're too late," Trevor said, his face pale beneath a lifetime's tan.

"Jesus. I wonder what's happened to the baby." They all stared back down the hill towards the small unmarked grave. "Surely not?"

Bex was crying, big fat tears slid down her cheeks. "Oh, my god, Gillian. Whatever happened to you?" She rocked back and forth in grief.

Theo slipped his arms around Rebecca and pulled her to her feet. "It's okay, I've got you. Bex. For what it's worth, Gillian doesn't look injured in any way. It wasn't a shark…maybe she died after giving birth, I don't know." He wrapped his arms around her and pulled her head down to his shoulder. Her loud sobs quietened down. Theo knew she had herself under some sort of control, and he admired her for it. It couldn't have been easy discovering your best friend lying dead on a Caribbean island, miles away from home. It was strange and completely out of place, but for some reason, in that instance, he knew he wanted to take care of Bex for ever. Theo knew no words could help her, so he let her cling to him until she finished crying. Finally, she stopped and looked up. She tried to give him a watery smile.

"There's a shack up there. Shall we go and look? We ought to check the place out. There might be some clues about what happened." He pointed after switching his glance from Gill's grey-tinged face and following the direction of the footpath. "We'd better look before we report back."

They carried on up and across to the wooden shack. Before going inside, they could see signs of a violent struggle. Blood smears across the veranda led to more indoors. Inside, they found the sofa and immediate floor covered in large pools of dried dark-red blood. A smell of copper pervaded above everything else. There was more gore in the bedroom. All three stared in horror. Outside, Gillian seemed relatively blood-free apart from a bloody face and hands, so this must have belonged to Harry. From the stuff lying around, it looked like the place had been inhabited by Gillian for some time. There was nothing of Harry's. Theo knew in that instant that Gill had been kept a prisoner and Harry had been her jailer. Jesus, what a shock. Trevor came out of the back room and shook his head. "Bedroom. Nothing much in there, but there are signs of a baby. Bottles, baby milk powder, nappies. Maybe someone came and took her before we arrived?"

Bex gave a cry as Trevor left the shack. "It must still be here. The boat's here, Gill too…where would she have put it? What happened, Theo? I can't bear to think that the baby didn't survive either."

Theo felt despair take hold. What if Gillian had killed her infant daughter as she realised she was dying and had little chance of survival? She wouldn't have wanted an innocent baby to suffer. The whole island was a gruesome mess. He guessed that when they dug into the small grave down on the beach, they'd find Harry or what was left of him. Theo just prayed the baby wasn't there as well. He drew an enormous breath; he didn't want to think about that and went to follow Trevor outside. As Theo stopped and took another desperate look around the room, he heard a tiny whimper. His heart leapt. He and Bex stared at each other and gasped.

It sounded like it came from under the rug.

Please Tweet/Facebook, *"Paradise Prison"* once you've finished and pass the word on.

To date Faith Mortimer has written and published:

'THE ASSASSINS' VILLAGE'. (1st novel in The Diana Rivers series). A murder mystery set in the Troodos mountains of Cyprus.

'CHILDREN OF THE PLANTATION'. (2nd in The Diana Rivers series), murder mystery, set in exotic Malaysia during the 1960's and 1950's and the present. Dark secrets threaten to destroy a family.

'THE SURGEON'S BLADE'. (3rd in the Diana Rivers series). This psychological thriller is tense and thrilling and guarantees to keep you on the edge of your seat!

'THE BAMBOO MIRROR'. An eclectic collection of short stories, covering subjects including: ghosts, murder, mystery, romance and greed.

'CAMERA-ACTION-MURDER!' The 4th novel in the "Diana Rivers" Murder Mystery series.

'THE SEEDS OF TIME - BOOK 1 of THE CROSSING'. Action-Adventure plus Romantic Suspense. (published June 2012).

'HARVEST - BOOK 2 of THE CROSSING' Continues from Book 1. Action-Adventure full of romantic suspense. (published July 2012).

'A VERY FRENCH AFFAIR'. Romance, Heartache and Suspense set on the beautiful south coast of France.

'CHILDHUNT' The 5th Mystery/Suspense Novel featuring Diana Rivers – Children are missing in the depths of an unusually cold Cyprus winter.

'ON DEVIL'S BRAE' – An Exciting Psychological Thriller set in the wilds of Scotland. – 1st "Dark Minds" Novel

'ON CHRISTMAS HILL *(A SEASONAL AFFAIR)'* – Romance blossoms at Christmastide.

'A DEADLY LEARNING' The 6th Mystery/Suspense Novel featuring Diana Rivers on "vacation" in Portugal

'SANDSTORM IN MY HEART' a Romantic Novelette

'A VERY ENGLISH AFFAIR' - A Romantic Novel in the Best Selling Series "A Very ... ... Affair"

'BEHIND A TWISTED SMILE' - A Psychological "Dark Minds" thriller

'NOT JUST FOR CHRISTMAS' - A Very Seasonal Affair

'A BRUTAL TRADE' – The 7th Mystery Thriller in the Best Selling "Diana Rivers" series

'THE GREEN ROOM'- A Psychological "Dark Minds" thriller

'A VERY DISTANT AFFAIR' – How far can love travel? A Romantic Novel

'PARADISE PRISON' – NEW

Faith Mortimer

All available as eBooks and Paperbacks from your favourite online bookstore

Find out more about Faith Mortimer and her books at:

www.faithmortimerauthor.com

www.facebook.com/FaithMortimer.Author

http://twitter.com/FaithMortimer

23955697R00184

Printed in Poland
by Amazon Fulfillment
Poland Sp. z o.o., Wrocław